PENGUIN BOOKS

FRENCH KISSES

Also by Jenny Ireland

The First Move

The Boy Next Door

Matched Up

FRENCH KISSES

JENNY IRELAND

PENGUIN BOOKS

PENGUIN BOOKS

UK | USA | Canada | Ireland | Australia
India | New Zealand | South Africa

Penguin Books is part of the Penguin Random House group of companies whose addresses can be found at global.penguinrandomhouse.com.

www.penguin.co.uk
www.puffin.co.uk
www.ladybird.co.uk

Penguin Random House UK

First published 2026

001

Set in 10.75/15.5pt Adobe Caslon Pro
Typeset by Six Red Marbles UK, Thetford, Norfolk
Printed and bound in Great Britain by Clays Ltd, Elcograf S.p.A.

The authorized representative in the EEA is Penguin Random House Ireland, Morrison Chambers, 32 Nassau Street, Dublin D02 YH68

A CIP catalogue record for this book is available from the British Library

ISBN: 978-0-241-72097-4

All correspondence to:
Penguin Books
Penguin Random House Children's
One Embassy Gardens, 8 Viaduct Gardens, London SW11 7BW

MIX
Paper | Supporting responsible forestry
FSC www.fsc.org FSC® C018179

Penguin Random House is committed to a sustainable future for our business, our readers and our planet. This book is made from Forest Stewardship Council® certified paper.

For Chris. *Je t'aime.*

Prologue

I still get nightmares about it.

The eleventh of February 2025, Ulster Schools Swimming Championship. Four-hundred metre medley relay. The last two lengths were mine. The memory is still so clear in my head. How I had to sit on the diving board because I felt like I needed to pee, even though I'd gone to the bathroom twenty minutes before. Nerves. Nerves that had been getting worse over the last few months. Twisted stomach and a buzzing in my ears that I'd never had before.

Swimming had always been my solace. The pool was where I knew who I was. The cool water around me, the ache in my muscles reminding me that I was exactly where I was supposed to be. Heaven. And I was good. Not Olympics good, but the best in the school and probably the county. Dad's face when I won. Like I'd just taken away all his stress and there was nothing wrong in the world.

It was our thing. Mine and Dad's. It used to be anyway.

'We've got this, Margot.' Priya squeezed a wet arm round my waist. She'd just finished her breaststroke, and she was out of breath, but still smiling. Priya was the only person I knew who was capable of smiling while competing. Even in the water, when we cheered before her turn for the next length, her toothy grin flashed white under the water.

'Shit. I don't know, they've got Paige Loughran.' I nodded over to the group of Belfast High School girls beside us, and let my eyes settle on Paige, who was stretching her long, muscular limbs while she stared straight up the lane. Focused. 'She's a machine.'

And instead of using this to drive me, like I usually did, the sight of her filled me with doubt. Doubts that had been planted a few months ago and had grown like weeds, taking over my thoughts, distorting them until I didn't know who I was at all.

Priya pushed my shoulder. 'What's got into you? You've *got* this. Now get warmed up, you're next.'

She was right. I *could* do this. I'd beaten Paige before. Twice. I could *do* this. I repeated it in my head over and over in the hope that it would make me believe it. Priya was always there for me. And I was there for her. We didn't hang out that much outside of school, but during those early morning and after-school sessions, Priya was my ride or die. There wasn't much time for anything else anyway.

I watched Ruby butterfly her way down the pool and my stomach lurched. Because that meant I was next.

I glanced over at the stands, like I always did just before my race. I scanned the crowd, looking for him. For Dad's eyes and the smile that would settle my stomach. But I couldn't see him. My eyes darted up, down and across the steps frantically until my gaze was drawn to a commotion.

A crowd forming, around Mum, Dad and my sisters, Rue and Wren.

My eyes fixed on Rue. Her splint was caught in the fold-up plastic seat, and she was screaming in pain. I watched as a man helped Mum release Rue's leg from its trap before she pulled her into a hug. Wren was crying while Dad thanked people around him.

'Margot!' Priya shouted in my ear. I looked down to see Ruby in the water below me, screaming something.

But I couldn't hear anything. I couldn't think. And I couldn't breathe. Not properly.

All I remember is Priya's mouth fall open in horror as I stepped back, away from the diving block. Our chance to qualify, and get a trip to Portugal, gone. Just like that.

All because of me.

I quit the team the next day. And I guess I quit Priya too, because we didn't see each other any more.

She sent me messages, and I ignored them the same way I ignored Coach Nichol's calls to see her in her office. The humiliation was too much.

Then I met Ari and Theo.

One Friday afternoon, when I'd usually be in the pool, I was walking home, and I felt a crushed can hit the back of my head.

'What the hell?' I spun round to see Ari and Theo looking at me. Ari Hamilton, who practically lived in detention, and Theo Burns, who'd been in my English class a few years ago. I wasn't in the mood. And I surprised myself with my hostility.

It was something new. Something that started after I quit the team. In those weeks that followed, when I didn't know what to do with myself.

'Oh, feisty,' said Ari. Her black hair was slicked back from her elegant face, her shirt untucked and her school skirt rolled up so high that it looked like she wasn't wearing one at all.

And even though it was Ari who was talking to me, it was Theo I was drawn to. The sheer size of him. Wide shoulders. Tall. Just standing there with his messy brown hair looking like he couldn't give a shit about anything. And it was that energy, the cool nonchalance that I'd grow to hate, that then made me say 'yeah sure' when Ari asked, 'Want to come to a party, swimmer girl?'

And I guess that was the start of it. My downfall. When Dad's looks of pride turned to disappointment, and then slowly to nothing at all as he focused all his attention on Rue and Wren. And it suited me. I started hanging out with Ari and Theo all the time, and it wasn't long until Theo and I became more than friends. I had an actual boyfriend. Even though I spent more time with Theo *and* Ari instead of just Theo. Time spent at parties Mum and Dad didn't approve of. Time spent drinking alcohol and smoking whatever Ari handed to me.

I was happy.

At least, I thought I was.

1

I'd hoped they'd forgotten about it that afternoon at the start of the summer holidays. But there it was, at the bottom of Theo's bed – the unopened Amazon package, sending me vomit vibes from on top of the navy duvet cover.

'Oh my God I can't wait for this,' Ari said, grabbing the package and ripping it open.

I sat at the top of the single bed, holding Theo's pillow in front of my face, breathing in the smell of him. Lynx Africa, musky, with a hint of lime. The scent that always calmed my heartbeat. But this time, it didn't work.

I shook my head. 'I don't think I can do it. You do it first.'

'No way, you drew the short straw, bitch.' Ari laughed and slid out the box, raising her eyebrows and giving me a deranged smile. She'd tied her poker-straight black hair up in a high ponytail, making her angles even more sharp. The total opposite to my blonde curls, round face and turned-up nose. Other than that, we'd morphed into each other over the last year. Well, I'd morphed into her. Black eye make-up, black nail varnish, chokers, piercings dotted the whole way up our ears. Even our clothes were the same. Band T-shirts, ripped jeans, skin-tight black lace and fingerless gloves. I even straightened my curls, despite Mum's protests.

'It'll be fine, babe,' Theo drawled, sitting on his desk chair in his oversized NFL hoody, blue-jeaned-legs splayed, scrolling through his phone.

'At least hold my hand.' I hid behind the cushion, a last-ditch attempt at convincing them, without actually having to say it, that I really, *really* didn't want to do this.

Theo didn't even look at my outstretched hand. He was laughing at something on his phone.

'Theo, hold her hand! Actually, even better, give her this.' Ari bent down to the floor and rifled in her bag. She pulled out a bottle of tequila.

'Where'd you get that?' I put down the pillow.

'My mum is dead into margaritas at the minute.' Ari shrugged and handed it to me. 'Dutch courage.'

I screwed the cap off the bottle, smelled it and almost retched at the scent. Like one of Dad's socks had been marinated inside. But I took a swig anyway, scrunching up my face and forcing the rancid liquid down my throat.

'We drinking?' Theo spun round, deciding to give us some attention. He smiled at me, wide and bright. I found his eyes. The same brown eyes that made me melt like butter every single time I lost myself in them. Which was a lot.

I pretended to hand him the bottle, then pulled it back. 'You doing it too? Only get to drink if you're taking part.'

'Oh really?' He launched himself on to the bed and kissed my neck, knowing it always made me laugh. I held the bottle up, trying not to let it spill.

'Just give it to him, Marge,' Ari said. The nickname I'd asked her a million times to stop using. It was funny the first time, but after that, it was just annoying.

Theo kept kissing and I kept laughing.

'Theo, Lav is texting you.' Ari held up his phone. 'And he says –'

And just like that Theo was up, snatching his phone from Ari, and sitting back down on his chair.

And now Ari was beside me, opening the box and sliding out the piercing gun. She dumped a bag on my knee and my stomach lurched. 'Choose one.'

My heart was racing again, and I felt like I was going to puke. It wasn't like I hadn't been pierced before. But it had always been at a jeweller's, or at that place at the back of the car park that was mad cheap. DIY piercing was a first. Mum and Dad had just about got used to all my ear piercings, so I'd no idea what they'd think of a hole in my nose. I inhaled, telling myself I didn't care.

I looked at the nose studs in my lap – sparkling diamanté, pinks, blues and clear. I picked up a tiny clear one. 'This one. What do you think?'

'It's *your* nose,' she said, shrugging. 'But yeah, it's nice.'

'What do you reckon, Theo?' I asked, but he was still looking at his phone.

'You ready?' Ari came closer, an alcohol wipe coming towards me. I backed away, my nose burning from the harsh bitterness of the smell.

'Ugh, you do it then.' She threw it on top of me.

I wiped my nose with it, taking way longer than I needed to.

'Theo, put your phone down. Marge needs you.' Ari slapped

his thigh playfully. I hated that I was jealous of the look he gave her. The arched eyebrow and the smile that turned up at one side. The smile that was usually reserved for me.

'It'll only hurt for a second, Margot. I promise.'

I closed my eyes and played him saying my name again. Slow, lazy, smooth. I reached for his hand, while Ari set up the needles.

He laced his fingers through mine. I stared at our hands. I'd always loved the contrast of the size of his hands against mine. He kissed my fingers and his shaggy hair brushed gently against my arm. 'I think it'll look really hot.'

'Really?' I asked.

'Ready!' called Ari, and she moved between us, breaking apart our hands. 'Sorry, I need to get in here.' She snapped the latex gloves, just to make the whole experience even more unpleasant.

I closed my eyes, blood rushing to my head, heartbeat in my ears.

'It'll just take a second.' Ari's finger on my nose, the smell of the gloves reminding me of the dentist.

Snap!

'Fuck!' It felt like someone had stuck a lit match up my nostril.

I reached up and felt the stud. 'Is that it? It's in?' I asked. I looked towards Theo.

'Wow, babe, you look even whiter than usual. Doesn't she, Ari?'

But their words sounded far away, and I was sweating. I needed a drink and felt like I was going to pass out.

Theo leaned in to get a closer look. 'Looks good.'

'Yeah?' I asked, instinctively touching my nose and feeling the metal stud.

'It's all good, bitch. But your phone has been blowing up for the last five minutes.' Ari dropped my phone on to my stomach, and I picked it up.

Six missed calls. From home. Shit.

'My mum and dad,' I said, pulling myself up. 'They're going to hit the roof when they see this.'

'Fuck 'em. We're eighteen. Adults!' Ari scoffed. 'And why are they so anal anyway? We've finished school.'

WhatsApp messages flashed up on the screen.

DAD: Margot where are you? You were supposed to be here an hour ago.

DAD: Come home now!

I sat up. Panicked.

'Shit. Rue's birthday,' I said. I reached up to touch the stud in my nose again, then pulled my hand away because it hurt. 'And I completely forgot. I better go.'

'Sucks for you,' Ari said, grinning.

I stood up and Ari air-kissed me goodbye. I held out my hand to pull Theo to the door with me.

'Don't worry about anything, babe. It'll all be cool.' He kissed me, slow and gentle. And I wanted to believe him.

But I knew nothing about going home right then would be 'cool'.

2

Mum, Dad, Rue and Wren were at the kitchen table eating dinner when I got in. I could smell the spaghetti bolognese from the hall. Rue's favourite. Obviously Wren wasn't eating that. She was eating her trademark chicken nuggets, waffles and beans.

And she was the first one who saw me. She turned in her seat and it was like she was trying to warn me with her big blue eyes to turn round and run back out the door. But I was too slow.

Rue turned round and grinned at me. 'She's home. Dad, you can yell at her now.'

'Girls, please take your dinner into the living room. Then we can have cake after.'

'OK, Dad.' Rue got out of her seat and picked up her plate. She threw me another smug smile and walked slowly and unsteadily across the tiles. Rue's cerebral palsy hadn't been diagnosed until she was three. The tightness in her legs made her unstable, so me and Wren were used to being careful around her. And I'd never admit it out loud, but right then I was ashamed to even think that I was tempted to trip her up and watch the spaghetti bolognese destroy the white walls.

Wren stopped beside me with her dinner. 'Dad's really mad,' she whispered. 'Tell him you didn't do it. Whatever it was. Mum's a little bit on your side,' she whispered.

I winked at her. 'Thanks. I owe you one.'

I heard Rue cackling at the TV from the other room.

'Sit down.' Dad pushed his reading glasses up his nose, like he meant business.

I'd barely sat down before he started talking.

'Family comes first, Margot. You know that. Rue's birthday? You know how much she's been looking forward to having everyone together.'

He was right. She'd been talking about it for weeks.

'Sorry. I forgot.' I shrugged, trying to channel Ari, trying to push back at the injustice. I was eighteen, for God's sake.

'You do a lot of *forgetting* these days. And I dread to think what you're going to get in your A levels. Honestly, Margot, you need to start taking your life seriously.'

I picked up a piece of kitchen roll and started shredding it on the table. 'I was just with my friends.' And that seemed to piss off Dad even more.

'Do you think these are the kind of friends you should have? Ones that are going to drag you down? This isn't you, Margot.' Dad shook his head.

And then I snapped. 'How would you know who I am?'

'Margot,' said Mum.

'I'm serious! Ever since I quit swimming, all you fucking care about is work, and Rue and Wren.'

'Margot! Language!' Dad's voice boomed and Rue stopped laughing from next door.

'You think *they* don't swear?' I pointed towards the living room. 'Rue's eight and is never done calling me a bitch.'

Dad slammed his fist on the table and Mum shot him a look. 'This isn't about them! This is about you! It's your future, Margot, and you're going to ruin it –'

'Margot?' Mum cut in.

I looked at Mum, who was staring at me. At my nose. 'What?'

Dad followed her gaze. 'What is it?' Dad asked her, completely oblivious to the sparkling stud, just like he had been to the multiple ear piercings over the last year.

Mum pointed at her own nose, and I watched his expression darken even more as the penny dropped.

'What is that in your face?' he said, seething.

Shit.

Before I could say anything, Dad stood up. 'Just get out of my sight, Margot. Go to your room. I don't want to see you again until tomorrow. I need to speak to your mother. And I've locked that window, so don't even bother trying to get out that way.'

'Fine!'

I stormed out of the kitchen and slammed the door behind me. My parents were ridiculous. I stomped my way up the stairs, lay down on my bed, shoved my head into my pillow and screamed. Then I pulled it away because it hurt my nose. And when I turned over, I saw Wren staring at me from the doorway, wearing the pink onesie that she got changed into every day after school. She was nine, but everyone treated her like she was younger because, unlike the holy terror that was Rue, she was so sweet. And I guess she leaned into it.

I probably would too if I were her. Her blonde hair hadn't darkened, not like mine and Rue's had. Ours was still light, but not the white blonde of Wren's curls.

'Are you OK, Gogo?' I bit my lip, trying to calm down before I spoke to her. That was Dad's stupid kid nickname for me, and it made my skin crawl every time he used it now. But Wren, Wren could use it.

'I'll be fine, just a bit mad.'

'At Mum and Dad?' She looked like she was going to cry.

'You know how you get mad at Rue sometimes?' I said, pulling myself up and patting the bed beside me. She walked over and curled up next to me.

'Yeah.'

'Well, it's kind of like that. It'll be fine again soon. Mum and Dad just need to get over their tantrum.'

'Like Rue,' she said.

'Just like Rue.'

'She said she's not wearing her night-time splints tonight.' Wren looked worried, an expression that wasn't unusual.

'She's such a brat. She *knows* they'll help.' It was shit that she had to wear them, and it wasn't like my heart didn't sink when she fell or couldn't join in with something, but I couldn't help getting pissed off at the serious favouritism that had existed ever since she was born more than two months early. And if Wren felt it too, she never let it show.

'I just don't think they're very comfortable. I'll go and see if I can convince her.' Wren left me alone with the rage that had been calmed slightly by her presence.

*

The next morning, I went downstairs to everyone eating breakfast at the table. Rue's standing frame was beside her, and when I looked at the anger that darkened her face, I knew it was going to be a huge fight to get her to use it. She was supposed to use it an hour a day. Something to do with posture. Mum was already reaching for the chocolate buttons, her usual bribe.

I sighed – as if I'd ever have been allowed chocolate at breakfast at that age.

'Rue, please. Listen, we're going on holiday tomorrow. Just try and use your frame as much as you can before we go.'

I left before Rue exploded, and just about made it back up the stairs and into my room before I heard her yelling. I phoned Theo.

I lay back on my bed and smiled when his beautiful face filled the screen.

'My mum and dad are freaking out at the minute. About my *future.*' I rolled my eyes. 'I need a hug.' I pulled a sad face.

'Well come and get one tonight. Ari is meeting some of the Birch ones up the Cave Hill, and it's better than listening to my mum yelling at Kobe.'

I could sleep to Theo's voice. Sometimes I played his voicemails on repeat at night, and within a couple of minutes I was drifting off.

'Yeah, I'd love to, but I better lay low tonight.' I wasn't about to admit that Dad had basically locked me in the house. 'They're away on holiday tomorrow for four weeks though, so I'll have a free house,' I said, smirking at him suggestively.

'Awesome. Can't wait to come and keep you company.'

‘Tell me about it.’ I smiled. I rolled on to my side and let my hair fall over half of my face.

‘Are you wearing those cute heart pjs?’ Theo asked.

I lifted the camera high above me and showed him.

‘Mmm,’ he said. ‘It’s a shame I’m not there, but listen, babe, we’ll have all summer together, and Kobe’s mate’s parents have that place in Portrush. We can go down there too, and I’ll teach you how to surf? Forget all about this PG school stuff.’

‘Surf? I don’t do water any more,’ I said, wondering if he would ask me to elaborate, but knowing he wouldn’t. It had been over a year since I’d quit swimming, and he’d never really asked why.

‘You can chill on the beach then, babe.’

A knock at my door.

‘Shit, got to go,’ I whispered and blew him a kiss. He winked into the camera and hung up.

Dad walked into my room, sighing like I didn’t already know he was pissed off at me.

‘Your mother and I had a chat last night. You clearly can’t be trusted to be left alone while the rest of us go on holiday. I’m not leaving this house to be destroyed for four weeks –’

‘I’m not going to Nan’s, she talks to that cat like it’s an actual baby. Super creepy,’ I cut in.

‘You think I’d make Nan have you? No, Margot, you’re coming with us.’

‘To *Eurocamp*?’ I could barely get the words out. He couldn’t possibly mean that he wanted me to go to France with them to Camp Loser.

'To Eurocamp,' he confirmed. 'You're going to spend time with your family and maybe you'll be reminded of what's important in life.'

And I waited until he'd left the room before I screamed into my pillow so hard my throat hurt, as the perfect summer I'd almost had flashed before my eyes.

3

Eurocamp. Could my life *actually* be more embarrassing? Eighteen, not eight. Mum turned round in the front seat of the too-small-for-five-people rental car and motioned for me to take off my earphones. We'd got off the plane in Bordeaux and were now squished into the car on our way to some campsite in Biarritz. The kind of campsite that we'd gone to every summer until I was about nine. And I used to love them. Ten years ago. I'd go to the kids' camps and spend days in the sun doing crafts and playing football, topped off by hours in the swimming pool or on the beach. Then Wren and Rue were born, and it just stopped.

I'd moved as close to the window as possible, but Rue's elbow was still digging into me.

I turned up the music that was blasting into my eardrums.

'Oh, Margot, what is that music?' Mum's face twisted in disgust when she heard it. 'Turn it down please, before they hear that.' As if the precious eight- and nine-year-old ears beside me would be scarred for life if they heard the word 'motherfucker'.

'We're here!' she said to the whole car.

Rue and Wren cheered, and I looked out the window.

Rows of pine trees, mobile home after mobile home, then

a few tents to break up the monotony. A blazing sun cast scattered pockets of light on the dusty lanes, and there were little children *everywhere. God.*

Dad slowed down and stopped at the entrance as some girl on a bike, with a huge smile, blonde hair and a Eurocamp hat spoke to him through the open window. Then we followed her, twisting down a million paths until we pulled up in front of our mobile jail.

'This is us. Home for the next four weeks.' Despite my music, I could hear Dad over it. *Four* weeks. The joy of having parents who were both teachers . . . Way too long to be away from Theo. But maybe that was deliberate. Dad said I'd *changed* since getting a boyfriend, but I think he was mistaking change with growing up. And anyway, I think he was just saying that to try to pretend he was actually still involved in my life. I think he was just mad that I packed in the swimming. And that was nothing to do with Theo.

I waited for them all to get out of the car and checked my phone.

ARI: Hey bitch, can't believe they kidnapped you

ME: I know, ffs.

ARI: Send me pictures

ME: Of what? Tents?

ARI: Wish my parents would kidnap me on holiday

ME: I'd rather be in Belfast. Seriously

Dad poked his head through the open door. 'Margot, give us a hand, please.'

I pulled my earphones down round my neck, so I could still hear the music, and got out of the car as slowly as possible.

Scorching heat hit me in the face, and I recoiled like a vampire. I could hear the chirpy Eurocamper explaining stuff to Dad.

I grabbed my bag from the boot and dragged it inside, wishing they'd just left me at home. I mean, technically, I could have protested more. I was eighteen. An adult. I didn't have to do what they told me. Four weeks was, like, totally excessive, but I guess I'd still have Theo when I got back and we could spend the rest of the summer together, and whatever came after that. My A-level results were going to be a disaster; that I *did* know. I pushed the thought away again, like I'd been doing for months.

'Margot, pick it up, you'll ruin it,' Mum complained. I hauled my bag up, making it look heavier than it was, then chucked it on to the little sofa, dust and all.

Mum sighed. 'This is going to be a long four weeks for everyone if this is your attitude the whole time.'

I winced at the shriek that came out of Wren's mouth. It was going to be an *unbearable* four weeks if I had to listen to those two squealing like banshees the whole time. And my room was right beside theirs. I glanced in as I walked past. Rue had Wren in a headlock. Oh well.

I lay down on the ridiculously small bed. Of course it was hard.

Dad stuck his head round the door frame, then pointlessly knocked.

'We're going swimming, Gogo. Want to come?'

'Don't call me that.' He really needed to let that name fucking go . . . go.

'At least take a walk or something – you've been sitting in that car for ages, we all have. Why don't you go for a dander and meet us back here for pizza at seven?'

I turned away from him on the bed and squeezed my eyes shut.

'Maybe. Might just sleep.'

'Well, suit yourself. I'll take the girls exploring.'

I sighed with relief when they left. Silence except for the sound of Mum pottering around the kitchen. But I finally had some privacy, and now I could FaceTime Theo.

He picked up after the fifth ring, in his bedroom, trusty baseball cap pulled down over his forehead.

'Hey, you,' I said, smiling. 'Well, I'm here. They actually did it. Kidnapped me.' I rolled my eyes and then stared into his, trying to work out if he was stoned or not, but I couldn't get a good look. He was staring at something else.

'Hey, babe,' he said, his voice even slower and more detached than usual. Definitely stoned.

'How was Tina's?' I asked.

'You know, same old . . . Ari's fucking mental.' He smiled like he was remembering something.

'What did she do?' I asked, desperate for anything to take my mind off this stupid holiday.

'Jumped off that pipe into the sea. At midnight. Fucking naked.' He grinned again and my stomach contracted so hard I thought I might throw up.

'Are you serious?'

'Yeah, man, we all did. But she started it. How's Spain?'

'France.'

'Oh yeah, France. Hey, babe, I better go, I'm still wrecked from last night, you know?'

'Sure,' I said, trying to keep the disappointment from showing.

'Bye, Margot.'

'Bye. The–'

But he was gone.

I felt sick. Ari was skinny-dipping with my boyfriend? What the hell?

ME: Ari wtf? Theo said you were all skinny dipping last night?

ARI: Chill, it was a bit of fun. Nothing happened. Possessive much?

ME: He's my boyfriend Ari

ARI: So talk to him about that. People can't be stolen Marge. Not unless they want to be

I could hardly breathe. How could this happen? Why the hell did I leave?

'Margot, why don't you help me clean? I'd like to give it a quick once-over before they get back,' Mum called.

'Nope.' I sprang out of bed, wiped my face, opened my suitcase and took out the first thing I saw. An AC/DC T-shirt long enough to wear as a dress. I got changed and looked in the mirror. I pulled my hair out of its ponytail, and it wasn't straight any more, but wavy in the heat. I tied it up again. I hated Mum right then. *Hated* her. If they hadn't made me leave, I'd have been at Tina's last night too.

'I'm away for a walk,' I said, sniffing away tears and keeping my head down.

'You sure you wouldn't rather stay with me?' Mum didn't even look up from her scrubbing.

'Yeah,' I said and walked outside. I put on my sunglasses. I'd been saving up for the Ray-Ban ones when Mum and Dad stopped my pocket money a while ago after I kept missing curfew, so I had to make do with ones from Primark.

I didn't know where I was going. I hadn't been paying attention when we came in. So I just walked. I swear to God there were kids everywhere. Literally everywhere. Like the worst kind of infestation. A ball came out of nowhere and hit me on the side of the chest.

'Do you mind?' I shouted and kept walking.

'*Pardon*,' a tiny French voice called, but I didn't look at who it came from because I knew they'd be cute, and I'd feel even worse. I was just in such a constant rage these days that not even adorable small people could get me out of it.

I kept walking in the blistering heat until I reached a restaurant/bar thing with red-and-white chequered cloths on the tables.

I sat down under one of the umbrellas and looked around. Everyone was about ten years younger than me or thirty years older. What was I supposed to do here for four weeks? I picked chipped black nail varnish from my fingers and stared at the drinks menu. I went over and over it in my head. What Theo had said. Ari's message. Was there something between them?

'*Vous avez choisi?*' a voice said. I looked up, over my glasses, to see a man standing there. No, not a man; a boy, my age, in a white shirt and black trousers. His hair was fair and wavy, and his eyes were light brown, with flecks of gold that had been missing from Theo's. I thought about taking off my sunglasses to look at him properly, but then he'd see my red eyes.

'*Vous avez choisi?*' he repeated, this time with a smile. The most perfect smile, which drew my eyes to his razor-sharp jawline.

'Sorry, *je ne comprends pas*,' I said, even though I kind of did *comprends*. I'd just done my A-level French exam. And even though the mark would definitely be shite, I'd loved it up until a year ago.

'You have chosen what you would like?' he said in English with that smile, and that *accent*. I tried not to keep looking at him and look at the menu instead, but it was hard. His shirt was fitted so you could see the outline of his biceps, square shoulders . . . that jaw.

'*Vin rouge, s'il vous plait*,' I said, hoping he wouldn't call me out, as if he could possibly know that I didn't even like or know anything about red wine. It was just easy to say in French.

'*Bien sûr*,' he smiled, and his eyes twinkled. I watched him walk away.

My phone buzzed and there was a message from Ella, some girl in my year at school. Why was *she* Snapping me?

I opened it and there she was, with Kylie, peace signs and tongues out. Must have been a mistake. I put the phone down on the table, but something made me pick it up again.

And I wish I hadn't.

I looked more closely at the photo this time. Theo was there, in the background, sitting on someone's couch with Ari sprawled on top of him in a tiny pair of shorts and a backless top.

I turned my phone off and put it face down on the table, then I clamped my hand over my mouth in case the bile that was churning in my stomach somehow made its way up my throat and on to the chequered tablecloth.

Then the tears started again. And I couldn't stop them.

4

When I saw that photo of Theo and Ari, it was like all my worst nightmares were being played out right in front of me. And what shocked me the most was that the intensity of the nausea wasn't just about Theo. Or Ari.

I wasn't *just* seething with jealousy that Ari had taken my boyfriend. The worst thing was that I felt stupid. And I *hated* feeling stupid. I kept getting flashbacks of so many other times we'd hung out. Other parties when Ari and Theo would be whispering about something. Were they wishing I'd leave so they could be alone? And the amount of time they *were* alone. I tried to force myself to stop thinking about it, but every single thought led back to them and the mess that was my life. I scrolled to our WhatsApp group messages, my hands shaking with rage. Me, Ari and Theo.

> **ME:** Well, Ella's Snap was a fun way to find out. Really classy doing it where everyone could see. Thanks for the heads up . . .

I posted a screenshot of Ella's message and watched as the ticks turned blue. Both of them had read it. I stared at the screen, waiting for someone to reply. But there was nothing. Not even any typing, and no private messages either. And just like that, I'd made myself feel even worse.

Almost without thinking, I scrolled to my last message from Priya. About a year ago, she'd sent me message after message, trying to convince me to come back to swimming. Until one day, the messages just stopped. Suddenly, I missed her. The way she smiled so much, making everything bad feel like it wasn't the end of the world.

I took off my sunglasses and squeezed my palms into my eye sockets, willing the tears to go away, because crying in public, alone, was almost as bad as feeling stupid. I took a deep breath and twisted an escapee blonde wave in my fingers. I glanced around at the couples, the families, speaking French, English, Dutch and wondered how they could all look so happy. It reminded me of Mum, Dad, Wren and Rue, how from the outside they just looked like this perfect little family. Wren and Rue with their blonde curls and the way Mum and Dad laughed so easily with them, playing games and talking about the future. And then there was me. I looked like I should fit. Long legs, blue eyes, blonde curls, just like them. But I didn't. I was the spare part that thought she was happy until Theo threw a grenade. I picked more nail varnish.

'*Vin rouge?*'

I glanced up to see the waiter looking down at me with a smile. I hid my messy nails under the table and his expression changed to concern as he studied my face.

'You are OK?' he asked.

'I'm fine,' I said, looking away. Despite how good-looking he was, I wasn't in the mood to talk. I just wanted him to go away.

But he wasn't going anywhere. 'Can I?' He motioned to the chair opposite me and set the glass of wine on the table.

I shrugged as he sat down.

'I can help?' he asked.

I shook my head and put my sunglasses back on. 'I'm fine, seriously.'

'You are sure?' he said gently. He leaned in close, bare forearms on the table, one knee touching mine underneath.

I nodded. 'I just got dumped.' I tried to laugh, but a strangled noise came out instead. I don't even know why I said it out loud. It was *so* embarrassing, but I had nobody else to talk to, and there was something about this place, his presence, that felt like shelter.

His forehead creased and he tilted his head in confusion. 'Dumped?'

'Ah sorry, my boyfriend ... We aren't together any more,' I explained, feeling a wave of nausea churn in my stomach. I mimed my head exploding and tried to force a laugh.

'Ah, I understand. *Se faire larguer*, we say in France.'

'Good to know, I guess.' I took a sip of bitter wine.

'What is your name?' He moved his chair closer, so he was beside me now instead of opposite. 'Sorry to be so close, I am trying to keep out of sight of Yves.' He nodded towards a man in his sixties with thick, dark hair and wearing an apron, then shielded his eyes and grinned at me with straight white teeth.

I noticed that he smelled like food and aftershave, lavender, vanilla, but in a masculine way.

'Margot,' I answered, barely.

'*C'est jolie*,' he said, 'like you.' And I couldn't help but smile. 'English?'

'Irish. Northern Irish actually,' I replied.

'I went to Dublin once,' he said. The same thing everybody says if you tell them you live in the North. 'How long are you staying here?'

'Four weeks.' I held up four fingers as if he wouldn't understand four even though he clearly spoke almost perfect English. 'What about you?'

He smiled. 'I work here, so, all of the summer.'

I was about to ask him his name when an angry male voice called from somewhere behind the bar.

'Felix!'

'*Merde*, he has found me,' he whispered, then smiled at me again. 'I must go. But maybe you will return? Tonight? I work until midnight.' He backed away, looking right into my sunglasses.

'Maybe,' I said, even though I had no intention of returning tonight. As lovely as he seemed, and looked, my head was filled with Theo and Ari, and it was hot with rage.

'Felix,' I whispered to myself. It was a nice name.

I finished my wine, left some Euros on the table, and got up from my seat. I thought about going back to the mobile home, but I wasn't ready yet, so I turned in the opposite direction, following a little wooden sign to *la plage*.

The air smelled different here. Hot, salty, the scent of the pine trees in the breeze. I could already hear the rush of waves on the shore. And even though I had been avoiding the water, *any* water since my swimming disaster, I'd always loved the sea.

It was further than I thought, down the sandy lane. But then I turned a corner and there it was. Miles of perfect beach. The sun was low and getting ready to set.

I watched kids running into the sea, couples sunbathing, topless women just walking about like it was entirely normal. Fair play to them. I don't think I'd ever have the balls to do that; I shuddered at the image of trying it and my dad somehow seeing.

I looked down the beach and saw a blue hut with multicoloured surfboards lined up outside. A guy was setting them on a rack. Even though he was far away, I could see how dark his hair was, and the tattoos on his bare chest. I sat and watched him until he disappeared into the hut and out of sight. Dad had mentioned something about this area being good for surfing, and like everything Dad said to me these days, it hadn't really registered, but there *was* something inviting about the coloured boards catching the day's last rays. Then I remembered Theo's offer of teaching me to surf, and it was like someone hit a dimmer switch on the sun.

I took out my phone and scrolled through the photos of me and Theo. Theo with his smooth brown hair and eyes so dark I got lost in them. Everyone fancied Theo. Including Ari clearly. I could feel the tears coming again, but I stopped them, pushing the sand hard with my foot, digging my toes into the warmth and staring out at the sun setting over the Atlantic coast. Then my phone buzzed.

DAD: Coming back Gogo? We have pizza

ME: 👍

I pulled myself to my feet and gazed out to sea again before walking back through the camp to try to find our mobile home.

Rue and Wren were kicking a football in front of our place. Rue was wearing her new Man United kit.

'You're shit, Wren,' Rue yelled at her.

Wren's face scrunched and she toe-poked the ball back in Rue's direction.

'Shut up!'

I messed up Rue's hair when I walked past her and kicked the ball from under her feet. 'You're shit too.'

'I am not,' said Rue.

'Pizza, everyone!' Dad called, way too cheerily, from the doorway. Mum had set the plastic table with knives and forks and glasses. There were boxes of pizza piled in the middle.

'I thought we could play a game,' Dad said when we sat down.

'No thanks,' I said, stuffing my mouth with pizza.

'What game?' Wren asked, a goofy, hopeful smile on her face.

'Why don't we all say something we're grateful for,' Dad suggested.

I pretended to retch.

'Margot,' said Mum.

'OK, I'll start,' said Dad. 'I'm grateful for being in southwest France with my lovely family.'

'Oh God, Dad. This isn't a *game.*' I cringed.

'I mean it,' he said.

'What about you, Wren?' Dad asked, looking at her. She glanced up from under the peak of her hat.

'I'm grateful for Rue and Margot, because I never get to see Margot at home, and here she might talk to me more.' And she meant it. Wren never said anything she didn't mean. And yeah, I felt shit. But it wasn't my fault Mum and Dad had left such a big age gap. Sorry, but I didn't want to spend my weekends hanging out with kids.

'She will, love,' said Mum, and Wren smiled so hard it must have hurt her face. Mum looked at me pointedly.

'Course I will. If you want to talk about how cool I am.' I stuck my tongue out at her and hoped she couldn't feel the fakeness of it all.

'My turn!' shouted Rue, then she almost knocked over her bottle of Orangina. 'I'm grateful for Orangina, because we only drink it on holiday, and it feels special.'

'That's nice, Rue.' Mum smiled at her.

'I'm grateful for this lovely weather,' said Mum. Coward.

'And you, Gogo?' Dad asked.

'I'm seriously *begging* you to stop calling me that,' I said, frustrated. 'What am I grateful for? I'm grateful for the fact that my parents have taken me away to a stupid campsite for *four* weeks. The kind of place that's impossible to enjoy unless you're Rue's age. Oh wait . . . I think I got the game wrong.'

I stood up and picked up a bit of pizza before walking away, back across the campsite, with Wren calling after me. I headed towards the Brasserie, because I didn't know where else to go.

What were they thinking? I never should have agreed to this. I kicked the stupid little bits of bark that lined the paths and got some stuck under my flip-flop.

It wasn't always like this. This weird disconnect with my family. Everything used to make more sense.

I kicked the ground again and kept walking away from the mobile home. Away from them.

I needed a distraction.

From whatever my life was now.

5

At the Brasserie, staff were clearing a space by moving chairs and tables out of the way, leaving a few around the edge. I stopped for a moment just to watch, tightening my ponytail hard enough to hurt. I lingered and listened to the voices around me. There was something soothing about the lilt of French speech, even if I didn't really understand what they were saying.

Then I saw him again. Felix. He was talking to a girl with the kind of brown hair that looked caramel in the evening light. Her hair matched his. I wondered if she was his girlfriend. Or sister maybe. Her limbs were long, graceful and tanned. The kind of girl that Ari would feel the need to point out a million non-existent flaws in just to make herself feel better. I struggled to see any at all. She was gorgeous. I watched them chat easily, moving tables, laughing and eventually hugging, before Felix spotted me and I had to try to pretend I hadn't been staring at them for the last few minutes.

I turned and walked away, planning to go to the beach again to watch the sun set over the Atlantic, where I could get lost in my thoughts. I shook my head in embarrassment and sped up. Then I heard footsteps behind me.

'Margot?'

I turned to see Felix standing there.

'Oh, hi,' I said with a stupid little wave.

'You would like to stay for the show?' He said it like a statement but raised his voice in question at the end. He pushed his hand through his wavy, sandy hair, looking away briefly before meeting my gaze again with soft brown eyes.

'The show?' I asked, confused.

'Yes, some nights, we have a show.'

I looked back at the Brasserie and a load of families with tiny children were walking towards it. A group of children were sitting in a semicircle in front of the cleared space.

'What kind of show?' I asked.

'For the children,' he replied. And he didn't look embarrassed or annoyed or anything like it. He actually looked happy.

'Are you in it?' I asked. Intrigued.

'You can wait and see?' he said and shrugged, smiling.

And I couldn't think of anything to say. *No, I can't because I'm too busy feeling sorry for myself and would rather go to the beach and be miserable alone.*

'OK,' I said, telling myself that I'd send a message to Mum and Dad when I'd sat down somewhere to tell them to bring the girls. They'd love this kind of thing.

'Great!' He grinned then, like he couldn't help it. And it felt nice. That something I said provoked a smile like that. There was a flash of Theo then. How, when I used to kiss him, I'd trace his jawline, feeling it move beneath my fingertips. 'Come,' he said and nodded his head back towards the restaurant.

'OK,' I said again, because it was better than any other option I had.

'I need to finish the set-up. Sit here. It is the best seat in the house.' Felix winked, then led me to a little table near the bar, where I could see everybody but not everyone could see me. Perfect.

'I can get you a drink?' he said.

I slid my hand into my empty pocket. I'd been in such a mood when I left. 'I forgot my purse. It's fine, I'm OK.'

'I will pay,' he smiled easily. 'Red wine?'

'Ah, *merci*. Could I maybe try something else?' I smiled with gratitude. It was such a stark contrast to nights out with Theo, who'd always 'forget' his wallet.

'*Avec plaisir*,' he answered, smiling. 'I will bring you a surprise.'

He left and came back in about five minutes with a champagne flute that was filled with something purple.

'Kir royale. It is *crème de cassis* and champagne. *Cassis* is blackcurrant.'

I picked it up and took a sip. The sweet, fruity bubbles were delicious.

'That is so nice,' I said, smiling.

Then he leaned down and whispered in my ear. 'But in exchange, you must stay for the whole show.'

His breath was hot, his accent making my own breath catch in my throat. I wasn't ready for this. My insides were still spiky and raw. Every thought digging something needle-like into my heart. But I couldn't help being intrigued by him and how openly nice he was. With Theo it had always been an effort. Just trying to get him to be nice to me so I could have this fabricated feeling in my stomach. The one I'd invented by a forced compliment.

'I'll stay,' I said, watching him as he walked away. I sipped the Kir royale, feeling my rage dilute.

I watched Felix as he bent over and picked up a table like it was nothing but cardboard. His sleeves were still rolled up and I found myself gazing at his forearms, where the tendons strained.

I listened to him shout something in French across the bar, then laugh at the reply. His whole face lit up, and I forced Ari and Theo completely out of my head.

The whole bar area was full now and they'd made a little stage. The staff had disappeared, including Felix. All the kids were talking to each other excitedly.

I scanned the crowd and spotted Wren on a little chair. I felt a flash of guilt that I'd forgotten to text Mum and Dad about the show, but here they were anyway. She was in the front row, and there was Rue beside her, looking sullen. Probably because she was sitting on a chair when all the other kids were on the ground. She hated anything that made her stand out like that. But Rue and Wren being here also meant Mum and Dad were here somewhere. I moved my chair even further back out of view.

Then the music started. Deep bass beats that vibrated the ground. Wren's face was a picture; she was so excited. She wasn't like me and Rue. We were cut from the same cloth. Wren saw all this fun and beauty in everything. Must be nice to be like that.

I only looked away because the staff had started to come

on to the stage. Well, I presumed it was the staff. They were all dressed up in ridiculous animal outfits. I tried to work out which one Felix was. The dog? The lion? The pig? Then I saw his trainers. The black-and-white checked Vans. The lion. And it was hilarious, watching him dance the way he did. They must have been so hot in there. I drank my champagne and watched the whole show just like I'd been told. And I didn't think about Theo or Ari once.

My phone buzzed.

> **DAD:** Where are you? We came out after you made a scene. Join us at the bar if you'd like to spend time with your family.

I ignored it and shifted my chair further away from the crowd. Felix was good at dancing, and the kids were absolutely loving it. I sat there until everybody started leaving, keeping my head down as I watched Rue and Wren get up and look for Mum and Dad.

> **DAD:** We're going back to the mobile home now, what are you doing?

I ignored his message again and picked up my glass, making my way behind the bar, out of the eyeline of Rue and Wren.

Then I felt a hand touch my waist, and I jumped.

'Wow!' I said.

'Did I scare you?' I turned round to see a lion talking to me.

'Felix?' I asked, cocking my head and trying to look through the little eye holes.

He pulled off his lion head and revealed a beautiful, sweaty, smiling face.

'You liked the show?' he asked, wiping his forehead with his paw.

'I did. I liked the dancing,' I said.

'You like to dance?' He took my hand and twisted me round, catching me off guard and making me smile.

'*Peut-être*,' I replied.

'Ah you *do* speak French,' he teased.

'*Un petit peu*.' I smiled, thanks to the champagne.

'You will come back tomorrow?' His eyes were wide. Eager.

'*Peut-être*,' I repeated, sticking to the words I was brave enough to use.

'I hope you will. I will be here, working. I think I must go and get out from this costume.' Felix sucked air in, filling his cheeks, and blew it out like a deflating balloon. 'I am very hot.'

Yes, he was.

I leaned against the wooden post that was attached to the bar and watched him as he peeled the lion costume halfway down. And then he was just standing there topless, and I couldn't help but stare. Toned, tanned, muscles more defined because of the sweat and breathlessness.

'Felix!' The girl from earlier appeared from behind and pushed him playfully. He turned and enveloped her in a sweaty hug, and I was surprised at how much I wanted them to separate. They were laughing and she was twisting her hair in her fingers. The worst part? She was even more gorgeous close up. And in a totally European way, which made it almost unbearable. Shiny brown hair pulled into the perfect messy bun, strands framing her heart-shaped face and from what I could see, barely any make-up. Her long, tanned legs escaped from tiny denim shorts, with delicate sockless ankles above trainers.

I obviously wasn't being very subtle because suddenly both of them were looking at me.

'Margot, this is Delphine. Delphine, this is Margot. She is from Ireland. Northern Ireland,' he corrected himself and I gave an awkward wave in Delphine's direction. She was looking me up and down, eyes settling on my AC/DC T-shirt.

She put her hand over her mouth and whispered something to Felix, who said something back to her in French.

'*Salut*,' I said awkwardly.

Delphine shrugged and walked off.

'Sorry about that,' said Felix, still half dressed. 'She is always like this at the beginning of tourist season. When the foreign girls come.' He rolled his eyes and pulled down the rest of the lion costume.

'Ah, OK,' I said, trying to take the disappointment from my voice. I was one of a million foreign girls – of course I was. And he was . . . I lost my train of thought as I glanced down. At the boxer shorts that left nothing to the imagination, at the Calvin Klein waistband and the dark hair of his thighs.

Then he pulled on jeans and a T-shirt as he continued. 'Delphine. She has a problem with, how do you say it . . . *jalousie*?'

'Jealousy?'

'That's it.'

'But what has she got to be jealous of?' I asked. Felix was now wiping sweat off himself with a towel. 'She is so beautiful.'

'Maybe she doesn't like me talking about you,' he said, shrugging.

'You were talking about me?' I asked, moving closer so I didn't have to shout over the music.

'Maybe. Just a bit.' He winked at me again, and I smiled, pathetically.

'Margot, there you are!'

I turned to see Dad staring at me, looking painfully serious.

'I was worried about you,' he said.

I felt my face flush with shame. I looked at Felix, who was tidying away glasses now.

'Dad, I'm eighteen.' I tried to laugh it off, but Dad wasn't laughing.

'Yes, Margot, I know that, but I'd still like to know where you are.'

'I'll be back soon,' I said.

'I'll wait up,' Dad said, before turning and walking away, leaving me standing there, humiliated, with Felix.

'So embarrassing,' I said, wishing he hadn't heard any of that.

'Your father? He just wants to keep you safe,' Felix said simply, as if it was completely reasonable.

'He thinks because I'm here he can treat me like a kid. It's so stupid.'

Felix shrugged. 'It is nice, I think. Do you want me to walk you back?' he offered. And it felt good. Different. But I wanted some time to think, even though I knew exactly where my thoughts would land.

I shook my head. 'I'll be OK by myself thanks.'

'I will see you tomorrow then?' He raised his eyebrows hopefully.

'*Peut-être*,' I said with a smile that he returned.

'*Je l'espère*,' he replied and pushed a strand of hair behind my ear. 'Sorry, it was in front of your eyes. You have beautiful eyes.'

It was too dark for him to see me blush. But I did. The whole way home.

6

'Croissant?' said a voice, pulling me from some weird dream the next morning. Someone was bouncing on my bed. I opened my eyes to see Rue about to land on my leg. And she was wearing her splints today so it would have been insanely painful if she succeeded.

'Get off,' I said and moved out of the way.

Rue launched a croissant at my face.

'We're going to the beach today and Dad says you're coming.' She slid carefully off the bed.

'Fine,' I sighed.

I knew there was no arguing with Dad when he was like this. And true to his word, he'd waited for me last night and made me promise that I'd spend some time with them. So I got up, had a shower and put on my black bikini.

'I can see your bum, you know,' said Wren when I walked into the kitchen to look for suncream.

'Lucky you,' I said, impatiently. Then felt bad. 'I like your swimsuit,' I said, knowing that Mum had finally given in to the pink Adidas one she'd been coveting for ages.

'Really? Thanks, Gogo.' She grinned.

I hung back as we walked to the beach. Mortifying. This big family walk together. Dad carrying a bag of towels and floats that were almost bigger than he was.

Passing the Brasserie, I saw Felix immediately. White T-shirt today with black jeans. His arms looked even more tanned in the morning light. He was talking animatedly to a table of people, and they were smiling back at him. I slowed down without thinking.

'Margot, come on!' Dad called.

I'd put on a dress over my bikini. And I told myself it was just because I liked the way the racer back exposed my shoulder blades, but I'd be lying if I said I hadn't been thinking of Felix too, and how I wanted to look nice in case I ran into him again. I remembered the way he'd looked at me yesterday. Slowly, like he was taking all of me in. The way he ran his eyes up my legs and how they hovered on my lips, making me wonder what it would be like to kiss him.

Hot sand seeped into the space between my feet and my flip-flops, burning me.

When I reached the end of the sandy lane, I took a minute to look out at the sea. Miles of beach. Way more crowded than yesterday evening. Kids *everywhere.*

I glanced over to see Rue and Wren walking towards the sea and Mum and Dad ambling slowly towards the sand dunes, probably trying to find some shade. I moved as slowly as possible after them, then changed direction and followed Rue and Wren to the water.

I stood at its edge and let the foam rush over my feet as the girls splashed each other in the shallows. I looked out at the waves and watched the surfers. The guy with tattoos from the hut yesterday was here again, in the sea up to his waist, instructing a bunch of kids on little multicoloured surfboards. He was laughing with them. I couldn't see his face, but I could hear him shouting good-naturedly in French. His tattoos almost covered his whole back, stretching over wide shoulders, tracing down his lean waist. Some with words I couldn't read, some just patterns.

'*Allez sur le sable!*' he called, and immediately the kids moved towards the shore, dragging their boards behind them once they reached the sand. I watched as he congratulated them, high-fiving each one as they walked past, and noticed how big their smiles were.

Rue and Wren had noticed them too. They came to my side.

'We want to do that, Margot.' Rue pointed at all the kids, lining up their surfboards on the rack beside the hut.

And just as she said it, he turned round. Dark hair, aviators, perfect child-friendly smile. 'You want to learn to surf?' he called. He walked over to Rue and Wren and bent down on his haunches. Rue's level.

'You can swim?'

'Yep.' Rue and Wren both nodded but he looked at me for confirmation. 'I'm really good,' added Rue.

'They can swim,' I confirmed.

Rue and Wren had gone to the same swimming club as me, but didn't do as much as I had, and it was different for Rue. She had a special coach and everything. But they *were* both good swimmers.

'And *you* can swim?' He was looking at me over his aviators and gave me a half smile. And the words were in my head, but they wouldn't come out. They couldn't come out. He was beautiful. The stubbled jawline, the intricate tattoos that decorated his hard chest . . . I found my eyes settling on one beautiful work of art before being drawn to another.

'Margot, why aren't you talking?' Rue said and punched my leg.

'That hurt!' I nudged her back but was glad of the distraction. 'Sorry, yeah, I can swim.' I shrugged.

'So, *les filles*, you want to learn to surf?' He was looking at Rue and Wren again, who both nodded enthusiastically. I tried to force myself not to look at his chest again, but the way the water dripped down off his hair and into the grooves of his abs made it impossible to tear my eyes away.

'*Bon! On commence demain.* Ten o'clock?' He looked at me as Rue and Wren walked off towards Mum and Dad.

'My name is Antoine. Tell them at reception you want to pay for surf lessons with Antoine. *Not* Delphine.' Delphine? I wondered if it was the same one as from the Brasserie.

'OK,' I said.

'And you?' he asked. The cheery tone that he'd used with Rue and Wren had disappeared into the searing-hot air. The way he spoke reminded me of Theo – unbothered, almost uncaring. It pissed me off.

'What about me?'

'*You* want to learn?'

'No.' My eyes flicked to the sea, bringing back memories of everything I'd left behind.

He made a noise. A sort of exhalation, accompanied by a

shrug before looking me up and down. 'Ah, OK, *Princesse*.' And when he smirked like he had me all figured out, fire filled my veins.

Ari called me Princess sometimes, and it had always annoyed me. Usually when I didn't want to do something, like drink Buckfast in the park or get my belly button pierced.

'I'm not a princess,' I said. 'And I can probably swim better than you.' I wondered why he had been so friendly to Rue and Wren and was treating me like this.

He grinned at that, then shook his head. 'I do not think so.'

'Well *you* think a lot of yourself,' I said, squeezing my toes into the sand. Hard.

He shrugged. 'I have experience.' He turned away from me and started to walk up the beach towards the little hut.

I couldn't believe what I was hearing. He'd just decided what I was like from looking at me?

'You don't know anything about me,' I raged to the back of his head.

'OK, *Princesse*,' he called.

I turned back towards the sea with a furious knot in my stomach.

I didn't follow Rue and Wren, who were sitting beside Mum and Dad; I pulled off my dress and sandals, threw them on to the sand, then walked deep into the water to cool down.

7

I didn't even hesitate as I felt the cool waves splash around my hot skin. Despite the fact I hadn't been in water since the day of that swim gala, the need to show this guy how wrong he was took over completely. I dived in and closed my eyes, enjoying the shock of the cold, my body remembering the water like I'd never turned my back on it.

How dare he speak to me like that. I swam out into the ocean with strong, sure strokes. Then I stopped, started treading water and looked back towards the beach. I could see Mum, Dad, Rue and Wren laughing about something. Then I glanced at the surf hut and there he was, just standing there, watching me from the sand. Who was he calling Princess? I swam along the beach, back and forth, careful not to go out too far. I did length after length along the same stretch, clearing my head, the anger diluting with every stroke.

When I finished, my muscles were aching in a familiar way. I emerged from the water and squeezed the salt water from my hair. I glanced up and saw the guy still watching me. I turned away, picked up my dress and sandals, and walked towards Mum and Dad.

'Looking good out there, Margot,' Dad said.

'Yeah, thanks.' I sat down on a towel on the sand beside Rue and Wren. I wasn't going to say it out loud, but I felt amazing.

'What's this about surf lessons?' Mum asked.

'Yeah, they do lessons here. That guy is going to teach the girls.'

'Oh yeah? I think that's a great idea,' she said, looking at Dad, who was looking out to the sea.

'You'll be with the girls, Margot?' he asked.

'I'll be with them.' I rolled my eyes. Like obviously, I wasn't going to send them off alone with some asshole, even if it did look like he was amazing with kids.

'You don't want lessons too?' Dad asked. I could tell by the softness of his tone that he was treading carefully.

'Nope,' I said simply.

Dad gave me his credit card, and I went via the camp reception on the way home. He'd offered to do it himself, but the swim had lightened my mood. When I got there, two blonde girls were laughing with each other in Eurocamp uniforms.

'Hello.' One of the girls gave me a huge grin when she saw me.

'Hi. Can I book surf lessons, please? With Antoine.'

'Of course,' she said, smiling, and the other one flicked something up on the computer. 'What is your name?'

'Well, actually, it's for my sisters. Rue and Wren Ryan. They're eight and nine.'

'Ah, OK. Antoine has space in his ten o'clock class – would you like this? One hour, Monday to Friday? You need to be there thirty minutes before each lesson.'

'Perfect.' I grinned, still buzzing from the water.

The second blonde girl typed something in the computer, took Dad's credit card details and I walked towards the door.

I headed back to the mobile home, found the key that Dad had badly hidden under a cup on the table and went inside. Dad had said they'd be right behind me, but I guess they were still at the beach.

A flash of disappointment consumed me, like I missed them or something. So I grabbed some Euros from the counter and went for a walk, and the feeling disappeared. Soon, I found myself at the miniature supermarket.

I hadn't been in a French supermarket for nine years, but as soon as I walked through the doors, it all came flooding back. The smells. The fish, the cheese, the sweet fruit that tasted so much better than it did back home. I picked up a paper bag and filled it with some peaches.

'You should smell them first,' said a voice behind me.

I spun round, and there he was. Felix from the Brasserie.

'Smell them?' I asked with a smile.

'*Les pêches.*' He reached into my paper bag and took out one of my peaches, bringing it to his nose and inhaling deeply.

'The ones that are ready have the best smell.' He put it back in my bag.

'Thanks, that's good to know.'

We ambled around the shop as I picked up pieces of fruit, smelling them just like he'd shown me. And now that he had, I noticed loads of people doing the same thing.

'You were at the beach? It was busy?' Felix asked, as he eyed my wet hair.

'Very busy. I signed my sisters up to do surf lessons tomorrow.' I picked up an orange and held it to my nose, breathing in the sweetest citrussy smell. I got another bag and put the orange in. 'Do you surf?' I asked when he hadn't said anything.

He just shook his head as he picked up another orange, examining it as if it was taking all of his concentration and he couldn't spare any for our conversation. The way he looked, lost in thought about an orange, made me smile.

And then he was back. 'How old are your sisters?' he asked, putting his orange into my bag. 'It is a good one,' he added, nodding at the fruit.

'Eight and nine.' I shook my head with a smile.

'It is nice to have sisters, no?' We'd found ourselves standing beside the bakery section. I walked over to the glass counter and looked in at all the perfect little desserts.

'Sometimes. Do you have any?' I hoped he'd look up at me with those brown eyes.

'No,' he said simply. 'My favourite is *le mille-feuille*.' He pointed at a rectangular iced pastry through the glass.

'It looks really good.' I salivated.

'*Deux mille-feuilles, s'il vous plait*,' Felix said to the woman behind the counter. She put them in a little brown bag for him and we walked again, moving out of the way for other shoppers in the little aisles.

'Do you surf?' I asked again, because I don't know, this image of us at the beach together just flashed in my head.

'I do not go to the beach. But you are hungry?' he said with a smile that made me immediately forget to ask why the beach was off limits.

'Starving,' I said.

'You will come to the Brasserie? I will make you whatever you like.' His smile was so inviting that it was impossible to say no.

'Sure,' I said.

We paid and walked back the way I'd come. When we got to the bar, Felix pulled out a chair for me and handed me a menu.

I stared at it. 'What should I have?' I asked.

'Do you like seafood?' His eyes sparkled when he looked at me and I had to catch my breath.

'I do.'

'*Moules frites*,' he said with certainty.

'*Bien sûr*,' I said, promising myself that I'd at least *try* to say something other than *merci* and *bien sûr* while I was here.

He disappeared into the kitchen and came out fifteen minutes later holding a steaming bowl of mussels and a plate of chips. He carried them to a table in the corner and I followed him.

'The orange.' He pointed to one of the brown bags I'd set on the table. 'You should eat it for breakfast tomorrow, with some coffee. But no milk.' He sat down opposite me. 'The contrast. It will make both taste better.'

'Oh my God, like Cécile!' From *Bonjour Tristesse*. That's what she eats. We'd read the Françoise Sagan book this year in class. I was delighted with myself, remembering something from a class I'd barely paid attention in for a year.

He looked pleasantly surprised at my outburst. '*J'avais dix-sept ans et j'étais parfaitement heureuse.*'

'I was seventeen and perfectly happy!' I grinned – at least I remembered the first line. 'You've read it?'

'Many times. *Cécile et sa voyage découverte de soi.*'

I cocked my head in confusion.

'Cécile and her journey of self-discovery,' he translated.

'Self-discovery. That's relatable,' I said with a laugh.

'What do you mean?' Felix immediately looked interested.

'I don't know. I think I've kind of forgotten who I am. Maybe, I don't know . . .' I shook my head, suddenly embarrassed.

'And where is better than the French coast to discover yourself again?' He smiled, with no judgement, sincere.

Then something in me relaxed. Something I didn't even realize was so tightly wound, that loosening it meant everything inside me felt . . . lighter.

'How long have you worked here?' I asked. His leg brushed against mine under the table, but he didn't move it out of the way, so I just let my knee rest against his, feeling the warmth of his skin against mine.

'Not long. Last summer, this summer. Before that, I worked at the market, but now I only help my mother sometimes,' he said.

'What does she do?' I asked, interested in a life so different to mine.

I chose a mussel and pulled opened the shell.

'She makes, how do you say, *du savon*?' His brow was creased in concentration.

'Soap! I know that one.' I smirked, and he laughed.

'Of course. She sells soap and I help at the market in Saint-Jean-de-Luz. It must sound very boring to you.' He looked down at the plate and put a chip in his mouth.

I nudged his leg under the table, and he looked up at me.

'It's not boring at all. It's so different to Belfast. I mean, the sun for a start. We spend so much time inside because it's so cold.'

He laughed at that. 'The sun is nice.'

My gaze landed on his lips as he ate a mussel, balancing the shell on his bottom lip and pulling it into his mouth with his teeth. I'd never been jealous of a mussel before.

He picked up a closed shell. 'Do not eat these ones. The ones that are not open.' He set it on the table and ate another open one. 'You are close with your family?'

'A bit. I don't know, we used to be closer. But now my parents think I'm a bit of a waste of space.' I shrugged and selected a mussel, focusing on the salt and garlic that exploded in my mouth.

'*Et mon cul, c'est du poulet?*' Felix said it loudly and I'd no idea what he meant so I just laughed.

'What?'

'In English, it translates as "My ass is chicken"? It means, "I don't believe you".' His brown eyes were sparkling again as he beamed at me.

'That's hilarious. And they didn't teach us *that* expression at school.'

'*Tu l'as étudié?*' he asked, pronouncing each word slowly instead of running them into each other.

'*Oui.*' I replied.

'Of course, you told me that you read Sagan. We must learn more. I will teach you.' Felix reached for my hand, with its chipped black nails and still painfully white skin.

'*La main*,' he said.

'I knew that one.'

He touched each of my fingers, gently. '*Les doigts.*' Then he turned my hand over and laid it on the table. Then he traced the lines of my palm. '*Les lignes de la main.*'

Then he took my hand again and raised the back of it to his mouth, kissing it gently. His lips warm and soft on my skin. 'And this? *Bisous*,' he said, looking right into my eyes.

'*Bisous*,' I repeated. And it felt different from the other French words I'd been saying.

'Or sometimes we say "*embrasser*".' He'd lowered his voice to a whisper. And he'd moved closer to me, leaning on his elbows.

'*Embrasser*,' I said, feeling the weight of each syllable melt on my tongue.

8

Then the moment was shattered by an angry French voice.

'Felix!'

We broke apart and Felix looked up. We turned to see his boss, Yves, yelling at Felix from across the Brasserie and waving his hands around.

'*Merde*,' Felix whispered. 'I have to get back to work.' He smiled at me apologetically. 'And I am working tonight, but tomorrow, I was thinking we could maybe go somewhere. For a date?'

'A date?' I said, more shock than a question. A grin escaped, and Felix matched it before Yves yelled across the Brasserie again.

'Felix!'

'I have to go.' Felix put his hands on my arms and kissed me on both cheeks before turning away briefly, speaking in French to Yves. 'But quickly. Give me your number and I will send you a message.'

We exchanged phone numbers, and then he jogged off towards Yves.

I watched him for a moment, how he spoke to his boss and the way Yves' demeanour changed as Felix talked to him. After five minutes, they were both laughing, and I couldn't help smiling in their direction.

As I turned away, I caught Delphine's eye. She was clearing a table of plates, balancing three of them on her arm. Her gaze flicked towards mine and I swear she rolled her eyes again. Whatever.

I walked back to the mobile home, where I could hear Rue shouting before I even went inside.

And I guessed what it would be about. Her splints.

Rue was mostly good about wearing them, but sometimes she just exploded about it, because sometimes they rubbed, or sometimes she didn't want to be different to anyone else. And I understood, we all did. But that didn't mean it wasn't a pain in the ass to deal with.

'I'm not wearing them!' Rue shouted and launched a splint across the tiny living room, nearly hitting me as I walked through the door.

'Rue, love, you'll be doing lots of walking, they help your legs.' Mum pleaded with her while Dad picked up the splint and Wren just sat beside her, looking sad.

'I don't care,' Rue said through tears.

This wasn't how Rue worked. You couldn't plead with her. You couldn't show weakness. Rue responded to deals.

I sat down beside her.

'What if I message Lexie to see if her boyfriend is setting up that disability football team at their club that she talked about?' I asked. Rue idolized our cousin Lexie.

And I could tell by the way her breathing changed that I had her attention. Mum, Dad and Wren were silent. Waiting for another explosion.

Rue crossed her arms furiously. But didn't say anything.

'And something else. Those exercises you have to do every day before you get your operation?' I felt queasy every time the operation came up. Not because I was squeamish – I just hated the thought of her having to go through it. The Selective Dorsal Rhizotomy. When the doctors would cut some nerve roots in her spinal cord to try to help with her mobility.

Rue flashed her blue eyes at me.

'You have to actually do them. *Without* complaining.' I nudged her and she didn't punch me back, so I knew I was getting somewhere. 'Is it a deal?'

'Only if you do it now,' she said, her voice still shaking from all the crying.

'Do what?' I asked.

'Message Lexie.'

'Fine.' I got out my phone and typed out a message to our cousin, before showing it to Rue, who nodded angrily.

'Send,' she said.

'Sent,' I confirmed, and stood up.

Mum took my spot. 'You know, love, we only keep going on about these things to help you. We don't do it to upset you. And hopefully, after your operation, everything will be a bit easier.' Mum took Rue's hand, and I watched as she didn't snatch it away.

As I moved past Dad, he put a hand on my shoulder and whispered, 'Thanks, Gogo.'

Then I left them to it. I went into my little bedroom, closed the door and took out the phone that had just buzzed in my pocket. My stomach lurched as I wondered if Ari or Theo had finally replied.

FELIX: I am looking forward to tomorrow already :)

ME: Me too x

And, just like that, the Ari and Theo rage disappeared. I looked at Felix's message again and stretched out comfortably on my bed, smiling as I did. I scrolled through my WhatsApp messages and stopped on Priya's name again.

ME: Hey . . . Long time no speak. I know it seems like totally out of the blue, and I know everything was all my fault. But I miss you P. Like really miss you. I'm on holiday, but would be great to catch up when I get home, you know, if you wanted to or whatever x

***PRIYA** is typing*

My heart was in my mouth. I held my breath, waiting to see what she'd say. *If* she'd even reply. She stopped typing. Then started.

Then stopped. And my heart hurt all over again.

I was half asleep when Dad knocked on my door.

'We're going for dinner in ten minutes. The girls want pizza,' Dad said with a roll of his eyes.

'Again?' I asked.

'Again,' he smiled. And it was nice to share a moment with him.

Rue didn't complain about her splints at all that night. Not even when we walked to the pizzeria, when the air was hot and they must have been rubbing against her skin. She brought a football with her, dribbling it with Wren along the path as we walked. She even said no when I offered her a piggyback.

'Are you excited to learn surfing?' I asked my sisters on the way back.

'Yep!' Rue said immediately. Wren was quiet.

'Wren?' I asked.

'What if I fall in? What if Rue falls in?' she asked, her big eyes even bigger than usual.

'So what? You can both swim,' I said, shrugging, trying to make her feel better.

'But what if the waves are too big?' she asked, and the fear in her voice was so real that I stopped her in the middle of the path.

'You don't have to do anything you don't want to do. And anyway, you won't be in big waves, not right away and probably not at all this holiday. OK?' I asked, and I watched the fear start to retreat from her eyes.

'Aw!' said Rue. 'I wanted the big waves.'

'What if the man isn't nice to us?' Wren looked at me, and

I had to adjust my face because I'd been thinking the same thing. There was no way his arrogance wouldn't spill over into the girls' lesson.

'He will be. I'm sure of it,' I said with as much conviction as I could muster. 'But I'll be there anyway. So don't worry. OK?'

Wren nodded, her blonde curls bouncing around her shoulders. 'OK.'

We played cards the rest of the evening and into the warm night. Rue wouldn't stop talking about the new football team she was going to join, so I just hoped that Lexie's boyfriend actually did get it off the ground. My cousin hadn't replied yet.

And Wren was happy, just because everyone was there. I flicked between not thinking about home at all, just daydreaming about Felix and the way he'd touched my hand, to my gut lurching with the shame of sending a message to Priya and getting no reply; it haunted me.

I took my hair out of its bobble and pulled at the strands that were turning curly again.

'I miss your curls, Margot,' Mum said, and I caught her eye.

'Me too,' said Wren.

'Me three,' said Rue. 'Looks better when you match with us.'

'Well *I* like it straight,' I said. But was that even true? Did I just straighten my hair to look more like Ari? Because I thought Theo would like me better like that? Is *that* what I was doing? It wasn't conscious, not really. But I thought back to how different I'd been before, how much I'd changed in one year – Ari and Theo the common denominators.

'Well, you've always had your own mind anyway,' Dad

added to the conversation, coating my doubts with a layer of my own disappointment.

'What's that supposed to mean?' I asked with a laugh, knowing exactly what he'd meant, because I used to love it when he said that. But this last year? I'd had anything but my own mind.

'Nothing.' Dad held up his hands. 'I just meant that ever since you were born, you've always known what you wanted and there's no point trying to argue with you. Just like Rue.'

Rue grinned like she'd just won a prize.

'Yeah, and like *you*,' I replied, teasing Dad.

And that interaction, and the laughter that followed, brought me back to the way things used to be, if only for now.

9

The next morning, I woke with sunlight streaming through the paper-thin curtains. I jumped out of bed and walked straight to the mirror. Here, I looked tanned. My white skin had a slight golden glow, and already there were new freckles on my nose. I'd washed my hair the night before and now it was an explosion of blonde curls that just about reached my jawline. I stared at the sparkling stud in my nose. It didn't look right here. Not without all my usual make-up. Maybe it never looked right. I took it out.

I checked my phone to see if Priya, Ari or Theo had replied. But there was nothing. So I left it on my bed, knowing that if I took it with me, I'd be checking it all day.

Everyone was still asleep. So I decided to go for a walk. My mind drifted back to Felix and the thought of our date later on. I'd noticed that so many of my thoughts brought me back to him. Like my brain was giving itself a soft landing after torturing itself with things from home. So, naturally, when I went outside, into the warm morning air, I found myself at the Brasserie.

It was busy already, with families getting breakfast and

single people at tables sipping miniature cups of coffee. I slowed down and looked for Felix. But I didn't have to look too hard. There he was, cleaning a table in his white shirt and black trousers. The shirt was rolled up at the elbows and I just watched him for a second. My stomach fluttered when the image of him kissing my hand yesterday filled my head.

'Margot!' he called when he saw me, his face all lit up. He pushed his hair back, as if he was trying to get a better look at me as he walked over.

'*Salut*,' I said.

'*Salut.*' Felix leaned over and kissed me gently on each cheek, lingering on the second one. I breathed him in. It was that smell again – lavender, vanilla, but with something deep and rich underneath that made me want to bury my head in his neck. But I resisted. 'You have come for breakfast?' he asked.

And I hesitated, because I couldn't explain why I'd come. I'd gone for a walk and ended up here. 'Yeah,' I said. 'Everyone in my family is still asleep.'

'It is their holiday, *non*?' Felix smiled, then held up one finger. 'One minute. Wait there.' Felix ran towards the bar and disappeared behind it. He came jogging back to me holding a paper bag. '*Un chausson aux pommes.* It was the last one. I hope you like apples. And also *des croissants, un pain au chocolat et un pain au raisin*. But you should have the *chausson*.' He handed me the bag and it was warm. The smell of pastry, sugar and sweet apple escaped from the paper, and I closed my eyes and breathed it in.

'It smells amazing. Thank you. And I'll see you later? What time?' I asked.

'I will be finished around seven if you want to meet me here?' he asked. I looked behind him to see Yves staring in our direction. I leaned in to kiss Felix on both cheeks before I left.

Rue and Wren were waiting for me outside when I got back.

'Margot! Are you excited to come surfing with us?' Wren asked with a big smile on her face.

'Of course.'

I wasn't. I was worried about that surf guy. I wondered how he would cope with Rue and her balance issues. He'd seemed great with those other kids we saw, but I don't think any of them had a disability. A visible one anyway.

'What's that?' Rue poked the bag I was holding.

'None of your business.' I snatched it away from her.

'It smells so good!'

I took the *chausson aux pommes* out of the paper bag and held it to my nose, breathing it in again before taking a huge bite. 'Oh my God, it's so good.' Pieces of pastry flew out of my mouth and Rue's face was a picture.

'Give me a bit.'

I handed them the bag and they dived into it like vultures.

'It won't be long before your lesson. Make sure you're ready in thirty minutes,' I said.

Mum was drinking coffee inside when I went in.

'I've been very lazy today, Margot. I'm only just up!' Mum smiled sheepishly.

'Sure, it's a holiday, isn't it?' I repeated Felix's words and smiled at Mum, before sitting down beside her.

'Are you having fun, love? I know this isn't the kind of holiday you want to go on at your age. Your dad knows that too. And I know you have your boyfriend at home, but it's just that we miss you and we'd like to spend time with you –'

'Mum,' I said, cutting her off. 'I *am* having a good time. I think. Sort of. And I might be going on a date tonight.' A smile appeared automatically when I said it.

'A date? With who? But wait, I thought you were – I mean, you and Theo?' Mum asked carefully.

I shook my head.

'Oh, I'm sorry, love.' She reached for my hand then seemed to change her mind and picked up her coffee cup again. I missed these moments with Mum. I used to come home from school and tell her all my gossip. We'd sit in the kitchen with hot chocolate and talk about everyone at school. I guess I just grew up.

'It's OK. Or it will be. But anyway, yeah, the boy from the bar, Felix. He asked me on a date. He's really nice, I think you'd like him.'

'He sounds handsome,' Mum said, with a raise of her eyebrows.

I burst out laughing. 'He is.'

'Maybe we could meet him?' she asked tentatively.

'He'd probably like that.'

I went into my bedroom and spent the next while lying on my bed, thinking about Felix and our mystery date. Maybe this holiday wouldn't be so bad after all. I picked up my phone. No message from Priya. I thought about sending another one.

And also thought about deleting the one I'd already sent when my phone buzzed in my hand.

PRIYA: Hey stranger . . .

I automatically put my hand over my mouth. She'd written back! My eyes filled immediately, which surprised me. I'd missed Priya. Of course I had, but even *I* didn't know how much.

ME: How are you? How is life? Update me!

PRIYA: Well, swimming hasn't been as good since you left, but I'm actually going out with Calvin now, so I guess that's kind of cool . . .

ME: OMG what? Can I call?

PRIYA: OK

I was shaking when I pressed the video call button. And then there she was. Her perfect Priya big brown eyes, black hair and white teeth filling my screen.

'Hey,' I said, because I didn't know what else to say.

'Hey. Where are you?'

'France, with my family. We're here for *four* weeks.' I rolled my eyes.

'Wish my parents would take me on a four-week holiday.'

Priya laughed but it was a guarded sort of laugh. Not like the way she used to.

'So . . . Calvin?' I grinned. 'When did that start?'

'Like six months ago. It's made practice way more interesting anyway . . .'

'Priya . . .'

'No. Margot, don't. Not yet.' Like she knew exactly what I was going to say.

I felt my face flush with embarrassment. 'OK,' I agreed. I had to take her lead, that much I did know. 'Thanks for not ghosting me.'

'I thought about it. It was actually Cal who convinced me.' Priya smiled slightly when she said his name. Like she couldn't help it.

'I guess we have a lot to catch up on . . .' I said, as sadness filled my gut.

'Yeah. Hey, I better go, my mum is calling me.'

'OK, P. Speak soon.'

'Bye.'

'Bye.'

And I didn't know how I felt. Empty? I thought if I just talked to Priya, everything would be fixed. But it was weird, and kind of awkward. I mean, I got it, of course I did. It was *my* fault. Not hers. I guess I'd made my bed.

I zoned out watching TikTok videos for a few minutes, then it was time to take Rue and Wren to the beach. I was kind of hoping Mum and Dad would take them, but Rue insisted that only I was allowed to go.

Rue talked non-stop on the way there. She was so excited.

It was quite a long walk for her, and Mum had convinced her to wear her splints, so they were probably rubbing in the heat, but you wouldn't know.

'You OK?' I asked.

'I'm fine!' Rue almost shouted back as we arrived at the beach half an hour before the lesson, like we'd been told. The sand was full of sunbathers and there were groups of kids learning how to surf in the water.

I squinted in the sun towards the beach hut by the sand dunes. Wren stood beside me as Rue walked on ahead. I could see the surf guy Antoine talking to some other dude, surrounded by kids messing around.

When we got to the hut, Rue could barely contain herself with excitement. She went straight up to Antoine and tapped him on the back.

He pretended to be scared, and she laughed. So did Wren, but she was still stuck to my side.

'My surfers are here!' Antoine grinned. I watched him glance at Rue's legs, where the pink splints stabilized her lower legs. 'One minute.'

Antoine looked up at me briefly as he came over. He was wearing black board shorts today with his aviators. That was it.

He bent down to talk to Wren. 'You are excited for your lesson?'

'I'm a bit scared,' Wren admitted, twisting her foot in the sand.

'Ah *non*! Do not be scared. I will be here all the time to make sure that you are safe. Safety is very important to me. The *most* important thing.' Antoine smiled so warmly that it felt like a completely different person who had been so rude to me.

'You promise?' Wren asked. I could tell that she'd relaxed from her smile.

'Cross my heart.' He traced over his heart with his finger. '*Croix de bois, croix de fer, si je mens, je vais en enfer.*' And Wren tried to repeat it.

'Are you ready?' Rue asked, tapping Antoine again, this time on the shoulder. He spun round.

'Almost.' He stood up, walked over to me, took my arm and led me a few metres down the beach. I thought about wrenching my arm away, but for some reason, I liked how it felt. The shock of some kind of current rushing through my whole body when he touched me. He let go when we were away from all the kids but surrounded by sunbathers.

'Your sister. She has *les attelles*.' Antoine motioned to his legs.

'Splints. She has cerebral palsy, they help stabilize her legs when she's walking. But she doesn't wear them in the water.'

'Ah OK, *la paralysie cérébrale*.' He stared at Rue, thinking for a second as she waited impatiently beside Wren. '*Bon.* We will adapt a few things. I will take your sisters myself and Sébastian can take the other children. You will watch from the sand.'

'Em. Yeah. Thanks,' I said, not happy about being *told* to watch from the sand, which I was going to do anyway, but so happy about the way he talked about Rue's disability. Or maybe it was because of the things he *didn't* say. Sometimes when I told people what she had, you'd get this sympathy face and stock phrases about things being 'so hard' or a million other variations of that. And maybe that would be OK if it was a different kid, but Rue didn't want people feeling sorry for her; she wanted to be the best at everything she could.

I leaned against the beach hut and watched their whole lesson. How Antoine helped Rue take off her splints and helped her and Wren on to big foam boards on the sand.

Sébastian was the guy he'd been talking to earlier. Tall, thin, with long, blonde, beachy hair and a goofy smile. He was on the other side of the hut with the other children, and they were all laughing about something he was saying, or maybe just laughing at him when he pretended to fall over, it was hard to tell. I turned back to Antoine and the girls.

He made them sit on the surfboards on the beach, practising balance. Then he got them to lie down, helping Rue gently. And she didn't complain when he did. Then he made them stand up beside the boards, while he scanned around him. Then his eyes landed on me.

'The sister. I need you for a second. Please.' He waved me over, and I looked behind me in case he was looking at somebody else.

'Who, me?' I asked as I got up and walked towards them.

'Yes. You. You are the sister? Lie down. Please.' The please an afterthought.

Antoine motioned to the board, and I replied with a shrug. And he just stood there and waited until I did what he said. I lay down face first on the board, feeling like a total idiot.

'OK. Girls, watch your sister. It is easier to watch someone try, so I can show you the mistakes.'

Ugh. And how was he so sure I was going to make mistakes?

'OK, move back so your toes are at the bottom.'

I shuffled backwards.

'Chin up. You need to see where you are going. OK, now practise the paddling.'

I could not have felt more stupid, pretending to swim on the sand. But I did what he said.

'More wide. And this?' Antoine grabbed my hand and covered the back of it with his. He squeezed it into a cup. 'Like this. Not flat. But you know already? From swimming.'

'Margot likes to swim a lot,' said Wren. Correction: I *did* like to swim.

I did what he told me – cupped my hands and pulled them through the sand.

'So it is like swimming, but you are pushing the board through the water, not just you. Do you see, *les filles*?'

'Yes, Antoine!' Rue and Wren said together.

The sun was hot on the back of my legs and neck, which was exposed by my high ponytail.

'OK, now the pop-up.'

I'd show him *mistakes.*

'Hands under your shoulders, like a push-up.'

Easy.

'OK and now you want to push up with both arms and slide your foot in between them. Right here.' Antoine tapped the space between my hands.

I took a deep breath and pushed myself up, sliding my foot in between my hands. I smiled, because I knew I'd got it right.

'OK, *Princesse*, good job. But maybe that was lucky? Try again.' He pointed back to the board, and I lay down again. I repeated the same motion about five times, and I got it right five times. And on that last time, I lifted my head and stared out at the sparkling water. And I felt something. Like a rush of warm nostalgia. Of a past that felt so far gone that I thought it would always be a distant memory.

Rue and Wren clapped for me when I pulled myself back up to standing. Antoine just stood there, eyes blocked by his glasses, so I couldn't even guess what he was thinking.

'You can stop calling me Princess now.' I brushed sand from my legs and tightened my ponytail.

'But you *are* a princess.' Wren smiled at me, then turned to Rue, like she was embarrassed she'd said the wrong thing. Which she had. But I forgave her.

Antoine just nodded towards Wren and shrugged, pulling a face and making her giggle.

'Let us try again, *les filles*.' Antoine clapped his hands and Rue and Wren lay down on a board each.

Then Antoine whispered something that made them laugh so hard that Rue almost fell off her board on to the sand.

At the end of the lesson, I watched as Antoine helped Rue put her splints back on. Both the girls went to the beach hut, where Sébastian was handing out little cups of water, and Antoine came over to talk to me.

'Your sister Rue. The smaller one. She is determined. More than my adult students. Stubborn. *La petite guerrière*,' he said. 'That means warrior. And Wren, the bird, *le petit oiseau*, she watches everything. I noticed how she would not relax until her sister was comfortable. She is the peacekeeper between you two, *non*? She puts out the fire?' Antoine said, a serious look on his face. I just stared into his black aviators, shocked that he'd picked up so much about the girls in so little time, and even more shocked by the state of my curly half ponytail hair in their reflection. I pushed rogue strands behind my ears.

'Do you notice this much about all your students?' I asked.

And by the way he looked down at me and smirked, I knew he knew what I was asking.

'Not all of my students, *non*. Just the interesting ones. Do you want to know what I noticed about you, *Princesse*?'

'That I'm *not* a princess?' I said, without half the conviction I'd intended.

'What I noticed was that there was a split second when you stood up on the board and I could see that you were not thinking any more. You were only feeling. Where everything around you disappears, and you had not even gone into the water. I am right?' He cocked his head and studied my face as I tried not to give away the fact that he could not have been more right.

'*Peut-être*,' I said with a shrug. I didn't smile. Two of us could play that game. He was just so sure of himself. And I wasn't giving him anything else to feed his ego.

'Maybe you do want a lesson?' he asked, looking down at me over his sunglasses.

'Why would I want a lesson?' I shot back, too quickly. Because behind the desperation not to let him be right, I couldn't ignore the longing. The one that tugged on something inside me, begging me to follow it. Into the water.

'It is up to you. But I will be here. Tomorrow. Early. Maybe six thirty?'

He let the question linger in the hot air. I scanned around to look for Rue and Wren, trying to buy myself some time. But by the time I'd seen them digging a hole and looked back at Antoine, he'd turned away from me and started walking back towards the hut.

I guess that was that then.

10

I spent the rest of the morning and afternoon chilling out with Mum and Dad. Well, really, I just sat there as Rue told them every single detail of her surf lesson with Antoine. And it was nice to see her so excited given that she had an operation looming over her. Maybe it was a little kid thing, or maybe just a Rue thing, but she didn't dwell on the heavy stuff, and she had more to deal with than any of us.

'I'm away for a shower,' I announced. Butterflies fluttered gently in my stomach when I thought about the date with Felix. I'd never actually been on a proper date with Theo. We'd just hung out. And more often than not, it was the three of us. I'd once suggested going for dinner somewhere, just us, and I cringed at the memory of his laugh, which played like a scratched record in my head. I shook the thought away and had a shower, washing away all the sand and salt that clung to my skin from earlier.

After, I lay on my bed and picked up my phone. I'd stopped myself from doing it since I'd seen Ella's Snap, because I knew I would hate whatever it showed me, but I broke. I went straight to Insta and on to Theo's account. His story was a shot of his Xbox with the caption 'When she says she doesn't game . . . then destroys you . . . 🎮.'

And as if the 'she' wasn't enough of a hint, I saw Ari's black leather cuff on the edge of Theo's bed.

I closed my eyes and breathed in deeply, trying to erase the picture from my head. Instinctively I opened WhatsApp and went to Priya's messages.

I sent her a picture that I'd taken of the beach earlier. It was beautiful. The endless stretch of the sand, the sparkling water, surfers on white-capped waves.

ME: Remembering our plan to swim across Belfast Lough that never happened . . . maybe this would have been a better plan.

Priya sent back an image of the outside of the local leisure centre – looking even more run-down than the last time I'd been there – under an overcast sky.

PRIYA: That looks amazing. Not jealous at all. You doing much training?

ME: Training? What's that?

PRIYA: That doesn't sound like the Margot I know . . . knew

ME: Nah. No lanes here. Just waves

PRIYA: Shame. I thought that maybe the old Margot was back.

And that stung. A series of pinpricks in my chest, like my body was making sure I didn't skim over her words. And I didn't even know how to reply. But I didn't have to, because Priya typed something else that made my throat tight.

PRIYA: How's Theo? Is he there too?

My mind flashed to the Insta story. To Ari's leather cuff. To the Snap of her straddling him, his hands round her waist, like they'd been doing that forever. Maybe they had. I took a deep breath.

ME: Actually, me and Theo broke up. Well, sort of. Ella sent me a snap of Ari all over him . . . It's so embarrassing . . . :(

PRIYA: Oh Margot, that sucks. I'm sorry. Are you OK?

ME: Yeah. I think so. I've kind of been hanging out with this French guy . . .

PRIYA: 👀 Tell me more!

ME: I will, but I've got to go get ready, for a date :)

PRIYA: You better report back! Bet it's more exciting than me and Cal's date to see the new Marvel . . .

ME: You always hated Marvel!

PRIYA: Still do. But I love that boy

ME: Cuteness overload. Talk later xxx

I locked my screen and held my phone to my chest for a second, smiling at the exchange with Priya. It felt so good to have her back. Sort of back, anyway. I stood up to look in the mirror.

I leaned towards it and studied my face. I looked different here. Even though it had just been a couple of days, I didn't feel like I needed foundation. The light tan made my blue eyes stand out even more, my hair looked lighter, and the salt air had made my curls look more defined than they ever had.

So I just put on some mascara, some highlighter and my

favourite perfume before pulling on a white summer dress that sat high on my thighs and had little spaghetti straps. I had no idea where we were going, so I grabbed a cardigan to take with me and put on my leather sandals, giving my sliders a break.

'Are you going somewhere now?' Dad asked when I emerged from my bedroom. 'We were going to play some boules tonight, and we could use your expertise.' Dad raised his eyebrows.

I laughed. I used to love boules, and on holiday when I was Rue's age we'd play every day with the multicolour boules set that Mum and Dad bought from the supermarket. 'Sorry, I can't. I'm going out with a friend,' I said simply, looking at Mum, who smiled knowingly.

'What friend?' Dad looked at Mum, confused.

'I'll fill you in,' she said, patting his hand.

'Her friend is a boy,' Rue said, and she burst out laughing.

'The plot thickens,' Dad said. 'In all seriousness, though, be careful, and keep your phone on.'

'I will.' I nodded before disappearing out the door and on to the deck.

When I went outside, Wren was sitting at the table with a bottle of Orangina and her iPad. She looked at me in shock from under a pink baseball cap.

'What's wrong?' I asked her.

'You look beautiful,' she said. Then her cheeks turned pink.

'Aw, Wren, thank you.' I smiled, the warmth of her words a plaster over the pinprick scratches.

'Why is your dress so short? It looks like it would fit Wren,'

Rue said from behind me, laughing. She was standing in the doorway, holding on to the door frame and swinging forward before pulling herself back.

'It's not *that* short.' I tried to pull it down a bit. I looked at the time on my phone.

'I need to go,' I said, sliding my phone into my cardigan pocket. My stomach flipped. I grabbed a piece of pizza from the table to eat while I walked.

The Brasserie was busy when I got there. Families getting ready to eat dinner. I'd finished my slice of pizza, but I was still hungry, and hoped Felix had factored food into our date.

He saw me before I saw him.

'Margot,' he called from behind the bar. Delphine was there too, with her usual look of contempt for me. I walked over and Felix finished pouring a drink.

'*Et voilà!*' he said. 'I am finished. We shall go?' His smile was wide and open, and he seemed genuinely excited. 'Just let me get changed,' he said, and disappeared round the corner of the bar as I stood there with an awkward silence hanging in the air between me and Delphine.

Felix emerged wearing a white T-shirt and blue jeans, and I couldn't take my eyes off him.

'Have you ever been on a Vespa before?' Felix asked as he came over. I shook my head as a rush of excitement rolled through my body.

'Nope.'

We walked to the car park at the entrance to the campsite and he led me to a silver Vespa in the corner. He handed me a helmet, and I pulled it down over my head.

'You are OK?' he asked, looking through the visor at me.

'I'm OK,' I replied. Then he put on his own helmet. He stepped on to the Vespa then turned and offered me his hand. I took it. And as I did, any nerves about getting on the back of a Vespa dissolved into the hot air.

'Hold on to me,' he said, taking my arms and pulling them round his chest. I clasped my hands together and could feel hard muscle underneath his T-shirt. Heat emanated through the cotton, and there was a rush of pure adrenaline through my veins as he revved the engine.

And we rode. Inland. The air was hot on my legs as he drove fast across rolling hills. It was breathtaking. We passed rows and rows of grapevines in impossibly straight lines. I'd always loved the French vineyards. On our holidays when I was younger, I used to look out the car window at the perfect spaces between each of them and feel immediately calmer. We drove through beautiful little towns that looked like they'd come straight out of another century.

And then we stopped in one of them. Felix parked on the street, pulled off his helmet and helped me off the Vespa.

'Oh my God,' I said, exhilarated. 'That was amazing.'

'You are hungry?' he asked.

I nodded as I removed my helmet. 'Very.' Felix took my hand, and I let him lead me to a little café on a corner that barely looked open. I sat down at a small table outside, and Felix disappeared indoors, emerging a couple of minutes later with two glass bottles of Coke and a menu.

He sat down beside me and leaned in close as we looked at the menu together.

'*Salade de chèvre chaud, le poulet Basquaise et le Gâteau Basque.*' He ran his finger down the French dishes and I leaned into his warm shoulder as I listened. 'It is a set menu, this is OK?' He looked at me and I sat up and looked straight back at him.

'Of course,' I said. 'I'm starving. What is *le poulet Basquaise*? Chicken and . . .' I shrugged and waited for him to fill it in.

'Your accent. It was perfect. *Poulet Basquaise* is chicken with peppers and tomatoes. And *Gâteau Basque* is *les cerises.* Cherries!' Felix smiled. 'I will order.'

'Sounds amazing,' I said.

Felix disappeared into the restaurant.

'*Alors*, tell me about you. I want to know more,' Felix said when he got back. His brown eyes were warm. Interested. 'You are enjoying Biarritz?'

'I think so,' I said. 'Although I've only seen the campsite and the beach so far.'

'Ah, but there is so much more! I will show you!' Felix smiled and reached for my hand across the table. And I didn't pull it away. I let my hand relax into his. 'You are OK? There is a sadness in your eyes.'

I looked into Felix's eyes. I thought I'd been doing a good job of hiding the emptiness.

'My ex-boyfriend is with someone else. Someone I thought was my friend,' I admitted.

'I am sorry. That is . . . hard, *non*?'

'*Oui.*' I tried to smile, but felt like I might cry. 'But it's fine, it wasn't serious or anything.' I took my hand back and pulled a curl gently, twisting it round my finger before letting go.

Saying the words out loud, it dawned on me: I'd just admitted the truth.

'But it is still painful?'

And I couldn't lie to him. Even though I wanted to brush away his words, the sincerity in his eyes, his face, made it impossible.

'Yeah.' I looked down at my hands as he took them in his, bringing them to his lips to kiss. And that made me smile.

The waiter arrived with our goat's cheese salads and set them in front of us. '*Bon appétit.*'

'*Merci*,' we both said, and the conversation shifted to lighter topics. Places in Biarritz that Felix wanted to show me, snippets of our lives flowing so easily it was like we'd known each other forever. Then, over our main course, Felix mentioned that he was going to study literature at university but had deferred his place.

'How come you want to stay here?' I asked, interested.

'My mother. I just wanted to be close to home for a while,' he said, and my eyes followed his hand to his hair, pushing it back, watching it fall back into place in thick waves.

'Is she sick?' I asked. I hoped he didn't think I was being rude. Since Rue was born, hospitals had just become an integral part of my life, and I was comfortable talking about illness and disability. But I guess that didn't apply to everyone.

'Ah *non*,' he said, then hesitated. 'I am sorry if I made it sound that way. And sometimes I think it is me? I worry that she will be sad if I leave.' He turned his head like he was embarrassed, then found my eyes again. 'It is not very sexy.'

'I think it's really sweet,' I replied. I reached for his hand this time, and he watched as I stroked the back of it with my thumb.

'Sweet.' He laughed. 'Tell me more about *your* family.' He picked up a piece of baguette and ate some.

'Em, both my parents are teachers, so that's pretty boring. Rue and Wren are super close to each other . . .' I hesitated, trying to think of what to say next, and then it just came out. Easily, like he had some secret key to the box of my innermost thoughts. 'I guess sometimes it feels like we all orbit around Rue. And it's not her fault. She has cerebral palsy. It's mild, but it kind of shapes everything, if that makes any sense.' I shocked myself. Saying that out loud felt wrong. Like I resented her or something. And I didn't. It was just the truth.

Felix nodded in understanding. 'And what shapes *you*, Margot?'

I loved the way he said my name. 'I used to swim. Competitively, I mean,' I said, and as I did, a lump appeared in my throat.

'Not any more?' he asked, and I shook my head. 'Do you miss it?'

I looked at my plate as a waiter took it away, surprised by the sudden swell of sadness in my chest. 'I do. Sometimes.'

The waiter brought dessert at the perfect time, and I was grateful for the chance to change subject. 'Dessert is my favourite.' I grinned.

'Me too.' Felix returned my smile, and we ate in silence. Hot sweet cherries and cherry coulis. The perfect conversation distraction.

'Do you trust me to take you somewhere as a surprise?' Felix asked after we'd finished and were walking back to the Vespa.

I scrunched up my face in faux uncertainty. 'Where?'

He tugged my hand and pulled me close to him. 'I cannot say, or it will not be a surprise.' And we were so close then. Standing on the cobbled street in the evening sun. My heart was in my throat, and I thought he might kiss me. And I knew then that I would let him.

'Please?' I whispered.

'No,' he said, smirking, as the anticipation of a kiss passed. Not in a bad way, but it was like the moment had settled into the air around us, becoming something else. Something safe and familiar. He reached over for my helmet and handed it to me.

We drove for about thirty minutes, through more towns, more vineyards, then Felix turned up a bumpy lane and kept riding. I held on tighter, digging my hands into his skin, hoping I wasn't hurting him. He drove higher and higher, up into the hills, and eventually, we stopped. We were completely alone. Felix pulled off his helmet and hung it on the handle.

'We have to walk a little bit, is that OK?' he asked. He held out his hand and I took it, nodding in agreement.

'Close your eyes,' he said.

'This sounds like the start of a horror movie,' I said, laughing, then regretted my joke. Because it didn't feel like that at all and I'd hate him to think that it did. There was just something about his way that made everything feel safe. The way he reached for my hand, how he found my eyes and listened to every single word I said as if each sentence held some kind of revelation.

So I let him lead me up a hill, the evening air still warm on our skin. Then we stopped. He spun me round and stood behind me. I leaned on him and felt the beat of his heart. Steady. Sure.

'OK, you can open.'

It was the most beautiful thing I'd ever seen. Fields of yellow that glowed golden in the low light.

'Sunflowers,' I whispered. Thousands and thousands of sunflowers everywhere. 'It's so beautiful,' I said. I moved my head to look up at him, and he was just staring out at the endless fields.

I turned to face him.

'*Les tournesols*,' he said. I wanted to close my eyes every time he spoke French, just so I could savour it.

'What?' I cocked my head, confused.

'Come.' Felix took my hand and he led me into the closest field, so we were surrounded by sunflowers, taller than us both.

'*Les tournesols*, that is what they're called. Because they turn towards the sun. *Tourne. Sol.*' He reached up and snapped one off, handing it to me.

'*Les tournesols*,' I whispered, stroking the narrow petals. 'That's beautiful.'

'*You* are beautiful,' he replied, not missing a beat.

And I really looked at him then. He appeared younger close up, the wide mouth and how his brown eyes seemed lighter in the golden glow.

'*Merci*,' I said, too happy to be embarrassed by his compliment. His fair hair was so thick and wavy and just asked to be touched. So I reached up and pushed it away from his forehead, before kissing him right there in the sunflower field, with the sun golden and low in the sky. The kiss was slow, and uncertain, a contrast to Theo's confident kisses. Theo, who took them whenever he wanted. Which is why I wasn't expecting for Felix to pull away, only slightly, and look into my eyes like he was making sure it was what I wanted, even though it had been me who kissed him. And it was as if he could tell just by looking at me, because he was kissing me again.

'You like the surprise?' he asked, smiling.

'I love it,' I said. 'Do you come here a lot?' I rubbed a sunflower petal between my fingers.

'I come here when I want to forget dark things,' he said with a sigh. 'I try to be like the sunflowers. Turn towards the light.'

'Dark things?' I asked, startled by the sadness in his tone. I turned to look at him and his expression matched his words.

'*Ouais*, like when you miss someone.' He shrugged and pushed a sunflower out of his way. 'You know, "I miss you" in French is *Tu me manques*. It means "You are missing from me", like you are part of the same thing. The same entity.' He looked through the field again, lost in thought.

'I like that,' I said, then added, 'for the right person,' when an image of Theo flashed in my mind before it disintegrated just as quickly.

'*Exactement*,' Felix smiled. 'The right person.'

'Who is missing from you?' I asked.

He looked at his watch. 'Maybe I should take you home now,' he said, ignoring my question entirely.

11

When we got to the campsite, it was almost dark, and the air was cooler.

Felix walked me back to the mobile home in almost silence. It was a comfortable silence, but was tinged with something else. Something that hadn't been said? Had something got lost in translation? But my worries evaporated when we reached my place and Felix tugged my hand to stop me, turning me round to face him.

'I had a really great time tonight,' he said.

'Me too,' I said, relieved. He kissed me gently on each cheek, and my stomach sank as it hit me how much I'd wanted him to *really* kiss me again. But I shook the thought away before it showed on my face. 'Thank you, for the sunflowers. *Les tournesols.* They were really special.' And I meant it. It felt like something I'd remember for the rest of my life.

'*Avec plaisir.* I will see you tomorrow?' Felix pushed his hand through his hair again, the way he did. A habit. Something else I'd remember. I loved that, after only a few days, I was noticing his quirks, his little nuances that exposed themselves one by one, like I was discovering all these separate parts of a patchwork quilt.

'I'd like that.'

'Goodnight, Margot,' Felix said, turning away and walking a few steps before looking back to smile, catching me staring at him.

'Night, Felix.'

When I walked through the door, muffled laughter made me look straight to Rue and Wren's bedroom. I walked over and pushed the door open. They were both hiding under bedsheets, trying and failing to stifle their giggles.

'We saw you kiss,' Rue said, and they both laughed. They pushed off the sheets and sat up.

'You didn't actually. He just kissed my cheeks. You know they do that in France to say hello?'

'They kiss?' Rue made a face.

'Just little ones.' I made a tiny motion with my fingers on her cheeks.

'I like that,' said Wren.

'Why aren't you asleep anyway?' I asked.

'We're too excited about surfing tomorrow,' said Rue.

'It does look fun,' I mused, and for the first time that evening my mind was back on the beach.

'Maybe you should do lessons too,' suggested Wren.

'Maybe I should . . .' I said as I closed their door. I took a few steps into my room, set an alarm for six a.m., and fell asleep with a smile on my face.

The next morning, I woke feeling full of energy, as if my body had decided to tell me to get up and go to the beach. And at swimming, I'd always been taught to listen to my body, so I jumped out of bed and put on a bikini, shorts and a T-shirt. I briefly looked at myself in the mirror, deciding to leave my hair as it was, a mass of blonde curls, instead of attempting to tie it back. I crept out, trying not to wake anyone; I'd be back before they'd even notice I'd gone.

I gazed towards the Brasserie on my way past, but it was empty.

The beach was empty too. But the water wasn't. It was dotted with surfers as far as I could see, riding sparkling waves in the morning sun.

I walked towards the surf hut and, as I got closer, my feet warmed by the sand in my sliders, I noticed how Antoine pulled down his sunglasses and looked at me. I swear I saw him raise his eyebrows too.

I stopped a few metres away and glanced into the surf hut where I could see a few others about the same age as Antoine.

'You are late,' Antoine said.

I pulled my phone out of my pocket. 'It's six twenty-eight. You said six thirty.'

'For surfing, on time is late.' Antoine picked up a black T-shirt that was drying in the sun on the back of a plastic chair and chucked it to me.

'It is a rash vest. It might be a bit big. You can change behind the hut.' He walked to the rack of surfboards and pulled one out as I walked behind the wooden building.

'Is this yours?' I called, after pulling the T-shirt down and realizing it was more like a dress.

'It does not fit me any more,' he called back.

I re-emerged wearing it and walked over beside him. 'Which one can I have?' I asked, tracing my fingers over a blue board with fiery waves up the side.

'None. Not yet. Come.' Antoine grabbed my arm gently and pulled me in the direction of the water. 'We watch first.'

I dug my bare foot into the sand when we stopped. I hadn't come here to window-shop. Antoine moved behind me, and instinctively I held my breath, as if breathing was something to be ashamed of.

'Look at the ocean.' He pointed over my shoulder at the glittering sea I was already looking at. '*Alors. Les vagues.* Sorry. The waves, they come in *des séries*. Sets. Come.' Antoine moved around me, then took my wrist and led me even closer to the water. He let go before I could object, but not before a rush of *something* tingled right the way up my spine, forcing me to close my eyes momentarily as it culminated with a thousand sparks fizzing at the back of my neck.

'OK, look at the horizon. You see?' He was behind me again, pointing over my shoulder.

I nodded.

'Watch for the sets. *Normalement* there are about seven or ten waves, and then *une accalmie*. A lull. And see? *That* is when you paddle out.'

We watched as the surfers paddled to deeper water.

'And you see where the waves are not breaking? Look, there is a calm bit right there.' Antoine's face was right beside mine now, making sure I was looking the right way, so close that if I turned my face, my cheek would scrape against the dark stubble that lined his jaw.

'I see it.'

'*Bon.* That is your *baïne*. Rip current. It can be dangerous. Sometimes people panic and they try to swim against it, but you must *never* panic. If you get caught, you must swim parallel to the shore. You know parallel?' Antoine asked. He'd moved back and was looking straight at me as if I was an idiot.

'Of course I *know* parallel. I'm not stupid.'

Antoine laughed. 'I did not say you were stupid, but there are many clever people who have been caught in rip currents, *Princesse*.' Then his demeanour seemed to change to something colder. 'The ocean is dangerous. That is why safety is so important.' He turned and walked back towards the hut.

I followed him and picked up the massive foam board that he'd left propped up against the wooden wall.

'Wow, where are you going?'

'Eh? The water?' I motioned to the sea.

'Not today, *Princesse*. First lesson is always on the sand.'

'Are you serious? I did this yesterday with my sisters. Remember?'

'I am very serious. Always. Yesterday was only a demonstration. If you want lessons with me, these are my rules. How long will you be here?' he asked and I dumped the board back down on the sand.

'Four weeks.'

'*Bon.* A lot of time.'

'I'm a swimmer, you know,' I said, just about stopping myself from crossing my arms in frustration. I put my hand in my hair instead, twisting a curl tightly round my finger.

'I know, I saw yesterday. But swimming and surfing are very different things. *Alors*, lie down.'

And we did the pop-ups. Again. Over and over, until my arms were aching, and I was ready to scream in frustration.

I stood up. 'Can we go in the water *now*? Please?' I begged.

'*Non*, but your lesson is almost finished, and then you are not my responsibility.' He shrugged, but I'd stopped listening and had turned to the water, where some surfers were paddling into a wave.

'They should wait, there's another set coming,' I said.

Antoine just stared at me for a second, then he looked out at the water, nodding. 'You learn quickly.'

I was about to try to convince him that I could go into the water when Delphine from the Brasserie, another girl, and Sébastian dragged their much smaller surfboards on to the sand beside us. They were all wet and wearing navy rash vests that looked like a uniform.

'*Salut!*' The black-haired girl Delphine was with gave me a huge smile, as Delphine spoke seriously to Antoine in French.

Sébastian lay down on his surfboard and looked up at me. His shaggy blonde hair fanned out on the white board beneath him.

'I sleep now,' he said, grinned and closed his eyes.

The girl kicked him in the side, and he folded over dramatically.

'*Allez quoi, Sébastian! Lève-toi!*' She laughed.

He groaned and looked up at me, his hand shielding his eyes from the sun. 'Lili is not kind to me. Delphine is not kind to me.' He gave me a sad face then bounced up to standing almost immediately.

'*Enchanté.*' Sébastian was at least a foot taller than me, with long, gangly, tanned limbs. He held out a huge hand towards me and I took it. Then he bent down and kissed both of my cheeks. 'I am Sébastian, *la victime* of Delphine and Lili, and who are you?'

I looked up at him and couldn't help smiling back at his grin. 'Margot. This is my first lesson.'

'First lesson! With Antoine!' Sébastian turned to Lili, who was squeezing salt water from her long, dark hair. I glanced over at Delphine and Antoine, who were still talking in low voices.

'Antoine is strict, *non*?' Lili looked at me with a warm smile. 'But he is good. He was the teacher of Delphine.'

Lili nodded towards them, but they were too deep in conversation to look up. Then, without warning, Sébastian launched himself at Delphine and pulled her over playfully.

'Delphine, *notre professionelle*!'

Delphine pulled herself away from him, but she was laughing. Then he started tickling her and Lili stepped towards them. '*Arrêtez!*' she said and grabbed Delphine's hand, pulling her close. Then they kissed, and an unexpected relief took over, as it dawned on me that Felix and Delphine definitely weren't together.

Sébastian walked over, slung his long arm round my neck and leaned in. '*C'est compliqué* here on the beach. Delphine is, how do you say, *la copine*?' Sébastian looked at Antoine.

'Girlfriend,' he confirmed.

'Yes. Delphine is the girlfriend of Lili. *But.* And it is a big but. She *was la copine*, sorry, the girlfriend of Antoine.'

Antoine was looking at me. I couldn't see his eyes behind his glasses, but I wondered if he was looking for a reaction.

'OK. I get it. And who is your *copine*?' I asked Sébastian.

'You?' He pulled me closer towards him. 'I joke. No, it is very sad. I do not have a girlfriend.'

Delphine said something to him, and he whispered in my ear. 'Help. I told you that they are not nice to me.' Then he laughed and released me.

Delphine and Lili were whispering to each other now and I walked over to Antoine. 'Delphine is a professional surfer?' I asked.

'She wants to be, but she needs to train harder,' Antoine said in her direction. She looked up and waved him away. 'There is a competition in September. *La Vague d'Or.* The Golden Wave. Last year she placed fourth in the girls' competition, and this year, if she comes in the top three, she will get prize money, sponsorship, invitations to competitions in Europe, maybe the world.' He glanced at Delphine, who was listening. 'If she trains harder, she might do it.'

'*Tu n'es plus mon instructeur*,' she said.

'*En anglais?*' Lili looked at her with big eyes and nodded at me as she pushed a strand of wet hair from Delphine's face.

Delphine rolled her eyes. 'Antoine, you are not my instructor any more. Happy?' Delphine said, turning to Lili and smiling.

'Margot,' Lili said. 'Are you coming to the bonfire tonight?'

I looked at Antoine, confused. 'The bonfire?' I asked.

'It is not for tourists,' I heard Delphine say.

'On the beach, we have a bonfire tonight, right here. For all the surfers. Do you want to come?'

'Oh, please come, Margot,' Sébastian begged beside me.

Felix flashed in my head. Our kiss. Our date. But maybe he would come too. A surfer party. I couldn't think of anything more cool.

'I'll be there.'

Then Delphine stormed off, mumbling something in French, followed by Lili, followed by Sébastian, who kissed my cheeks again before he ran after them, leaving me standing on the sand with Antoine.

'Delphine. She is complicated.' Antoine flicked his head in their direction.

'I can see that,' I replied.

'I will see you soon? With your sisters?' Antoine asked.

'Yep, I'll be back.'

'Perhaps I will let them in the water,' he said, grinning at me, and I pushed him playfully.

'You better not. See you later.' I turned and walked back towards the campsite, and I felt Antoine's eyes on me the whole way down the beach.

12

Back at the beach with Rue and Wren later that morning, I sat alone on the sand, just watching Antoine with the girls. He'd taken them into the water today, and was so good with Rue, helping her balance, making her laugh. He made it look so easy. I remembered when Mum and Dad asked me to help teach Rue how to ride her bike and we almost killed each other.

'Did you see me?' Rue pushed soaking-wet hair from her face as she walked up the beach towards me with Wren an hour later.

'Yeah, you were brilliant.' I smiled. 'And you too, Wren.'

They wrapped themselves in towels and chased each other while Antoine came over to talk to me.

'You were up early. I thought you might have changed your mind and be resting now,' he said. He sat down on the sand beside me, so close that I could feel the coolness of his T-shirt from the water. Millimetres from me, both of us staring out at the ocean.

'I said I'd be here. Anyway, I wanted to see if you were so strict with everyone, or if it was just me.' I turned away so he didn't catch my smirk.

'Different methods for different students,' he said.

'So you're saying I need the drill-sergeant approach?'

He grinned at that. Briefly, before being serious again – of course. 'I think you have potential. And potential can be wasted if there is too much . . . being gentle.'

'But how do you know? I haven't even been in the water yet.'

'I do not need the water to see a surfer.' Antoine pulled himself up. 'The bonfire. You will be here?' I nodded. He held out a hand to help me up. I took it, and I felt his touch surge through my body like electricity. 'You should not stay out too late. Serious surfers do not stay out late before dawn sessions.'

And that surge of electricity? It hit a power cut, as the irritation of him telling me what to do again took over.

'*À bientôt,*' he added before he left, giving me no chance to reply.

I stared after him for a second before letting my eyes find my sisters.

'Rue! Wren! Time to go.' I was ravenous, and was desperately hoping that Mum and Dad had bought a fresh baguette from the shop.

As we walked past the Brasserie, I heard my name. But it wasn't Felix.

'Over here, Margot!'

I scanned the crowded bar, and there were Mum and Dad, sitting at a table with tiny cups of coffee in front of them.

I walked over, followed by Rue and Wren.

'Fancy an early lunch here today, girls?' Dad smiled and stood up to look for more chairs. 'We were watching out for when you came past.'

'I'm starving!' said Rue. Dad pushed a chair in behind her, pleased.

'Me too,' said Wren.

'Me three.' The restaurant was already buzzing, and I glanced around briefly to spot Felix. I saw him talking to a family, waving his hands and talking enthusiastically. Those hands that held me as we kissed. My stomach did a rollercoaster flip. I turned just in time to see Rue taking the piss out of me by doing a ridiculous kissing face at Wren, who burst into laughter.

I sighed dramatically, while Mum looked at them endearingly. 'So how was surfing?' Mum clasped her hands together and stared between Rue and Wren.

'Amazing!' Rue said. 'Antoine said I was a natural, like Margot.' Rue beamed with pride.

I couldn't suppress my smile – for both of us. 'He said that?'

'Yep. I *am* amazing. He said that there are special competitions for people with disabilities too.'

'That's wonderful, love. It is safe, isn't it?' Mum looked at me and I nodded, still basking in the glow of what Rue had said.

'Antoine is with them the whole time, they don't go deep,' I reassured her.

'You were surfing too?' Dad took a sip of wine and found my eyes.

'Yeah, I mean, just on the sand so far, but I think I'd like to keep doing it.' I looked down at the menu to try to hide the blush that was threatening to engulf my face.

'You are ready to order?'

That *voice.*

Felix. Soft and warm, with the most perfect accent. I looked up to see him, eyes on me, white shirt pulled up at the sleeve, exposing tanned forearms. He smiled.

'Felix, this is my family. Rue, Wren, my mum and dad,' I said, more awkwardly than I'd wanted. 'Mum, Dad, this is my friend Felix.'

Felix shook Dad's hand, then proceeded to kiss the cheeks of mum, Rue and Wren, who dissolved into giggles.

'You are enjoying Biarritz?' Felix asked Mum and Dad.

'Oh yes, it's lovely, although we haven't done much exploring yet,' Mum replied. She pushed some hair behind her ear. Was Felix making her nervous? I sat back and watched the exchange.

'Oh you must explore. I will give Margot the name of a restaurant in Bayonne for you. It is perfect.'

'Well that would be lovely, but with the girls, we tend to eat in restaurants that serve pizza,' Mum said, laughing.

And then it just came out. 'Maybe you and Dad could go out and I'll stay with the girls?' I offered.

'And Felix can stay with us too,' Rue added, and I felt my face flush. 'He can teach me French.' Rue grinned at him and Felix smiled.

'*Bien sûr.* Of course,' he said, translating for her.

I looked at Mum and Dad, who seemed delighted with the plan.

We ordered our food, and while we were waiting, Felix tapped me on the shoulder, before leaning in to whisper in my ear. 'Can I speak with you a moment?'

I stood up and followed Felix to a quiet space beside the bar.

'I am sorry if that was too much, meeting your family and telling them about the restaurant.' Felix's hand was in his hair, and I reached up and took it, bringing it down and holding it in mine between us.

'Don't worry, Rue has already invited you to our house and I think my mum and dad were *enchantés*,' I said. 'Oh, and I had my first surf lesson,' I added, and I couldn't help myself from smiling at the memory of impressing Antoine with my ocean-watching. I'd been looking forward to telling Felix all about it.

'Oh yeah?' Felix moved to wipe a table. And that hollowed-out feeling of disappointment was back. The one that showed up when I expected someone to react differently. Like I'd had it all decided in my head, then it was the total opposite.

'Yeah. Just on the sand, but maybe tomorrow I can go in the water.' I was struggling to keep up the excited tone I'd led with.

'Are you sure this is what you want?' Felix asked, still not looking at me. What was this? Was he not interested? In the surfing . . . or me?

'Yeah, I loved it. But some girl, Lili I think her name was, she invited me to a bonfire at the beach tonight with the surf school. Maybe we could go together?' I felt weird now. Uncomfortable, self-conscious. He was wringing out the cloth in his hands. Hard. So hard the muscles in his forearms tensed.

'Antoine Laurent's surf school?'

I nodded. 'You know him?'

'Biarritz is not a big place. But those parties, they can be *un peu intense.*' He made a face to himself that I couldn't read and shook his head.

'Oh, OK. Are you sure?' I asked, my stomach lurching at the 'no' he'd given me so quickly. 'It's not until later, so maybe you'll change your mind.' I smiled playfully.

'Not tonight. Sorry,' he said simply.

'Is everything OK?' I asked, struck by his sudden change of mood.

'Tomorrow, I have time off work. If you are free, I would like to show you Saint-Jean-de-Luz, the town where my mother sells soap, if you remember?' Felix looked at me hopefully.

'I'd like that,' I said. It made sense about the party, I guess – he'd have been working all day and evening. He'd probably be too tired. He'd asked me out tomorrow. It was fine.

'I should get back to work. But I will see you tomorrow? At ten?'

'You will see me at ten,' I said, nodding. 'Meet here?' He grinned, and his uncomfortable reaction to the bonfire felt like a distant memory.

'*Bon.* And, Margot? There was something else I wanted to say to you.' He scanned the restaurant, before turning to me again.

I inhaled and looked into the brown eyes that were flecked with gold. 'Yeah?'

'Last night at *les tournesols* . . . I have lived here my whole life. I have seen so many sunsets. But not one was as beautiful as it was when you were with me . . . and I know you are only here for the summer, but I want you to know that you are already important to me.'

I couldn't help but feel elated as the words flooded my body, filling the hollow with a relief that cascaded right through me. I took his hand again and squeezed it, had a brief look around to make sure Mum and Dad weren't looking, then kissed him gently, my hand on his jaw, and I felt him relax into me, our mouths in sync, the buzz of the restaurant fading into nothing.

'And, Margot,' he added again, like he'd forgotten something. 'I am not asking for promises. I know better than that. I just do not want to waste the time we have, pretending that it is just for the summer. It already feels like something more to me.'

Worry filled his eyes. Like he'd said something horribly wrong. But his words made my whole body warm, a warmth that had nothing to do with the heat of the sun. It was a heat that grew from inside, spreading through my veins like an antidote to a sickness.

'Margot!' Rue's voice called across the restaurant. 'Food!'

I looked round, before looking back at Felix.

'It feels like that to me too.' I kissed him gently again, squeezed his hand and walked back to my family, knowing in that moment that something had changed. The warm air fizzed with excitement. With possibility and understanding. Whatever happened next, we could discover it together.

13

The sun had already set when I followed the path to the beach for the bonfire that evening. It looked different in the dark. Less like paradise, more like the murder spot in a crime documentary. I walked faster.

I heard a '*Merde!*' but couldn't see anything. Then, when I turned the corner, there was Delphine, hunched down on the sand, fidgeting with her flip-flop.

'Are you OK?' I asked.

'*Mes tongs sont cassées*,' Delphine replied without looking up at me.

'Your flip-flops?' I bent down beside her. 'I have spare ones at the mobile home. I could get them if you like?' I offered, ignoring her cold tone and deliberate French.

She hesitated, like my niceness had shocked her. It had shocked me too. The rage that had consumed me at the start of the holiday had completely faded. Delphine stopped fidgeting with the flip-flop and looked like she was considering her answer. 'Thank you, but no, it is OK.'

She took off her flip-flops and threw them into the darkness to get lost in the reeds.

We started walking again. And the silence was uncomfortable until she broke it.

'*Tu es avec Felix?*' She didn't even turn to look at me when she asked.

'Now?' I clarified. I looked around to show her that he wasn't there.

'*Non.*' She shook her head. Irritated. 'You and Felix. It is serious?'

What was I supposed to say to that?

'I don't know,' I said awkwardly. I wished he was here tonight. I'd thought about sending him a message and asking him again to come with me, but I remembered how he'd shut it down so quickly before, so I didn't. I settled on sending him a gif of puppies instead, before immediately cringing at how immature it looked. But he sent one back, right away, even cuter than mine.

'Why do you not know?' Delphine asked.

'Why are you asking?' I said, irritated. She was with Lili so I had no idea why she was so concerned about me and Felix.

She muttered something in French and all I could pick out was 'Antoine' and *les filles de l'été*. Summer girls.

'And *you're* with Lili?' I clarified.

She snorted. '*Oui.*' She extended the *oui* like I'd said something really stupid.

As we turned the corner, I saw it. The fire burned bright orange in the night, and there were teenagers everywhere – sitting on the sand, standing in groups, huddled around some guy with a guitar. I took a photo of the silhouettes and sent it to Priya as Delphine walked on ahead.

ME: French beach parties / Irish beach parties? Hope you're doing something fun tonight x

I couldn't believe I was here by myself. This wasn't the kind of thing I usually did. I'd spent the last year doing things as a trio with Ari and Theo. But here? It was like a different world, and I was so intrigued. By the beach, by the surfers, by Antoine. I didn't even want to think it, not after my date with Felix, and our kiss, but there was something that drew me to Antoine. Kind of like the first time Ari had given me beer. I hated it. Horrible. Bitter. Couldn't stand it. But when I tried it again, there was something I liked about it, and there was something about it that kept bringing me back. As I walked towards the bonfire, I could just see the surf hut down the beach. I scanned the crowd for him, but could barely make out anyone specific in the darkness.

'Wohoo!' Delphine shouted and ran towards the group, who cheered when they saw her getting close. I hung back, walking slowly, starting to feel less brave.

'Margot!'

A figure bounded towards me. Big, skinny, loud. 'Margot!' Sébastian.

He had a huge grin on his face when he reached me. 'I am so happy you came to *le feu*,' Sébastian said. He threw his arms round me, then let go. 'This is how you say hello in Ireland? A hug?'

I laughed. 'Sometimes.'

Then he leaned forward and kissed both my cheeks. 'And we do this in France.'

His blonde hair was tied in a top knot, and he was wearing shorts and a black shirt that was open the whole way down.

'Is Antoine here?' I asked as we walked slowly towards the bonfire. It had just come out. I hadn't planned it. But it made sense that I'd look for him as, out of everyone here, he was the one I knew the best.

'Of course Antoine is here. *Le flic de la plage.*' Sébastian, unfazed by my question, nudged me and I stumbled. 'Margot, I am sorry! We will walk like this instead.' Sébastian threw one arm round my shoulders and pulled me close to him.

I laughed. 'What's *le flic*?' I asked.

'The cops. Police! Antoine thinks he is beach police,' he explained.

'Is that why he's so strict about not going into the water during first lessons?'

'Yes. But Antoine is boring. I am much more *intéressant*,' Sébastian said.

'Oh yeah?'

'Yes!'

We were so close to the bonfire that I could feel the heat of it on my face. The guy with the guitar was singing as well as playing. Something in French. Sébastian took my hand and made me spin in the sand.

'Dance with me, Margot!' he said, and I hated dancing but couldn't help but laugh as he gave me a big goofy smile.

'*Arrêtez de traumatiser la nouvelle!*' Lili appeared beside me and grabbed my arm, pulling me away from Sébastian. 'Are you OK, Margot? He is like a little puppy. Too much excitement. *Le surexcité.*' Lili smiled at Sébastian, who laughed back.

'*C'est pas ma faute. Je suis irrésistible!*' he called.

'He is not irresistible,' Lili whispered in my ear. 'And it is always his fault!' she shouted back at him.

Lili took my hand and led me towards a little group of teenagers. One that contained Delphine.

'*Laissez-moi vous présenter Margot!*' Lili said. I hadn't noticed earlier because it had been wet, but her hair was even curlier than mine and sat in dark ringlets on her shoulders. She was wearing denim shorts and a T-shirt with the surf school logo.

A few of the group gave me a nod and Delphine whispered something to the boy she was standing beside. He laughed.

'*Bon!*' Lili said. She reached down to a cool box at her feet and handed me a can of beer. I opened it, thankful for something to concentrate on.

'*Tu es canon dans cette robe.*' Lili flicked the lacey part at the bottom of my dress.

'*Canon?*' I asked.

'Hot,' said a voice behind me. A familiar voice that sent a shiver up my spine. 'She said that you look hot in that dress, *Princesse*.'

I turned to see Antoine looking at me, words stuck in my throat and butterflies from nowhere filling my stomach. White shirt wide open, board shorts, dark hair sticking up like it had just dried after being in the sea.

Lili leaned up and whispered something in Antoine's ear, but he didn't take his eyes off me as she did.

'*C'est pas mon problème*,' Antoine said as Lili walked back towards Delphine, whose group had moved to the other side of the bonfire.

'*Alors, Princesse.* Welcome to your first beach fire party. I hope you have a good time.'

And he did something to me. Scrambled the thoughts in my head, and I couldn't get any words out.

And with that Antoine walked away towards the beach hut, leaving me standing there, alone, with my beer.

14

I took my drink and looked for Sébastian. It wasn't hard to find him because he was so tall. He was standing with a group of kids I hadn't met, so I walked round the outside and poked him gently on the arm.

'Ah, Margot! You are OK?' His face lit up when he saw me.

I nodded and gave him a smile.

'*Margot apprend le surf avec Antoine.*' Sébastian put his hands on my shoulders, and I sipped my beer as the group stared at me. Four pairs of French-boy eyes.

They laughed and talked between themselves, and I could only catch the name Antoine.

Sébastian shook his head when he saw the name had caught my attention. 'Antoine never parties with us. Not any more. He likes to keep an eye on the ocean. I told you, *le flic de la plage.*'

I was trying to work out why Antoine would hide from the party, when the guy with the guitar started playing another song and everyone erupted in a cheer and moved towards him.

Then I found myself alone again. I looked down the beach, at the surf hut that seemed so lonely in the darkness, and without really thinking, I walked towards it.

The wind had picked up, and I was so far from the bonfire that I felt a bit cold for the first time since I'd got to France. I pulled my cardigan round me and gazed out at the waves that were crashing against the sand.

'*Les vagues*,' I whispered into the night. And I found myself walking towards them like they were calling me.

I slid off my sandals and walked into the water. I stared up at the blanket of stars above me and wondered why I never saw this many in Belfast. I took small steps into deeper water, enjoying the coolness of the waves that swelled against my legs, then took another sip of my beer. I breathed in the salted air, closing my eyes to really get lost in it.

And I nearly dropped my beer when a voice said out of nowhere, 'What are you doing?'

I turned round to see Antoine on the sand, hands in the pockets of his board shorts, looking at me with a serious expression on his face.

I gave a small laugh. 'Em, I was just looking at the stars.'

'The stars are in the sky, *non*?' Antoine pointed upwards. 'So why is it that are you in the water? You need to come back to the sand.'

I was about to wade back but changed my mind. Why should I?

'I'm in the water because I *want* to be in the water.'

'Because you want to?' Antoine repeated.

I turned round, taking a sip of beer and enjoying the view of the whole ocean.

'The ocean is dangerous. I thought we had talked about this,' Antoine said.

'I'm not swimming,' I said.

'Not yet. I have seen it before. *Les mecs, les filles* who go into the water when they drink alcohol. It is stupid. It is dangerous.'

I squeezed my hand round my beer can then turned back to him. 'So you think I'm just going to go for a swim right now? Why would I do that?' I demanded.

'I do not know. I do not know you,' Antoine replied. 'But I would like it if you came out of the water.' He didn't move towards me, just stood in the same place.

'What's in it for me?' I asked playfully, thanks to the beer.

'I will show you my hut,' Antoine said. He didn't return my smile.

'What's so special about your hut?' I asked, stumbling slightly as a wave smashed into the back of my legs.

'Come and find out.'

And then a million reasons flashed in my head about why I *shouldn't* go into Antoine's hut alone with him. Felix being one of them. And I don't know why I didn't just shut it down right there.

'OK,' I said and left the water, watching his shoulders visibly relax.

'I can make you coffee?' he offered.

'I don't like coffee,' I replied.

'*Chocolat* then. I have a feeling it is going to be hard work to teach you.' He sounded more chilled-out now. The clipped tone from a few moments ago had morphed into something marginally softer.

'Deal. I like hot chocolate.' I picked up my sandals and we walked towards the hut.

'Please no alcohol near the water,' Antoine said.

I shook the almost empty beer can. 'I don't really like this beer anyway,' I said. And I caught his smile as he tried to hide it by looking away.

When we got to the hut, Antoine unlocked it.

He pushed the door open, and we walked inside. He flicked on a light, then hit another switch. Fairy lights twinkled around the edges of the windows. There wasn't much apart from that. A bed. A tiny kitchen with a mini fridge. A rusted locker, a sofa with worn-looking blankets and a corner full of floats, wetsuits and other surf paraphernalia. The windows went all the way around the hut so you could see the entire beach.

'Do you live here?' I asked, scanning the room again. It looked lived-in, but it was tiny.

'Yes. Well, I stay here most of the time. I like to be close to the water.' He walked over to the little kitchen.

I put my beer can down and sat on the sofa, the sounds of singing at the bonfire in the distance. There was something charming about living on the beach. And it just added to the whole mystery of Antoine.

'Cool,' I nodded, thinking how fun it must be to live alone with nobody telling you what to do.

'*Chocolat?*' Antoine asked again and I nodded.

'*S'il te plaît.*'

Antoine made the hot chocolate on the little stove and handed it to me in a mug before sitting down beside me, leg against mine.

And it was the first time I'd seen his eyes. They were usually hidden behind black sunglasses, but here, in the soft light of the hut, they were a warm, deep blue, outlined with thick, dark lashes. Like a tide pool surrounded by water-soaked rocks.

'It is nice?' he asked, nodding at the mug.

I dragged my eyes away from his and blew on the hot chocolate before trying some. It was sweet, and rich, and perfect. Who knew an arrogant surfer held the secret to the best hot chocolate in the world.

'Amazing – what's in it?' I asked. It was sweet and spicy and creamy all at the same time.

'A secret. A secret family recipe,' Antoine said before leaning back on the sofa. It was the most relaxed I'd seen him.

'Sébastian and Lili are nice,' I mused.

'They are very special to me, they are my family,' he said, and I could tell that he really meant it.

I'd turned to look at him and had let my knee keep leaning against his, but moved it when I had Felix *déjà-vu*.

'And Delphine?'

'Ah – Delphine. She is a bit more complicated. But underneath? She is who you want to save you if you are in trouble,' Antoine said. He was looking right at me now and it was like I could feel his gaze, like some imaginary laser beam that ignited this heat inside my chest and made my heart race.

'She's good at surfing?' I asked, knowing the answer.

'She is more than good. She could be great, but she needs to do more training,' Antoine said seriously, as if she was there to hear it.

'Cool,' I said. I thought about asking him why she was so cold towards me but didn't want to ruin the mood. 'When do I get to go in the water?'

'Have you been practising at home? Your pop-up?' he asked me matter-of-factly.

'What? No, I don't have a board.'

He shrugged and said something in French that sounded more like a noise than a word. 'You do not need a board to practise.'

'My sister would jump on me!' I laughed.

'Which? Rue? I would like to see that,' he said, then laughed too, as if he was imagining it.

Then he stood up quickly. Like he'd sensed something or heard a noise that I hadn't. He looked out the window.

'*Merde*,' he said simply, before opening the door and running down the beach towards the water.

15

I rushed out of the hut and on to the beach, where Antoine was racing towards the water. There were kids dragging surfboards into the waves, while others stood and watched from the sand.

Antoine was yelling in French.

I jogged after him and watched as the people in the water stopped what they were doing.

'*Sortez de l'eau!*' he shouted. Furious. As if there was an imminent shark attack or something. The groups on the beach just watched him and when the surfers didn't listen, or maybe didn't obey him quickly enough, he went into the water himself, up to his waist and screamed at them again.

They listened this time, and I watched as surfboards turned round one by one and they all paddled towards the shore.

I was about to go and see if Antoine was OK, but I was beaten to it by Sébastian, Delphine and Lili, who had surrounded him in the sea. Sébastian patted him on the shoulder and Lili hugged him from one side.

Antoine didn't leave the water until everyone was on the sand. And they stood there and listened to him talk like he was the teacher of a disruptive class.

An awkward silence at the end of his speech filled the air with tension. Then Lili shouted, 'Let's party!'

They all walked back towards the bonfire, and I took my chance to talk to Antoine. He was just staring at the ocean when I reached him, taking deep breaths that seemed to synchronize in time with the tide. So I just stared out at the water too.

'Are you OK?' I asked.

He hesitated before speaking. Before even moving. Like he was stuck in some kind of trance.

'The water. It is dangerous,' he said, and I wasn't even sure if it was to me. Eventually he turned to me. 'You want to party?' And he didn't give me time to think of an answer, he just grabbed my hand, and we walked towards the bonfire.

The way he took my hand was gentle. Not tightly like I would have expected. His skin was rough, I assumed from years of feeling their way round surfboards, but his touch was soft, like he didn't want to crush something delicate. And I didn't pull away, even though Felix's face filled my head and guilt pooled in my stomach. I liked it. And I didn't want it to stop.

When we got to the bonfire, Sébastian greeted us, followed by Lili and Delphine. I saw Delphine glance at our hands before I pulled mine away, reaching up to push hair behind my ear.

'*Une bière*, Margot?' Sébastian handed me a can of beer. 'I told you he was *le flic*.' Sébastian grinned at me and Antoine said something to him in French that made him laugh.

Delphine started talking to the group in French when Antoine stopped her. 'We should all speak English. *Pour notre invitée*.' He glanced at me as he said it and I smiled gratefully.

I knew a bit of French, but it was too fast to catch and as soon as I'd managed to translate a word they'd moved on to something else.

Delphine rolled her eyes. 'OK,' she conceded.

We walked down the beach a bit. Not too far that we couldn't feel the heat of the fire, but not too close that the singing drowned out our voices. Then Delphine and Lili dropped to the sand, leaning against each other comfortably. Sébastian sat beside them, then me, then Antoine, in a circle.

'*Alors*, Margot. Tell us about you, have you wanted to learn to surf for a long time?' Lili sipped on her can of beer and smiled at me. There was something warm about Lili, like an aura that drew you in and made you feel immediately welcome in her presence.

'Oh, no. Not at all.' And as soon as it came out of my mouth, I knew it was the wrong thing to say. Delphine made a noise, half laugh, half snort. Lili elbowed her. 'I used to swim. Competitively,' I said, trying to pull it back.

'Ah, a swimmer,' Sébastian said. 'Antoine was a swimmer too.' He nodded towards Antoine, who didn't say anything.

'Oh yeah?' I looked at him to elaborate.

He didn't, only saying, 'Bastian, tell Margot about your first surf competition.' Antoine grinned at Sébastian.

'Oh no, Margot, you do not want to hear this. It will make you not want to surf at all.' Sébastian put his face in his hands and shook his blonde head.

'You have to tell me now,' I pleaded.

'OK, you win. The Biarritz Junior Open.' He jumped up on to the sand in a surfer's stance and Lili groaned. 'The sun was shining. The waves were perfect. I paddled my little arms out so hard.' He made a paddling motion.

'You have never been little.' Delphine actually cracked a smile when she said this.

'OK, I paddled my big eleven-year-old arms out with the confidence of Antoine. I was ready. The horn, it goes off and I see this perfect wave. The most beautiful wave you have ever seen. I got up, and I raise my arms in victory before I had even caught it, fell off backwards and knocked myself out with my board.'

Sébastian mimed a thud, then sat down and looked sad.

'Oh, poor Sébastian.' Lili leaned over and kissed his cheek.

He smiled and pointed at his forehead. 'Five stitches and they have called me *le clown des vagues* ever since.'

I leaned over to see the scar on his head.

'That *is* a very sad story,' I said, playing along.

'But it was not that sad because in the hospital was the most beautiful woman I have ever seen. A nurse who did my stitches. I was in love.' Sébastian winked at me, and I laughed.

'Delphine, tell Margot about *La Vague d'Or*,' Antoine prompted.

She shrugged. 'There is nothing to know. I came fourth.'

'You were amazing,' said Lili, stroking Delphine's leg.

'Amazing is winning. I lost.' She shook her head. And it was the first time that I felt like I was on the same page as Delphine. This was exactly how I'd felt when I was swimming. To win was everything. Ecstasy, euphoria. Second place? Might as well have come last.

'You did not lose!' Lili protested.

Delphine took a drink of beer. She shook her head. 'This time, I will win.'

'Yes!' Sébastian leaned in and clinked his drink against hers. '*Et*, Antoine?' Sébastian looked at him and Antoine smiled before pushing his hair back off his face.

'My first competition? I was thirteen.'

'*Les Jeunes Vagues*?' Lili asked.

'*Ouais*,' Antoine nodded. 'I had been training for months. Everybody expected me to win. And I did well. I had the highest score when I went into the finals. But during the final, I saw a kid who struggled with the current.'

Everyone was silent as Antoine told his story. There was no laughing like there had been for Sébastian, or encouragement like for Delphine, just silence.

'And nobody else noticed. And he was getting tired trying to paddle. Then I helped him out and missed my heat.' The way he said it, like he was so desperate to make it sound as if it was no big deal, made me think it had been the total opposite.

I watched Antoine, who wasn't looking at anyone now, just staring into the sand.

'To Antoine.' Lili held up her drink. We all did, except Antoine, who didn't have one.

'What about you, Lili?' I asked, interested to know her story too.

She grinned and glanced at Delphine before looking back at us. 'Not my first, but my favourite. A year ago. I had been surfing maybe for three years, and I still was not good.' Delphine nudged her in support.

'*C'est vrai!*' Lili laughed. 'I had no business being at any competition. And I wiped out in the first heat. But I stayed to watch the finals. And this girl?' She turned to Delphine. 'She was riding the waves like she owned them.'

I smiled at the story. 'And that was when you started going out?' I asked.

Lili snorted. '*Non*, then Delphine went out with Antoine.' Lili flicked sand towards him.

'And then Lili stole my girlfriend,' Antoine said.

'You were never meant for each other, and I did not steal, it was at least a month after you two broke up. *Your* true love is still to come.' Lili smiled, then turned and kissed Delphine gently on the lips.

'I think it is time to go,' Antoine said. Then he stood up.

'*Le flic* returns,' Sébastian said before standing too. I pulled myself off the sand and watched as Antoine yelled across to the bonfire.

'*C'est l'heure. La marée monte.*'

Sébastian was standing beside me. 'He is telling everyone to leave because the tide is coming in,' he translated.

'Ah OK.' I expected it to be like parties at home where nobody listened and just kept on drinking, but they didn't. They all started to make their way down the beach, away from the dying bonfire.

When everyone else had left, we helped to tidy up the beach.

Sébastian offered to help put out the fire, but Antoine shook his head and picked up a metal bucket that he took towards the water. I jogged to catch up with him.

'Do you want help?' I asked, leading with that before I thanked him for this evening.

'You should go home now,' Antoine said. His tone was cold. Serious. I watched him bend over and fill up the bucket of water before turning and walking back towards the bonfire, while I just stood there, unsure of what to do with my hands.

'I'll see you at my lesson tomorrow?'

'Six a.m.,' he replied. Any of the softness he'd shown in the hut felt like a distant memory.

'That's very early,' I complained, trying to tease it back.

'Six is when the real surfers catch waves. Unless you are not serious about learning?' He looked at me briefly.

'I'll see you at six,' I said, and he nodded his head.

'*Tu jeu avec le feu.*' Delphine said in my direction when we got back. She glanced at Antoine after she'd said the words, which were slow and clear enough for me to translate.

'You're playing with fire.'

I wasn't 'playing' with anything. I was getting surf lessons. And even though at that moment Felix's lovely face filled my thoughts, I chose to ignore what she'd said.

On the way back towards the campsite, before they branched off on to another path, Sébastian chatted away excitedly about surfing, but I was only half listening. I couldn't get Antoine out of my head. The way he'd held my hand out of nowhere, how he'd looked at me, how his mood had suddenly changed into something darker.

And then there was Felix, and the sunflower date that felt like another life altogether.

16

I'd woken at five a.m. the next morning, ready for my lesson with Antoine. Just so I wasn't 'late'. And today, we'd gone into the water. I'd been so excited about the fact I'd stood up on my first go (and every time after) that I told Antoine I'd see him at my sister's lesson.

It wasn't until I got back to the caravan, exhausted and happy, that I realized. I had my date with Felix in Saint-Jean-de-Luz.

'Margot, Margot! Did you go into the water today?' Rue asked as soon as she spotted me. She was sitting at the table outside, eating breakfast in her pyjamas.

I nodded. 'I did. And I stood up. First time.' I held up a finger.

'Awesome. Do you think I could stand up?' Rue asked.

'You'll have to do what Antoine tells you. And it might be that you stay lying down for a few more days, but he'll show you what's safe,' I said.

'But you could just ask him?' She didn't miss a beat.

I took a deep breath and looked at Mum and Dad. 'Mum, Dad, would you mind being there for their surf lesson today? I made plans with Felix and I completely forgot. Sorry.'

'You're not coming?' Rue shouted before Mum and Dad could answer.

'I'm sorry, I can't. Not today.'

'That's fine, love,' Mum said. 'It's your holiday too, you should enjoy yourself. Where are you going?' Mum and Dad seemed to have chilled out here. And I don't know if Mum had spoken to Dad, but even he had been giving me a break. A serious contrast to the way we got on at home.

'Saint-Jean-de-Luz,' I said.

'With your *boyfriend*,' said Rue, who was in a major mood now.

'Yes, Felix happens to be a boy. So, their lesson is at ten but you need to be there for half nine,' I said.

Rue went inside and tried to slam the door shut but hadn't pushed it hard enough, so it swung open on its hinges, ruining the effect of her sulk.

I walked in after her and knocked gently on her open bedroom door, and found her lying on her bed.

'You OK?' I asked.

'I'm not talking to you,' she said.

'Why not?'

'You promised to spend time with us this holiday,' she said sulkily.

'I am. And I have been. Didn't I set you up with the lessons in the first place?' I asked. 'And haven't I been to them so far?' I risked sitting on the edge of her bed, aware that her foot was in kicking distance of me.

'Yes, but I was going to show you how good I was today,' Rue said, and my heart sank at how sad she sounded.

'But listen, think how much more special it will be when you've been practising without me and then I see all the improvement?' I offered, and she sat up like she was considering it.

'You'll come tomorrow?'

'I promise,' I replied.

'You better,' she said, narrowing her eyes, then she launched herself at me for a hug, and I let myself breathe in the smell of her curls. Strawberry. That kid shampoo that transported me back to childhood.

'Ugh, you smell like the sea,' she said and wrenched herself away.

'You will too soon.' I stuck out my tongue and went to have a shower and get ready to see Felix again. I took my time, planning my outfit. Denim shorts, strappy white top, grey cardigan. I liked how the grey looked with my blonde hair and blue eyes. I played some cards with Wren and Rue, who had almost forgiven me until I beat her at Jack Change It, then was angry at me all over again. And soon it was time for the girls to go for their lesson. I waved them off, ate a leftover breakfast croissant, and looked in the mirror again before I walked towards the Brasserie.

When I got there, he was already waiting for me, sitting at the edge of the restaurant, scanning the pathway that led to my mobile home.

'Margot.' He stood up to take me in. 'You look *très jolie*,' he said before kissing both of my cheeks.

'Thank you. You too,' I replied, thinking that *jolie* was the perfect word for him. He *was* pretty. His cheekbones sat high on his face and his jawline was defined without being too prominent. And his hair! The fair waves had the kind of shine that I'd been coveting for years. He was wearing loose denim jeans that were ripped at the knees and a khaki T-shirt that made his skin look even more tanned than it was.

'Come on!'

We walked to the Vespa where he handed me a helmet, put on his, then took my hand and pulled me on behind him.

I knotted my fingers round him and felt the warm, hard muscle of his chest again as we drove through the French countryside, vineyards blurring as we passed and the sun blazing on our skin.

He drove us through a town then stopped beside a harbour. I took off my helmet and smelled fish in the air as multicoloured boats bobbed up and down in the port.

'We are here!' Felix said.

I walked across cobblestones to look at the town. The white buildings with coloured shutters against the impossibly blue sky looked like something from a movie.

'It's beautiful here,' I said.

'*You* are beautiful here,' Felix said smoothly. 'But you are beautiful everywhere.'

I laughed and took the hand he offered to me and threaded my fingers through his.

'Do you mind if we go to the market before we go for lunch? I need to speak to my mother for a moment.' Felix looked at me as if he really was asking for my permission, that if I said I was too hungry, he'd just abandon the market altogether.

'Of course,' I said, trying to hide the fact that nervous butterflies were attacking each other in my stomach.

The market was in a building that looked kind of like a barn. A barn that was packed with tables and colours and so many people. And the *noise*! French voices everywhere. I let Felix lead me through the crowd.

'Felix, *kaixo*!' someone shouted, and Felix pulled me towards a stall that was selling cheese. There were huge wheels of cheese everywhere and a man who looked around eighty smiled at Felix.

Felix talked away to him and, still holding on to his hand, I gazed around the market, completely mesmerized by this other world. When Felix tugged me gently, we walked away.

'*Kaisho*, what's that?' I asked loudly, to be heard over the hum.

'*Kaixo*. It means hello in the Basque language. Sometimes you will see it on signposts, and some of the older generation still speak it. But I only know a few words,' Felix explained.

'Wow,' I said. This world, it was so different from mine. I was so utterly intoxicated by this place, by this boy.

'Here we are,' Felix said, and led me to a stall with towers of home-made soap, decorated with dried flowers, and little baskets. It smelled like heaven and I breathed it in, trying to calm the feeling of impending doom of meeting Felix's mum.

'Felix!' A woman came round from behind the table and kissed Felix on both cheeks. She was small, thin and elegant. She had dark hair and was wearing an apron over a cream blouse.

'*Maman, c'est Margot*,' Felix said, grinning, and his mum

looked at me with deep blue eyes that sparkled in the rays of sun that cut through the gaps in the wooden roof. And just like it was with Felix, I felt immediately accepted, safe.

'Margot. *Enchantée.*' Felix's mother came towards me and kissed both my cheeks. She even smelled like soap.

'*Enchantée*,' I replied awkwardly. She looked at me the way her son did sometimes, like she didn't want to miss something. She smiled. '*Si, si belle.* You are very, *very* beautiful,' she translated.

'Thank you,' I said, pushing hair behind my ear.

Felix started talking to her in French and I looked at the stall, running my fingers along the towers of soap, picking some up to smell.

'*Lavande.*' A girl's voice.

I looked up to see a teenage girl in an apron behind the stall. 'It is the favourite of Marie. I think she will give you some. She has a good instinct for the girls who are with her boys,' the girl said.

I put the soap back and looked at Felix, a bit confused, but he was still deep in conversation with his mum, so I turned back to the girl.

And I just couldn't help myself. 'Are there a lot of girls with Felix?' I asked her.

'With Felix? *Non*,' she said, making a Jenga tower of soap. 'But –'

'Margot, you are ready?' Felix called over to me.

I walked away, bemused, but figured it was just something that got lost in translation.

'For you,' Felix's mum said. She handed me a brown bag

filled with soap. I lifted it to my nose and breathed it in. '*Lavande*,' she said.

'*Merci beaucoup*,' I said. Yet it felt tainted after what the girl had just said. Delphine's remarks about tourists flooded my mind too. But I smiled gratefully.

We walked away and I followed Felix out into the blazing sun.

'I am sorry,' he said. 'Maman, she likes to give soap to people.' He shrugged and looked embarrassed.

'I love it,' I said simply, and he smiled with such relief that I leaned forward and kissed him right there, outside the market, and the moment was so nice that I decided to shove the 'other girls' out of my head.

'Can we eat now?' I asked.

'*Bien sûr!*'

17

We walked through the narrow streets hand in hand, and it felt like we were proper grown-ups. Like we'd come on our own holiday and were exploring the town. I took so many photos. Usually I'd put them straight on Insta, but I was still trying not to look at it after seeing Theo's post.

Felix led me down a side street and I almost tripped on the cobblestones, but he pulled me up and pushed my hair behind my ear as I laughed.

'Sorry,' he said. 'Sometimes the best restaurants are in these hidden streets,' he explained.

'You mean away from all the tourists?' I pretended to be offended, hoping he'd say something sweet, and hating the fact that Delphine's words from the start of the holiday had really got under my skin.

'Yes.' Felix smiled. 'I want to show you the real France, not just what the tourists see.' And then he kissed me, taking all of my doubts away.

We ambled up the almost empty street looking for a restaurant when Felix stopped suddenly. A song filled the air. He had let go of my hand and had just frozen, right there in the road, looking at a man playing what looked like some kind of flute up the street.

'Felix, are you OK?' I asked, even though he clearly wasn't.

'The txistu,' he whispered. Not to me. It was like he was in a trance. I took his hand again, but he didn't respond. It was heavy, lifeless.

'I need to . . . can we . . .?' Felix turned to me with panic in his eyes and this time he did take my hand, pulling me back down the street the same way we'd come, back down towards the harbour, where he found a bench to sit on.

We sat and Felix bent over his knees, putting his head in his hands.

And I didn't ask what was wrong again, I just put my hand on his back and waited for his breath to calm and his heart to stop racing.

Finally, he sat up and just stared out at the harbour.

'Sorry, Margot.' Felix shook his head but still looked out at the boats. I put my hand on top of his.

'Don't apologize,' I said gently. I knew what it felt like. Like there was no air, like your chest was tight and sore and ready to explode, like you might die. That day at the swimming pool. I'd felt it too.

'I just . . .' Felix hesitated, and I could tell how painful he was finding whatever it was, so I stopped him.

'You don't have to explain if you don't want to. We can just sit here if you want?' I offered.

I squeezed his hand, and he squeezed mine back, then looked at me with what I swear were tears in his eyes.

'You know, there's this song,' I said, taking a breath, because it still hurt to think about it – how *she* couldn't breathe. 'This Irish folk song. "The Irish Rover". And Rue loved it because in the version she'd heard, there were bad words.'

I glanced at Felix and watched him attempt a smile, breathing heavily, so I continued.

'So anyway. She got pneumonia. With Rue's cerebral palsy she's more prone to respiratory infections. And this time was really bad. So when she was stable, I got on her bed beside her and played the song over and over again, holding her little hand, and it probably didn't help at all, but I knew it made her happy. And now? I can't listen to the song any more, it brings back memories of how scared she was, and just how unfair it all was.' I was shocked by the tears that filled my eyes now, just by talking about it, but I forced them away. I was just trying to let him know that I understood.

'Will she get better?' Felix asked, more normally now, like he'd come back to life.

'She'll always have cerebral palsy, but she's having this operation in September that will hopefully make things a bit easier for her.' I shook my head. 'She has these injections all the time, and they used to bother her. But now? She just lets them inject her without even saying anything. She's incredible.' I inhaled the salty air and turned to Felix.

'Music can make us feel too much sometimes. Too many memories.' He brushed hair away from my cheek. 'I promise I will explain what just happened. But the words are not here right now.'

'Felix. It's OK. I understand,' I whispered. 'I've felt like this too. Last year I had a panic attack at a swimming competition.'

I looked at my lap as I let the memory in. Felix reached for my hand as I continued. 'It just came out of nowhere, like I couldn't breathe, I couldn't move, it was horrible. And I let so many people down.' I shook my head and blinked back tears.

I felt his hand under my chin, raising it gently to look at him.

'I am sorry you have felt this way too,' he said.

I leaned into his palm, which was now on my cheek, and gazed into the comfort of his eyes.

And then he kissed me, slow and gentle, his hand on my jaw and my hand at the nape of his neck, twisting my fingers in his hair.

'I know a good place to get pizza. Just over there.' Felix pointed.

'With all the tourists?' I asked. Shocked.

Felix rolled his eyes and smirked. 'As long as my favourite tourist is there to protect me.'

I stood up and offered him my hand. He took it and we ate pizza in a beautiful little pizzeria looking out over the harbour, surrounded by Americans.

After lunch we walked around the town and Felix bought me a bracelet. It reminded me of the friendship bracelets that me and Priya used to give each other in primary school. This one was blue and black thread twisted together. I loved it. And it only made me want to go to more tourist shops.

For the next couple of hours, I followed Felix around the lesser-known parts of Saint-Jean-de-Luz like I was trying to keep up with a tour guide. But I loved it, soaking it all in. And of course we stopped for ice cream. *La glace.* The shop had about a million different flavours. Felix made me order by myself to help my French, and I was so proud when I managed to tell the guy behind the counter exactly what I wanted.

'I am impressed,' Felix said outside. I even ordered his for him too.

'You owe me some for that.' I reached over and managed to lick his ice cream before he pulled it away.

And then we kissed in the street, ice-cream-cold tongues colliding, happiness radiating from our sun-kissed skin.

We had savoury crêpes at the side of the street. Then more kissing.

The streets were illuminated by the golden glow of the sun when Felix asked if I wanted to see his house.

At that moment, I couldn't have thought of anything more perfect. There was something so calming about being with Felix, like I knew he would never do anything to hurt me.

We got back on the Vespa and rode past vineyards and fields of sunflowers for about twenty minutes before Felix turned to our right and drove up a long, dusty pathway.

At the end of the road there was a house. The cutest thing I'd ever seen – white stone, blue shutters, with vines growing up the walls.

I climbed off the Vespa and removed my helmet.

'This is beautiful,' I said, taking it all in. The house backed on to endless trees, and there was a ripped football net in one corner of the little front garden. And it reminded me to tell Rue that Lexie had replied about the disability team. I said I'd give her a call about it when I got home.

'I thought I would show you where I grew up.'

'It's so French!' I laughed, and that made him laugh too.

I followed him inside. Into the kitchen that was painted white with dark wooden beams on the ceiling, and pots and pans hanging from hooks on every wall space.

'My mother. She likes to cook,' Felix said when he saw me looking at all the utensils.

'Do you want to see my room?'

I nodded, following him.

I had no idea what his room would be like, but when he led me into the first room on the left down the little hall, it just made sense. Floor-to-ceiling stacked bookshelves filled one wall. Against another was a narrow bed with plain blue sheets and white pillows. Against a third, a desk, nestled underneath shuttered windows, and walls covered with posters of French movies and bands I'd never heard of.

I walked over to the desk and pushed the shutter open gently, letting a streak of light into the dark room.

'Not too much, you will let the heat in.' Felix pulled the shutter back a bit then sat on the desk in front of me. I stood between his legs and looked into his eyes.

'Thank you for earlier. For telling me your story about your sister, and when you felt the same.' Felix looked so sad that I thought about asking if he wanted to talk about what had happened to him earlier, but I didn't want to ruin the moment. The sound of the breeze outside, the creak of the shutters, the old smell of the books on the shelves, the coconut suncream on my skin. Just being there. Together.

'Of course,' I whispered, then leaned in and kissed him. Gently. But I let my lips linger on his, pressing them harder against him to let him know what I really wanted.

And I didn't need to explain myself, because he reached for my T-shirt and pulled it gently over my head. I reached for his hand and pulled him towards the bed, where I lay down.

He just looked at me for a second. And I wasn't embarrassed. Like I used to be when it was Theo. Like I was always doing the wrong thing and making everything awkward. Felix made me feel beautiful and it was like there would be nothing I could do that was wrong.

I watched him take off his shirt. And his trousers. Tanned skin and muscles that I was desperate to touch. I mirrored him, taking off my shorts and lay there on the bed.

'You are sure?' he asked, lying on top of me and taking his weight on his elbows. I stroked his biceps gently and looked into his eyes.

'I'm sure,' I said. Then I pulled him closer, his mouth was on mine again, and as we kissed, I could feel him grow hard against me. He reached for a condom, and I smiled as I watched him struggle with it before I took off my underwear.

Having sex with Felix felt different than it did with Theo. With Theo I was always in my own head, doubting myself, hoping it felt good for him and not giving my own pleasure a second thought. It made me hate seeing it on television, or reading about it in books, because the sex I was having was so far removed from the way it was on screen. Slow and romantic, like they were telepathic and knew exactly what to do to make each other feel good.

But with Felix? That's exactly how it felt. Like every single movement of his hips had been prompted by a thought that I'd sent him through the ether. I buried my face in his shoulder and breathed him in, raising my hips and gripping on to the soft waves of hair at the back of his neck as I relaxed into rhythmic waves of pleasure before feeling him do the same.

'Margot,' he whispered, hot in my ear. 'You are perfect.'

I gave a shallow, breathy laugh. 'I definitely am not, but *that* ... *That* was perfect.' I bit my lip and he kissed me, releasing my lip from my teeth and finding my tongue again. And we lay there for a while, tracing each other's skin with our fingertips. He discovered a vein on my inner elbow and followed it down my arm with the lightest touch, before lifting my wrist to his mouth and kissing the delicate blue line.

'*Les veines*. Back to the heart. They can take this too.' He kissed my arm again, and I closed my eyes, savouring the feeling of his soft lips on my skin.

We didn't get dressed properly. Felix put on his boxers, and I pulled on the khaki T-shirt that he'd left on the floor.

'That looks good on you,' he said before guiding me back down on to the bed, his arm circling me protectively.

'Oh yeah?' I replied.

'Yes.' He planted tiny kisses on my exposed neck. 'But everything looks good on you. And nothing looks even better.'

I laughed gently and gazed around his bedroom as I imagined him growing up here. So idyllic. Surrounded by vineyards, by sunflowers, so close to the ocean. It must have been the perfect childhood.

I felt his heartbeat against my back, steady and strong as he traced invisible patterns on my hip. For the first time since I'd got to France, I felt still. Like my mind was only thinking about one thing, and I was there. In the moment, and it was perfect.

'You are hungry?' Felix sat up, slowly, like he didn't want to disturb me.

'Thirsty,' I said.

'OK, give me one minute.' Felix got out of bed and left the room. I stood up and walked to the window, opening the shutter that he'd pulled closed. The evening sun was warm on my skin.

I looked down to the desk and picked up a book that was sitting on top of a pile.

Le Grand Meaulnes by Alain-Fournier. I tried to read the back, but I could only translate a few words, so I flicked through the pages, fanning them on my flushed face and inhaling the book smell. Then something dropped on to the table. A bookmark. No, a photograph. I picked it up and put the book down. It was Felix – he must have been about thirteen. His hair was lighter and wavier. His smile was wide and open, and beside him was another boy. Smaller, younger, dark-haired, with the same smile, except bigger. A cousin maybe? He was wearing a shark's tooth necklace. The same kind I'd begged for when I was nine, when I saw them at a market stall in one of the French towns. But we had to rush to get our flight home, and I never got one.

'*Et voilà!*' I heard from behind me. I spun round, photograph in hand, to see a smiling Felix holding a tray carrying a jug of water, glasses and some pastries in the doorway. Then his smile disappeared as his gaze fell on the photograph in my hands. And there it was again. The same look on his face that was there in town when we heard the music.

'Sorry, I was just looking at your book and this fell out . . .'

I let my words tail off as Felix walked towards me, put the tray down on the table and gently took the photograph from my hand.

'It is fine.' He put the photograph in a drawer and closed it.

'He looks like you. Is that your cousin?' I asked, remembering that he said he had no siblings.

'My brother. Gabriel.' Felix's voice was quiet. Weak.

'Brother?' I asked.

'He *was* my brother.' And the past tense wasn't lost on me. My stomach dropped and I froze. 'He drowned three years ago.'

'Oh, Felix.' I covered my mouth, then reached out and touched his shoulder. 'I'm so sorry, I didn't mean to –'

Felix turned away from me and walked to his bed where he started pulling on more clothes.

'It is OK . . . Maybe I should take you home, it is getting late.'

I just stared at him for a second, not knowing what to do. Then, in the room that had made me feel so close to him, I suddenly felt like an intruder. I took off his T-shirt then pulled my own clothes on as quickly as I could.

We didn't speak until we got back to the campsite. The sun had set, but there were still people walking about in bikinis and swimming shorts.

I watched Felix take off his helmet, hang it on the bike and hesitate before turning to me, his jaw tight.

'I am sorry, Margot. I am not good at talking about Gabriel.'

'You don't have to explain,' I said, even though I wished he would.

'I do . . . I will. Just not tonight,' he said before leaning across and kissing my cheek in a way that felt like a promise and a goodbye at the same time.

And as I walked back to our mobile home, silent tears rushed down my cheeks. For Felix, for his brother, for his mother, and also for me. It felt selfish to even think it in the same breath, but I had opened myself up to him in a way I hadn't to anyone else, while he kept part of himself hidden. Like he showed me this version of himself and censored the things he didn't want me to see. The words from the girl at the market pierced new holes in my head – the 'girls'. And Delphine's words came back again, all of them like flashing red sirens that I'd chosen to ignore.

I walked into the mobile home quietly in case everyone was in bed. My phone buzzed with a message.

FELIX: I want to tell you about Gabriel.
Please give me time.

ME: OK

And it felt genuine. Just as it had while I was lying there in his arms.

Another siren. Loud and flashing so bright, I didn't even want to look at it.

I'd always thought Ari and Theo were genuine too.

So I guess I couldn't even trust my own thoughts.

18

Mum and Dad were still up when I got home, drinking wine on the decking. But I wasn't in the mood to talk so walked straight past them and opened the door.

'Margot! Did you have a nice day?' Mum asked, her tone overly cheery from too much wine.

'Yeah, it was nice,' I said, not turning round.

'Come and talk to us,' said Dad.

I walked back outside and stood beside them at the table. 'How was the girls' lesson?' I threw a question at them before they could ask me more about my day.

Mum looked at Dad for an answer.

'It was good. The boy with all the tattoos, he's very good with them, and the girls love it, but I'm not sure it's the right thing for Rue at the minute.' Dad took a sip of wine, and I looked at him in shock.

'What? Why?' I asked, anger spilling seamlessly out of my mouth.

'Why?' Dad replied, like it was obvious. 'She has cerebral palsy, Margot.' And he said it like I hadn't been in the same house after she got her diagnosis or held her hand when she got her injections. Rue *loved* it, I knew she did, and he was going to take it away from her?

'Yeah, Dad, I know. *And?*'

'And it's not the same for you and Wren as it is for her. It's too much. She was exhausted after her lesson today.' Dad looked at me sadly and Mum reached for his hand.

'Of course she was, because she's using muscles she doesn't usually use. Let her sleep after! She loves it. Do *not* take this away from her. Do you know how horrible that would be? How terrible she'd feel? And Antoine, he said she had more determination than any of his adult students.' The emotions from earlier were so close to the surface. Rage made my stomach tight and my jaw clench. 'He adapts things for her. Did you not notice how he takes the girls alone and someone else takes the other group of children?'

'They did seem to love him,' admitted Mum.

And I couldn't stop. It just seemed so unfair. 'But this isn't about surfing, Dad, it's about letting her try and maybe letting her fail, the way you used to do with me. Let her have the same opportunities as everyone else,' I said through gritted teeth.

'She's *not* the same as everyone else,' Dad countered. I knew he was frustrated and that this was coming from a place of love. But the injustice of it all, and the thought of Rue's face if he told her she couldn't surf any more. I just couldn't bear it.

'You're right. She's not. She's better.' It was like all my feelings about Felix were spilling over and tangling up with something else.

I left them to it without saying anything more, and on my

way to my room I stopped outside the girls' room and looked in at them, asleep, peaceful, and I silently promised I'd do all I could to stop them ever being disappointed, because I couldn't bear it. I couldn't let them feel the way I did right now, like something precious had been taken away from me.

The next morning, I was at the beach early. Before six. I was dying to get into the water. To feel it again, the freedom of being on the board. To forget yesterday. The perfect day that had been turned on its head by the realization that nobody was ever the way they seemed.

When I got there, Antoine was outside the surf hut wearing his black rash vest and when he caught sight of me, he chucked a T-shirt in my direction. I walked behind the hut to get changed.

'You did not want to watch your sisters yesterday after all?' Antoine called.

'I was in Saint-Jean-de-Luz yesterday,' I said, then emerged from behind the hut. Antoine was waxing a surfboard. I stood over him, watching the muscles in his back move underneath his top with each scrub of the wax on the board.

'Saint-Jean-de-Luz. Nice town. You were there alone?' he asked, still not looking up at me.

'I went with a friend.' I didn't want to talk about it.

Antoine jumped on to his board and looked at me, up and down, the way I'd got so used to.

'Nice Lycra,' he said, stroking my shoulder with a finger. And I wished that he hadn't, because I didn't want to feel like every single nerve ending in my body was alive, exposed and defenceless.

'*Bon.* Today we will learn the bottom turn,' he said, then pulled me on to his board as he moved on to the sand and my breath caught in my throat.

'What's that?' I asked.

'It is, how do you say, the building block for everything in surfing. When you drop down the face of the wave, you get speed. Then you use that speed. OK, show me your stance.' He walked around me on the sand.

I moved into the surfer stance, bringing my mind back to the beach.

'*Bon.* Now you need to put your weight on your back foot, press down, look where you want to go and let your shoulders lead.' Antoine was behind me now, hands on my shoulders, turning them towards the water and I had to stop from closing my eyes.

'And now you must get low. Knees bent.' Then Antoine took my arm and traced his fingers down to my hand, which he placed on the sand. 'This hand. It can touch the water. It gives you control.'

'I got it,' I said frustratedly. I was desperate to get into the water and clear my head.

'Oh yes?' Antoine laughed, but it was a nice laugh.

'Yeah,' I said, jumping off the board and going to the rack to look for the one I used yesterday. I found it and pulled it out. 'Can we go in the water now?'

'*Bien sûr,*' he said, and waved me on to lead the way.

The sun was rising, and the water glittered as we walked in together. We stopped for a moment, looking out at the other surfers.

'It really is beautiful,' I said.

'Beauty can still be dangerous,' he mused, and I looked at him, but he was just staring at the water.

I pulled my board in and jumped on, followed by Antoine on his.

We swam out and turned to face the shore.

'Show me,' Antoine challenged, and I could feel my jaw set in determination.

I waited for the right wave, then just went for it. I wasn't in the mood to hang back or be hesitant. I popped up, bent low, felt the speed and leaned on my back foot. I looked towards the waves and let my shoulders rotate. And it felt natural, letting my hand drop back and touching the water. I couldn't hear anything except the rush of the water and my heartbeat in my ears. Adrenaline shot through my veins as the board responded to each and every tiny movement I made. And it wasn't until I'd finished, until I'd emerged from the wave still standing, that I heard Antoine.

'Margot!' I let myself fall into the water, exhilarated, and when I surfaced, Antoine was looking at me with a smile that matched mine. He sat on his board, legs either side of it, and pushed his hand through his hair. 'That was . . . It was like a textbook. Like you have been surfing for years.'

His shock made me laugh. Pride filled my chest

'You are sure you have not been practising in secret, *Princesse*?'

'No practice. But I felt it. Like the board was a part of me.' I stroked the board that floated beside me. 'I haven't felt like that since . . . well, it's been a really long time.'

We did it again, and again, and again. And by the end of the lesson, I was exhausted. We walked our boards up the sand to the surf shack and Antoine took it from me.

'I think you are done with this board. I will find you a more responsive one.' Antoine walked over to the rack, pulled out a white one, and handed it to me. 'This was my first board, a hard board. Use it and get a feel for it.'

'Thanks so much!' I grinned, and I think I shocked him with my enthusiasm because he laughed.

'You will be back soon?' he asked. 'With your sisters?'

I looked at him and smiled.

19

After a breakfast of croissants and *pains au chocolat* at the table outside, I chilled out in my room, going over and over Antoine's lesson in my head, replaying each wave and desperately trying to recreate the feeling. By the time I emerged from my room, it was almost time to go back to the beach. But I had to speak to Dad first.

I found him inside, making coffee while the girls got changed in their room.

'Dad. I'm sorry for getting so angry last night,' I said, because I knew it wasn't all on him, my reaction. A lot of it was from all the shit with Felix. I watched as he put down his coffee cup. He sighed and turned round, his expression soft.

'I am too. And you were right. The girls, they really do love it. I just worry, you know?'

'I know.' I nodded. Of course he did. We all did. 'You know you can come and watch?' I offered.

Dad laughed. 'Rue won't let me. She's adamant it has to be you.'

'Well, I am pretty cool.' I grinned, and Dad smiled as he poured his coffee, then walked outside with it.

'Tell me what you did this morning, Margot,' Rue said as she came out of her room wearing her swimsuit, followed by Wren. The excitement on her face was photo-worthy.

'It was so cool. I learned this thing called a bottom turn, it was incredible.' I told the girls all about my lesson with Antoine.

'Do you think I could do it?' Rue asked, her eyes wide and hopeful, and the guilt was like a gut punch. It was tactless, saying stuff like that, when I knew that Rue probably wouldn't be able to do it in the same way.

'No way,' I teased – it was always the best way to diffuse Rue.

'Why not?' She folded her arms and narrowed her eyes, and I had to double take, because it was like I was looking right back at myself ten years ago.

'Too small.' I shrugged, and she threw a pair of goggles at me.

'It sounds too complicated,' said Wren. 'I like what we're doing.'

'Wren's right. You'll do something way better,' I said.

We passed Dad on the way out. 'Going to the beach?' He looked at his watch.

'Yep,' I said.

'Ruthie, Wren, come here a wee minute,' Dad said, calling them over. He sat on the steps, where he was eye level with them.

'Promise me you'll tell Margot if it's too much or you want to stop?' He said it to them both, but it was really for Rue. And I could call him overprotective, but he knew Rue as well as I did, and that she would push herself as hard as she could. Too hard sometimes. And maybe I knew her because I knew me.

How hard I pushed myself during swimming training, and with Antoine.

They nodded and he hugged them both, making Rue groan.

'I'll be there, Dad,' I promised.

'Have fun, girls!' Mum called from the doorway.

The beach was packed with people when we arrived.

Rue was fizzing with excitement, while Wren was stuck to my side.

'You OK?' I asked her.

'I'm fine,' Wren said, smiling in the way she did when there was clearly something up but she didn't want to say. I always got the feeling that Wren would say she was fine when she didn't want to add anything 'extra' to the situation.

'Well just tell me if you're not, *petit oiseau*.'

She giggled. 'What does that mean?'

'Little bird. It's what Antoine called you.'

'He did?' And her grin took up her whole face. 'I like him.'

'I like him too,' I said, staring towards Antoine's hut for the second time that day. Well, I liked *parts* of him. Not the arrogant part that told me what to do, but the softer part. The part that made me hot chocolate and the part that made his face light up when my technique was right.

I didn't have to stare too hard; he was where he always stood, beside the rack of boards, looking out to sea. And then he was being tortured by kids, grabbing at him, throwing balls to him. I laughed.

'Ah, *la princesse, la guerrière et le petit oiseau.*' Antoine smiled at us and Rue rushed towards him, stumbling on the sand.

'Wow,' he said, lunging forward to catch her. 'You are OK?' he asked.

'Yep! What did you say? What's a guer . . . and a . . .' Rue scrunched up her face and cocked her head, making Antoine laugh.

'*La princesse.* Princess.' He pointed to me. '*La guerrière.* The warrior.' He pointed to her, and she could not have looked more proud. '*Et le petit oiseau.* The little bird,' he said, gesturing to Wren, who smiled into my side.

'What are we waiting for?' Rue asked.

'Delphine.' Antoine replied to her but was looking at me and I didn't know what to say. 'I think I should stay with Rue by herself today and I wanted some help for Wren.'

Wren's disappointment was palpable and I hoped that Delphine would be nice to her.

And then there she was, walking up the beach like something out of a movie, her legs looking even longer in the tiny shorts she was wearing and her hair hanging dark and wet round her shoulders.

'Ah *les filles*!' Delphine smiled and Wren immediately grinned back at her, dissolving my worries. 'I have heard you are brilliant. Do you mind if I teach you?' she asked Wren. And I felt her move away from me easily, like she gravitated towards Delphine. And I probably would as well if she was that nice to me.

Delphine held out her hand to Wren and she took it without hesitation.

'And you. *La guerrière.* You are with me.' Antoine pointed to Rue, and she nodded.

'Good.'

'Margot!' I looked to my right, where Sébastian was surrounded by the rest of the children.

'Yeah?'

'I need your help. Antoine said you did an amazing bottom turn this morning? This is true?' he asked. '*Arrête!*' Sébastian shouted at a kid who was throwing a football at him.

'*C'est vrai*,' Antoine called over to him and I shrugged back in his direction.

'Please, Margot. Show these monsters what they might be able to do. One day. In the future,' he pleaded.

'I could try?' I said. I walked to the rack of surfboards and reached for the board Antoine had lent me, turning to him to catch his eye before I took it out. He nodded, then turned all his attention to Rue.

I walked to the water with Sébastian, and the kids stood beside us.

And it surprised me that I wasn't nervous. That I remembered everything from earlier that morning, and I felt like I knew exactly what I was doing.

I caught the perfect wave and felt the same adrenaline rush through my veins. And when I emerged from the water and walked on to the sand, Sébastian was standing there clapping, while the kids were messing around beside him.

'Margot! That was *génial*!'

I smiled. '*Merci*, Sébastian. I loved it. I can't wait to learn more.'

'Can you teach *me*?' he asked, and I pushed his shoulder.

I looked over at Wren and Rue, who were in the water with Antoine and Delphine. They were both laughing. I walked over as Antoine pulled Rue on her board out towards a wave. I watched him encourage her to paddle and then she stayed on her stomach as she rode the wave all the way to shore. She pulled herself up awkwardly, then turned to me and I don't think I've ever seen her look happier. It was like she felt it too, the adrenaline rush.

I watched the rest of their lesson, my eyes mostly on Wren and Delphine. I couldn't believe how different she was. She was warm, constantly smiling, and Wren was laughing when she fell in the water instead of the tears I'd half expected.

And when they finished, the girls looked so happy, even though they must have been exhausted. Especially Rue.

'Did you see me?' Rue asked excitedly as I packed up their stuff and put it into a bag.

'I did, you were amazing. You too, Wren.'

She smiled back at me. 'I didn't think I could do that. Delphine is so nice.'

I didn't reply to that but when I looked up, Delphine was standing there, and her smile had vanished. I braced myself for whatever she was about to say.

'Your sisters are great,' she said.

'They are,' I agreed, shocked at the compliment. I kept getting ready and was about to leave when Delphine stopped me by touching my arm gently.

'That bottom turn you did. It was not terrible.' It looked like it actually hurt her to say it.

'Thanks,' I said and moved to head off but she stopped me again.

'Try to keep your back shoulder even lower than you think.

And watch your front arm, it needs to stay parallel to the water,' she explained. I looked around to see if there was someone else she was talking to, because this was actually really helpful.

'Thanks,' I said in surprise.

She shrugged. '*La Vague d'Or*, they take away points for raised arms.'

I was about to respond when she walked away. But just before she got too far, she turned. 'Antoine is not a bad teacher, but sometimes he is too nice.' She nodded, like she'd said everything she needed to say, picked up her surfboard and walked back towards the sea.

La Vague d'Or. She didn't think I wanted to compete, did she? She didn't think I could, did she? And hold on . . . *Too nice?* Not the Antoine I'd met.

But before I could call after her and ask her to explain, Antoine had come over, pushing his hand through his wet hair. 'You have some more time? I want to show you something. Meet me back here in thirty minutes?'

I nodded, but it didn't feel like a question. Definitely not one I was going to say no to anyway.

20

I walked home with the girls, still buzzing from their lesson, and left them to tell Mum and Dad all about it.

'I'm just going back out for a bit. See you later,' I called, and took off again in the direction of the beach before they could ask me any questions. I turned to look at them as I walked away, but I needn't have worried. Mum and Dad were immersed in whatever Rue was telling them, and I was too distracted to be sad or jealous. Nervous energy fizzed in my stomach, electric butterflies colliding with each other again. The feeling sat low in my abdomen and I put my hand there to try to calm it.

The butterflies turned to guilt as I passed the Brasserie. I did my best to keep out of sight, wondering if Felix had thought about me today at all. All I'd said in reply to his text about needing time before telling me about Gabriel was 'OK'. And it had made sense at the time. I'd been so frustrated, so confused. And now I wasn't sure, in the clear light of day, if it had been a bit cold. He hadn't replied. But there was nothing to say.

So I just kept my head down and walked faster. To the beach.

Antoine was waiting by the hut when I got there. I watched him check the locks and say something to Sébastian, who waved at me when he saw me coming.

'Let's go, *Princesse*,' said Antoine. I'd weirdly grown to like the nickname. Even though it was stupid . . . he'd come up with it just for me.

Antoine picked up both our surfboards and I followed him down the beach and out on to a secluded path, where a van was parked.

'Where are we going?' I asked.

'I want to show you *real* surfing. Not the tourist stuff. You are good.' Antoine fixed the boards to the roof then opened the door for me. My chest swelled with pride before I was hit with the smell of salt and oil, with a hint of board wax. The latter a smell I'd come to know well after the half-hour demonstration from Antoine on how to wax a board properly. There were shells on strings hanging from the mirror and the van rattled as Antoine started the engine.

He drove with the confidence of someone who'd been doing it for years. He put his hand on my head rest and turned the van, spinning the wheel round, and I caught a glimpse of a tattoo I hadn't seen before. A wave, which emerged from under the Lycra sleeve that clung to the inside of his bicep. A wave that shattered into little pieces of glass. And there was something written underneath it, but the word *pour* was all I could see. 'For'. For what?

He spotted me looking at it.

'Your tattoos. Did they hurt?' I asked.

He inhaled. 'Everything hurts if it means something.'

Something caught in my throat when he said it. His tone was serious, sad, and reflexively I wanted to ask what it meant, but before I got the chance, he turned on the radio and we didn't speak again until we got to our destination.

When he stopped the car and opened the door, all I could say was 'Wow.'

He'd parked beside a rocky headland. And the view was mesmerizing. It was like I could see the whole ocean. The strength of the salted air threatened to make me stumble as I walked closer to the edge. I just stood there, gazing out at the beauty of it all.

When I turned to walk back to Antoine I almost lost my footing, but he was already there to grab my hand.

'Never stand too close to the cliff.' He tugged me gently away and nodded his head towards a little path. Antoine carried the boards, and I followed him down to a little cove, where the waves were bigger and more powerful than anything I'd seen before. The nerves were back. And not the good kind that warmed my stomach, but the kind that made me nauseous. The ones that had haunted me for the last few months of swimming.

'We're going in there?' I asked, my voice filled with fear.

'Not yet. Come.'

I followed Antoine on to some rocks, and we sat down, so close that his leg leaned warm and heavy against mine. 'Watch first. Read the waves.' Antoine pointed to the water, to the waves that crashed over each other in wild peaks. 'Do you see the third wave in each set? That is where it is magic. But it is also where people get hurt if they are not ready.'

'Do you think I'm ready?' I squinted up at him in the sun. But he kept looking at the water.

'I think that you could be.'

'Delphine mentioned *La Vague d'Or*,' I said, testing his reaction.

He made a disapproving noise with his exhale. 'Competitions make surfing about winning instead of just understanding the water. The beauty. The strength. The danger.'

'But can't it be all of that? And winning too?' I asked. Before he could answer, I continued. 'I used to compete. In swimming. I know what it's like to lose the joy in something because of all the pressure, and to regret walking away . . . but I also know how good it feels to win.'

'Why did you quit?' he asked, his eyes on me, not the water this time.

'I don't know. I guess I let it get bigger than me. I forgot about the love of the water, and I let everything else get in the way. Pressure. Family. Rue. I don't know, maybe it felt like I was taking up too much time when she needed my parents. Maybe I just got scared of failing.' I shrugged in the warm breeze. 'I don't really know.'

Antoine inhaled, gazing at the water again.

'Do you miss it?'

'Yes.'

'Everyone who loves the water must decide if fear or love is stronger. Come on, let us see what you choose.' Antoine stood up and took my hand.

He helped me off the rocks and we picked up our boards.

Everything felt different in the water here. The waves were

so much bigger. More powerful. I let Antoine guide me into position and listened to every single word he said.

'Feel that pull? Do you feel it, Margot?' Antoine was right beside me, his hand on my board, steadying it. His fingers brushed the top of my thigh. And I felt that too.

'I feel it.'

'Then use it,' he said, and pushed my board. I paddled hard. Standing up was trickier than it had been before. But when I did, it was like magic. The water felt like it was alive, like it was a lion I was taming. The ride was cleaner, longer, and a thrill surged through my veins like nothing I'd ever felt.

And when I paddled back out towards Antoine, he smiled. 'Good. Now try one without my help.'

Good. I repeated it in my head. Every compliment, every piece of encouragement from Antoine made me desperte for more. So I pushed myself even harder the next time, drunk on the look on his face when I did better than he expected.

Afterwards we sat on the rocks again, our bodies soaked and muscles aching. 'Do you bring all your students here?' I asked.

Antoine shook his head.

'Why me?'

'You remind me of why I started surfing,' he said simply.

'And why is that?' I asked, nudging him.

'I have seen the look on your face after the wave. You light up.' He stared at the sea.

'You don't any more?'

'Not like that.' He smiled sadly. He stood up and offered his hand to pull me up. I took it.

‘Can we come back tomorrow?’ I asked.

‘Your lesson is on the main beach.’ He lifted the boards and we walked towards the van. He handed me a towel and a bottle of water, which I took gratefully.

‘You did well today,’ he said, and started the engine.

His words sent a tingling heat through me.

‘Thanks,’ I said, watching how his muscles flexed as he changed gears. ‘The waves are different here.’

‘They are. They are more honest. Less forgiving, but everything makes more sense here,’ he said. And when he spoke, he found my eyes and held my gaze before turning back to watch the road, as heat rose in my cheeks.

On the way home, the silence was charged. Not awkward, not uncomfortable, but like the air just before a storm.

‘Same time tomorrow?’ Antoine asked as he pulled into the campsite to drop me off.

‘I’d like that,’ I said, ignoring the storm warning completely.

21

I tried not to dwell on what had happened with Felix. But he hadn't written back after my last message, and it really pissed me off. I was a pushover with Theo, and look where that got me. Well, I wasn't going to be the same with Felix. *He* could apologize.

So I didn't even feel guilty that I spent the whole of the next week with Antoine, surfing early mornings at the main beach, supervising Rue and Wren at their lessons, which they'd loved so much that we booked more, surfing with Sébastian, Delphine and Lili, and late afternoons surfing at the cove with Antoine until the sun was setting. At the end of the sessions we'd sit on the rocks, eating ham-and-cheese baguettes and watching the sun go down. I basked in Antoine's encouragement, which had become more frequent and more complimentary with each lesson. I didn't give myself the space to think about Felix's silence, or Ari and Theo and whatever they were doing at home. I didn't care about any of it. I was focused, the way I used to be in the pool. At least that's what I told myself anyway. And there was something else. Something that hung in the air between me and Antoine. It was in the way he looked at me when he thought I wasn't watching, and in the way his fingers lingered just a few seconds longer when he was showing me a new technique. And that electricity? It hadn't disappeared. If anything, it was getting harder to ignore.

And on one of those evenings, staring at the blurred gold horizon on the sparkling water, sitting beside Antoine and dreaming about competing in *La Vague d'Or*, my phone buzzed.

FELIX: Can we meet? There is something I want to show you. Tonight?

I froze and just stared at the message as if I was trying to translate it. And I guess I was.

'Everything is OK?' Antoine looked at me, concerned. Over the last few days I'd noticed how observant he was. If I'd a pain somewhere, it was like he almost knew about it before I did and demanded that we rest. When I was quiet because Rue had cried when I told her I was going out again, he teased it out of me almost immediately. So when I replied, 'Yeah . . . just family stuff,' I knew he knew I was lying. And he didn't push it or ask again. But it was there, in the air, when the atmosphere changed from something easy to an awkward silence.

I hesitated before replying. I'd deliberately stopped myself from thinking about Felix, but when I let him in, my gut response wasn't to be cold or unresponsive, it was to give him a chance.

ME: OK. Where?

FELIX: I'll pick you up at 9. Dress warmly

The message from Felix was just something I couldn't ignore. There was so much we needed to talk about. That day, at his house. How perfect it had been until everything fell apart. But there was this uneasiness, like I was betraying whatever this was that I'd built with Antoine.

When Antoine's van pulled into the campsite, he didn't turn off the engine.

'OK, thanks. See you later?' I asked, trying to force some cheeriness into my tone.

'Later?' he replied, like he was demanding clarification.

'Later, like tomorrow?' I offered, tailing off as my own awkwardness closed in on me.

'You should take your board,' Antoine said, then got out of the van. I followed him, then loitered a few metres away, tracing the dusty ground with my sandal.

His jaw was tight when he brought me my board. And that was it, just a handover, like he was the teacher and I was the student. Professional. But cold. Then he got back into his van and I watched him drive away.

Back at the caravan, Mum, Dad, Rue and Wren were playing Jack Change It outside.

Wren grinned when she saw me. 'Margot! Come and play too! Rue keeps cheating.'

I leaned over to look at Rue's cards and motioned to Wren to try to change direction. She smiled at me.

'You playing, Gogo?' Dad asked hopefully.

'I can't. Sorry. I'm meeting Felix. He'll be here any minute, and I need to get changed.'

'Felix? You haven't mentioned him all week,' Mum said.

'He was asking after you today when we had lunch at the Brasserie.' I knew what she was doing, trying to tease info out of me. But Rue changed the subject.

'Told you she wouldn't play,' she said angrily.

'We'll hang out tomorrow?' I offered, hoping Mum and Dad would jump in and save me. But they didn't.

'She means it,' I heard Wren say as I walked inside.

I had a quick shower, washing the salt from my hair before putting on shorts and a grey hoody.

My hair was still wet when Felix arrived. There he was, talking to Mum, Dad, Rue and Wren, who looked a lot happier than they had when they were talking to me twenty minutes ago.

When I walked outside, he looked up immediately and smiled. And there it was. The Felix that had made me feel so wanted, when all I wanted to do *now* was cry. I gave him a half smile, because that was all I had. There was still so much in the way. My head was a mess. He'd hurt me with his silence. I'd opened up about Rue, about my panic attack. I'd had *sex* with him. And I guess I just thought we were worth more than this weird silence.

Then there was Antoine.

And I didn't even know how to explain that to myself.

'I won't be late,' I said to Mum and Dad before following Felix down the path.

We walked through a part of the campsite that I hadn't explored yet. In silence. So many times, it felt like someone was going to say something, just for nothing to come out.

The lane opened on to a coastal path. And that's when he spoke.

'Careful.' He turned to me and reached for my arm, but I

moved it before he could touch me, making it look like I was just fixing my hair. I wasn't ready, not after I'd given so much of myself to him. 'It is dark,' he continued. 'You must watch your step. Hold on to me if you like.'

He walked ahead and held out his hand behind him. And he wasn't wrong. It was dangerous. The path was tiny and when I stumbled on a rock, I reached for his hand and felt the comforting warmth of his skin as he closed his fingers round mine.

We walked until we reached the clifftop.

'*Voilà*,' said Felix.

And there it was. The whole of the main beach. I could see Antoine's hut, the length of the sand and of course the ocean, which was a deep midnight blue now, matched by a sky that was dotted with stars.

But no, he couldn't just do this. Bring me here, like it was going to fix everything. And I knew he was hurting, but that didn't mean I wasn't hurting too.

'You hurt me, you know. The silence, after . . .'

His hand was in his hair. 'I know. I –'

'We shared something special. I don't just do that with everyone. It was important, at least it was to me anyway, and then you just disappeared.' Angry tears stung my eyes, and I wiped them away.

'I did not want to hurt you. That day, it was important to me too. I just . . .'

'What?!'

'It is hard for me to let people close. It feels like it will be OK, and then I panic. I get scared that they will be taken away . . .' He let the words hang there in the air, leaving me to catch them and feel them and work out what I was going to do with them all at once. And I got that. The terrible tragedy that he'd been through, of *course* I understood the panic. And I think that's what hurt the most, that he couldn't trust me to understand.

'You can't lose me by caring about me, Felix,' I said, wrapping my arms round my body to try to protect myself from the breeze that had picked up, and from whatever words were coming next.

'I can. You will be gone at the end of the summer, and it will be worse than being alone. I will know what I will be missing. You are so special, Margot.'

My stomach turned. The way it did when Rue had to go for another appointment or injection. Like I desperately wanted to protect him but couldn't. I reached for his hand and felt it tremble. I didn't have a solution. It didn't feel like it was just a summer romance. When I thought of those, I imagined a kind of wild, fleeting passion that burned intensely before fizzling out as summer ended. It wasn't like that. It felt deeper than that. Like coal that still glowed with warmth, underneath the ashes.

'We don't have to ruin the time we *do* have,' I said quietly, scared my voice would shake.

He laughed gently. 'You make it sound simple.'

'It's not. But pushing me away just means you'll lose me now instead of later,' I said as I hunkered down on the ground against a rock and held out my hand for Felix to sit too. We sat there for a minute, staring at the beach, at the ocean, up at the stars. 'You can see everything from here,' I said. And then it hit me. 'You watch the beaches . . .'

Felix cleared his throat. 'Every morning. Early. Before I go to work. I have to watch.'

I hooked my arm through his and leaned my head on his shoulder.

'Gabriel drowned on the fifth of August. Three years ago tomorrow. On that beach.'

I sat up. 'Oh, Felix. I'm so sorry.'

Felix stared out at the water. 'It was my fault. I was with him. But I couldn't . . . I just couldn't save him.'

'The ocean is so dangerous, and you were so young. It wasn't your fault. I'm sure of that.' I said it with as much conviction as I could muster.

He just shook his head and looked at his feet.

'That's why you watch? To protect people?'

He shook his head again. 'I try. I phone the coastguard if I see someone in trouble. I tell myself that it is the perfect place to keep people safe. But really? I think it is just because it is safe here. A safe distance. I cannot be close enough to fail all over again.'

We sat in silence. Our fingers threaded together. Looking out over the ocean.

'I should have told you earlier. Because I knew earlier . . . that you were special.' His voice almost lost in the wind.

'You're telling me now,' I said, an empty hollow of guilt in my gut as Antoine flashed in my head.

'I do not want to waste the time we have left.'

'Then don't,' I replied, turning to him. I looked into his sad eyes before kissing him. The kiss was soft, desperate, like both of us were searching for something.

I pulled away and leaned my forehead against his. And in that moment, none of the other stuff mattered.

22

Felix and I talked until after two a.m., when the sky had deepened in darkness and the stars were at their brightest. The night became cold, and I walked home with his arm round me. Something felt new. Like I'd walked through a door I couldn't close. He'd opened up so fully to me. Late, maybe, but he did it. And it must have been so hard to tell me all that about his brother. I'd felt it in his kiss, the desperate longing to be understood.

I fell asleep thinking about Felix, about the kiss, about all the things we'd shared, and then I thought about being with him. How I'd shared more of myself than just words, and how perfect it had seemed.

When I woke after only a few hours' sleep, everything was different. But only in my head. All my thoughts felt weighted. Like every thought of Felix came with one of Antoine and vice versa. The chemistry with Antoine I couldn't deny, this craving that came from somewhere I'd never felt before. And it wasn't just physical; it was a need to hear him praise me. To impress him. This urge to be better for him.

I walked slowly to the beach, tearing off pieces of buttery croissant and letting them melt in my mouth, thinking.

My stomach flipped in anticipation. I couldn't wait to see Antoine. But the way we'd left things yesterday . . . And then I felt guilty. This tangle of thoughts that made me ashamed because I wasn't just thinking about the anniversary and how difficult the day was for Felix. And I was, of course I was. But I couldn't control the other things that came into my head.

When I got to the end of the lane and it opened on to the beach, I'd expected to see Antoine's silhouette, as I usually did, beside the beach hut. But he wasn't there.

I carried my board to the hut. Put it down and looked through the windows. There was nobody there. And it was locked. The weight of disappointment shocked me. It left me rooted to the spot for a second. I just stood there, looking around, as if Antoine was going to appear out of thin air. Then I saw a note taped to the wall near the door.

Princesse,
I am sorry. Cannot teach today
Do not surf alone, wait for Delphine's group lesson at 10.
Antoine

Right then, I wished we'd exchanged numbers. But it had never come up, and although I'm sure he must have one, I never saw Antoine with a phone. He was never walking around staring into a screen like everyone did back home.

The condescension stung. *Do not surf alone* – as if all the lessons, all the praise, all the chemistry meant nothing, and I was just some tourist who'd taken one lesson. No explanation. Just orders. Had the connection all been in my head? Those lingering touches. Was I imagining everything? The electricity? The way him touching my hand felt like he'd lit a match in my veins and my whole body was on fire? But what if . . . it was just me who felt this way?

I pulled the note from the wall and crumpled it in my hand, leaving it on the sand in front of the door.

I turned round and dug my foot into the sand in frustration. I stared out at the waves. Small. Manageable. *Do not surf alone.* Ugh! I wasn't about to let Antoine tell me what to do. Not when he wasn't even here. He didn't *own* the beach.

I took off my denim shorts and sliders and walked towards the sea with the board under my arm, the cord round my ankle.

I put it down in the water and took a deep breath. I jumped on the board and paddled out, just like I'd done yesterday and the day before *and* the day before. And it was easy, catching the little waves that rushed to the shore. The adrenaline was back, turning my body into something charged with electricity. I sat on the board and stared out at the ocean. At the sun that was rising, at the other surfers in the water, who were so far down the beach that they were barely visible. Something about this moment just felt *right.*

So I went deeper, hunting for a bigger wave.

I watched them come in. The sets. Let myself float over the first few, waiting for one that felt right.

And there it was, the perfect wave. I paddled hard, pulling my cupped hands through the water, chin up. I popped up, leaned on my back foot and did everything Antoine told me. I used my speed and let the feeling take over entirely. I was hooked.

I caught another wave, and another. Soon my arms and legs were aching. I wasn't ready to stop. But when I looked back to the shore, I had to squint. It was further away than it had been. Like *a lot* further away. I looked down the beach and couldn't see the other surfers at all any more. I was drifting out. I tried to paddle back towards shore, but I was barely moving, and my arms were so tired.

Shit.

What did Antoine say about rip currents? I squeezed my eyes shut, trying to remember. And then I was there, standing on the sand, with Antoine so close behind me I could almost hear his heartbeat.

'And you see where the waves are not breaking? Look, there is a calm bit right there . . . That is your baïne. *Rip current. It can be dangerous. Sometimes people panic and they try to swim against it, but you must* never *panic.'*

Calm. I had to calm down.

I tried again, paddling towards the shore. But I just wasn't moving anywhere. I thought about Mum, Dad, Rue and Wren asleep in the mobile home.

How could I be so fucking stupid?

'Help!' I called. To who? I couldn't see anyone and the shore was getting further and further away.

Parallel.

So I turned my board, tried to regulate my breathing and started to paddle across instead of head on. But, just as I did, a huge wave smashed down on top of me like a ton of bricks and I was dragged under the water.

I couldn't see. I couldn't breathe, and all I could hear was the roar of the water around me.

It was too strong.

I couldn't compete with the waves.

23

I woke with a surge of nausea, followed by a gasp for air. My eyes were open, but my vision was blurred. I coughed and felt a hand on my back. A person. People around me in orange vests, but I couldn't make out who they were. My head ached.

I gulped the air, reaching out with sudden, jerking movements, as if I was falling.

'It is OK, Margot.' A voice. A voice I knew.

I looked to my right and Antoine came into view. He was leaning down beside me. I glanced around at the other faces looking down at me. Sébastian, Lili and Delphine.

'Breathe, Margot. *Les sauveteurs* are here. Give her some space,' Antoine said, and everyone who didn't look official moved out of the way as I coughed again. And I don't know how long I lay there and coughed, but eventually, with an aching chest and sore throat, someone helped me sit up.

A blanket was wrapped round my shoulders, and it was Antoine who hunched down beside me.

'What happened?' I asked Antoine when I'd finished another coughing fit.

'You almost drowned,' he said, and his voice cracked as he said it.

I found his hand in the sand and grabbed hold of it. 'You saved me?' I asked, looking up at him.

He shook his head. 'I was too late.' Antoine looked down the beach at something. He stopped to listen to the two guys in orange talking French.

Then one of them knelt down at my side.

'Can you tell me your name?' he asked.

'Margot Ryan.'

'And you know where you are?'

'Biarritz. The beach.'

'Good. Any pain anywhere? Your neck, back, head?' He gently examined my head.

I shook it. 'I don't think so.'

He took my pulse and asked me questions about my breathing. When he was satisfied, he stood up.

'There is an ambulance on its way.'

'Was it you who saved me?' I asked, my voice weak and cracked. Antoine had come back and was listening to our conversation.

The man shook his head. 'We got the call, but by the time we got there you were on your way out of the ocean, so we took you from there.' He smiled.

'But who then?' I looked at him for answers.

'I don't know, he disappeared when he realized you would be OK. Good swimmer. Probably a local who did not want to do the paperwork,' he said. 'But it was lucky that they were here.'

'Margot! We were not at the beach this morning. Antoine, he phoned us.' Sébastian held my hand and cried, like he just couldn't help it.

'It's OK. I'm OK.'

Most of the spectators had disappeared after Antoine's order, but Lili and Delphine were still there, just holding each other on the sand. Lili's head was buried in Delphine's shoulder.

The coughing fits had died down. 'I need to find out who saved me. I need to thank him,' I said, my throat sore.

'Delphine,' Sébastian choked out.

Delphine came to my other side, out of breath, and laid her hand gently on my shoulder.

'Oh, Margot.' Then she hugged me, and I could feel the shake of her body as she did. 'I am so happy you are OK.'

'Me too,' said Lili quietly.

'Ah, here is your family, I ran to get them,' Delphine said and pointed down the beach. I saw Mum dashing towards me.

'Margot, oh, Margot.' Mum dropped to the sand as Sébastian, Delphine and Lili moved out of the way.

Tears were streaming down her face. She took my face in her hands and just looked into my eyes. 'I love you so much, don't ever do that again,' she said, kissing my forehead.

And then Dad came with Rue and Wren. And it was Rue who hugged me first. So tightly I thought I might throw up.

'Ruthie, careful, love.' Dad's voice, but it didn't sound like him.

Wren sat by my side with a tear-stained face. I reached out my hand to find hers and squeezed it. 'I'm OK,' I said.

I could see Dad talking to Antoine.

Rue released her grip, and I could breathe more easily again. 'Mum and Dad thought you were going to die. But I knew you wouldn't do that to us,' she said, her face red from where she must have been crying.

'I wouldn't,' I said.

And then I was surrounded by French paramedics, lifted on to a stretcher and carried towards an ambulance.

Mum came with me and Dad said he'd follow with Rue and Wren.

And through the open door I saw Antoine standing there. He was examining something. A necklace on a blue cord. One that looked like a shark's tooth. Like one I'd seen before, but I couldn't place it. I couldn't think properly.

And Antoine looked like he'd seen a ghost.

24

The hospital was a blur of doctors and nurses talking to each other in French, then speaking to me in English. Not that I remembered any of what they said. I kept thinking of my last memory. Paddling out for bigger waves, then getting stuck in the rip current.

And then in between doctors, and nurses, and tests, it came back to me. Gabriel. The anniversary of his death on the same day as my near drowning. Part of me hoped that Felix wouldn't find out, but the campsite wasn't a big place, and after what had happened, I didn't think there was any chance of it staying quiet.

Eventually the doctors said I could go home that evening if I remained stable.

Which I did.

Mum, Dad, Rue and Wren took me home, and I spent the next day at the mobile home with someone constantly at my side. If it wasn't Mum bringing me croissants and reading me the paper, it was Dad showing me something on YouTube, or Rue and Wren making me watch their cartoons. But it was nice. My muscles still ached, and there was a tightness in my chest, but it was slowly getting better.

'Felix came over to see if you were OK,' Mum said later that morning.

'Oh, that's nice. Did anyone else come? Delphine or . . .' *Antoine.*

'Just Felix,' Mum said. I tried to hide the empty feeling of disappointment that filled my gut from showing on my face when Mum didn't add another name.

'I asked him if he wanted to see you, but he said he was in a rush. He seemed quite upset.'

My stomach sank, and my heart ached for him.

'What do you mean, how did he seem upset?' I asked.

Mum looked up to the ceiling like it would help her remember. 'Oh, I'm not sure. He was talking very quickly. He said that the water was *wrong* that morning. That the current was pulling north. But he was rambling, and his English was mixed up with French.'

I sat up. Desperate to know more. 'Did he say anything else?'

Mum shook her head. 'He just said he was glad you were OK and that he had to go.'

He saw the water that day. Had he been on the cliff? On the beach? Had he been the one who dragged me from the water?

Breath caught in my throat and Mum put her hand on my shoulder. 'Margot, are you OK?'

'I'm OK,' I assured her. But I needed to know.

That night, after Rue and Wren went to bed, Mum and Dad sat down either side of me.

'I think we can all agree, no more surfing,' Dad said, as if it was something obvious. He took a sip from a glass of whiskey, which he only drank when he was stressed.

'What?' I couldn't believe what I was hearing.

And I don't know why I had such a strong reaction. The thought of getting back in the water right then *was* terrifying. But something boiled up inside me and came out of my mouth before I could even think about it. 'No!'

It was like it was just at that moment that I realized what it meant to me. This wasn't just a holiday activity – it was so much more than that. For the first time I really understood it. The ocean. How powerful it was. And the surfing gave me something that I hadn't felt in a really long time. Like I was finding myself again.

'We can talk about it tomorrow,' Mum suggested.

And it would probably have been a good idea, because I was so tired. My body ached, my eyelids were heavy and my throat was sore, but this had woken me up, and I wasn't about to go to sleep without making my point.

Dad shook his head and took another sip of his whiskey. 'Margot, you almost *died*.'

'But I *didn't*. Dad, you're the one who taught me that water isn't something to fear, you're not taking that away from me.' I felt my jaw clench, and I didn't look away when he turned to me, so he knew how much I meant it.

But he didn't say anything, so I just got up and went to bed. But before I went to sleep, I sent a message to Priya.

ME: Hey . . . I need to tell you something . . .

PRIYA: Ominous . . .

ME: I kind of nearly drowned yesterday . . .

PRIYA: WHAT? Are you OK? What happened?

ME: I'm fine now, but it was pretty scary. I was out surfing and got caught in a rip current.

PRIYA: Jesus, you could have died!

ME: Yeah . . . my parents are freaking out

PRIYA: I'm not surprised!!

ME: They want me to stop surfing. Like forever

PRIYA: Can you blame them?

ME: I mean I get it . . . but P . . . I can't stop. When I'm out there, I feel like me again. The waves. It's like I'm the me I was when I was swimming. The real me

PRIYA: Yeah but . . . can't you find the real you on land too?

ME: I kind of thought you'd be on my side with this one

PRIYA: What? I AM on your side. But I'm also on the side of keeping you alive

ME: You think I should quit?

PRIYA: I'm just trying to be a good friend. Sometimes that means telling people what they need to hear not what they want to hear

ME: Wow thanks for the support. Maybe we always were on different pages

PRIYA: Maybe . . .

I slept on and off all the next day. Mostly tossing and turning, frustrated at Priya and her total lack of understanding. Then I got upset about our argument and wished I hadn't said anything at all. Rage still simmered in my gut from my conversation with Mum and Dad. And then it was as if I'd opened the floodgates to every negative thought that existed in my head. How it might have been Felix who pulled me out of the water, and I'd probably traumatized him even more than he already was, how Antoine hadn't even bothered to check on me. And to top it all off, I scrolled through Insta, just to torture myself by studying Theo's stories. Staring at them just long enough to spot some kind of Ari reference, making the rage intensify.

I stared at the ceiling after that. Until my eyes got heavy and the explosive thoughts began to fizzle out.

I woke the next day, with a ray of sunlight warming my face through the gap in the curtains. I looked at my phone. It was almost the afternoon.

I lay for a moment as Felix filled my head.

Did he see the beach that morning?

I pulled myself out of bed and when I went into the little kitchen, I was greeted by Rue and Wren, who wrapped themselves round me.

'Mum made us let you sleep. But we wanted to wake you up,' Wren said.

'I've done my exercises already and everything,' said Rue.

'That's brilliant, Rue.' I hugged them back. 'Where are Mum and Dad?' I asked.

'Outside,' Wren answered.

I grabbed a croissant and walked outside.

'Good morning, how are you feeling?' Mum asked.

She looked tired. Like she hadn't slept at all, and that even the smile was an effort.

'I'm OK,' I replied. 'I'm a bit sore but I think it's just muscle pain,' I said.

'You need to give yourself time to recover,' Dad said, before walking back inside to make more coffee.

'I'll take it easy,' I called after him. I wasn't about to get back into our argument right then. 'Felix,' I said, as I remembered the revelation.

I sat down beside Mum, noticing her worried eyes.

'He's a nice boy, Felix. Gentle,' Mum said. 'I think he's been good for you, Margot.'

'Yeah?'

'He just seems so different to your friends at home. I've noticed the way he looks at you.'

'What do you mean?' I asked. I was genuinely curious. Mum was like Wren – both of them saw things that the rest of us didn't.

'He sees you the way we do. He sees how special you are.' Mum found my eyes and smiled, putting a lump in my throat.

'Mum –'

'It's true, Margot. And two days ago, we thought –'

'Mum, don't,' I cut in. 'I think I'd like to go and see him maybe?'

'Sorry, you're right. Go, tell Felix we say hello.' She cleared her throat, and I leaned in to give her a quick hug.

I made my way to the Brasserie in the afternoon heat. When I got there, it was just the same as it always was over lunchtime. Busy.

I scanned the tables for Felix. Then I saw him. Chatting to a family, using his hands to speak like he always did. I just watched him, taking in every piece of him.

It wasn't until five minutes later that he saw me. He was taking glasses back to the bar. He stopped in his tracks and just stared at me. I gave him a little smile and a wave. He held up a finger and disappeared towards the bar before emerging again a couple of minutes later.

He stopped about a foot away from me, like he was scared to touch me.

'Can we talk?' I asked.

He nodded. 'I will tell Yves I am taking a break.'

When he came back the second time, I felt it. A strange tension in the air. One that had never been there between us. We walked aimlessly down lanes of the campsite lined with other people's mobile homes. He seemed worried, and there was a change in his breathing, like the air around him was thin.

'I am so happy that you are OK, Margot.' Felix's hand was in his hair, but he wasn't looking at me. He was looking at the path as we walked.

'It was stupid,' I admitted. 'Going out alone.'

Felix didn't say anything to that. Probably because there was nothing he could do but agree.

'Felix?' I asked, holding his arm and stopping us both in the middle of the lane. 'Was it you? Were you the one who saved me?'

Felix started to shake his head, then abandoned it and looked down at his feet. 'I am not sure what –'

'You knew the tide was wrong, that it was dangerous. You were watching from your spot.'

Felix's breathing sped up and he was taking short, shallow breaths. He closed his eyes. I put my hand on his shoulder. 'Felix?'

Then he opened his eyes and looked at me. And all I saw was terror. Like he was experiencing it all over again. 'I couldn't . . . I saw you . . . I watched you go under . . .'

I threw my arms round him, and he held me so tightly I thought my ribs might break. And when we separated, his eyes were glistening.

'You saved my life,' I whispered. 'You saved my *life*, Felix.' And it was like it came out of nowhere, the pressure that built up behind my eyes, then days' worth of tears streamed down my face. And I'm not sure if he pulled me in or I collapsed into him, but then we were hugging again, my head buried in his shoulder, my chest heaving. And I thought I felt him tremble as he held me, but it might just have been me.

'Come,' he said. Felix released me then took my hand and led me off the path to the edge of a little children's playpark where there was a bench. We sat down.

'I saw you from the hill. I was up there.'

'But it was so early,' I said. 'If you hadn't been there . . .' I shook my head as I thought of the possibility.

He held my hand and stroked the back of it with his thumb. 'But I was. I was there, Margot. The night before the anniversary, I couldn't sleep, so I went even earlier than usual. If it hadn't been the anniversary, I am not even sure if I would have been in that place. And then . . . then what would have happened?'

I squeezed his hand. 'Let's not think about what could have happened. I'm here, I'm alive. Thanks to *you*.' I blinked back the tears in my eyes as he did the same. 'I didn't see you after it happened. Were you OK?' I asked. I hadn't thought about it, how hard it must have been on *his* body too. Maybe he should have been checked by doctors as well?

He looked away then, just for a second. 'I am OK. My body

is OK. But I broke the promise I made after … Gabriel. I swore that I would never go back into the ocean after he died. But I could not let you … I could not fail again.' He shook his head and looked down at his knees.

'You didn't fail, Felix. You were a child.' My words were choked with tears.

He shook his head. 'I did not see the current change. I should have seen.'

And the guilt that consumed him was palpable. Like it surrounded him with this big, black cloud.

'You were just a child,' I said again. 'And you saved me, Felix. Without you, I wouldn't be here right now.'

And he cried. Right there. Proper tears that shook his body and made me wrap my arms round him, because I couldn't bear his pain.

'Have you told anyone that you went in the water? It's a really big deal,' I said when he'd calmed down.

'No, I would not know who to tell. The only person who would really understand what it meant … we do not speak any more,' he said sadly, choosing to scan the playground instead of looking at me.

'Well, I can be that person now.' I took his hand. 'Why don't you come round tonight? My mum and dad could probably do with a night to themselves after what happened …'

'I would like that,' he said with a smile.

25

I sat there for a while watching kids play in the park, then I found myself walking to the beach. My breath caught in my throat as I turned the corner and saw the sparkling blue ocean that almost ended my life.

I headed towards the hut, dodging round all the sunbathers and kids playing football. I could see Antoine talking to a group of kids, waving his arms about and pointing at the water. Like nothing had changed.

But everything had changed.

When I got close to them, I stayed out of the way, leaning against the surf hut in the shade under the overhanging roof, just watching. And then he saw me. He looked over his sunglasses, then looked down the beach. 'Sébastian!' He called something to him in French and I watched Sébastian bound up the beach towards him. It looked like he was complaining about something. But then he saw me too and his face lit up with a smile. Sébastian ran towards me, arms outstretched. He pulled me into a hug and picked me up.

'Margot!' He squeezed me then put me down. 'Sorry. Did I hurt you? I am so happy to see you.'

'You too, Sébastian,' I said.

'Really? You are happy to see me?' He put his hand on his bare chest and grinned.

'Very happy,' I said.

'And now I am even more happy,' he said, laughing.

'Sébastian!' Antoine called again.

'*J'arrive!*' Sébastian shouted back. Then he leaned in and kissed both my cheeks before walking towards Antoine and taking over his group of kids.

My stomach flipped when he walked towards me. His chest was bare today and his board shorts hung low on his hips, showing even more of the deep V that outlined his abs. He came right over and kissed each of my cheeks. And although it sent fireworks through my veins, it felt weirdly formal. He never greeted me like that. 'We will go inside?' he asked.

I followed him into his hut and sat down on the little sofa.

'Would you like something? Water? Something to eat? *Du chocolat?*' he asked, putting things away as he did.

'No, I'm OK, thanks.'

'*Non*,' he replied. 'You are not OK. That morning. It was intense. You must rest and take care of yourself.' Antoine sat down beside me. He was so close that I could feel the heat from his body without actually touching it.

'Two days ago. You scared me.' He pushed his dark hair back.

'I scared me too,' I said.

'But I can ask you a question?' Antoine looked right into my eyes, the blue of his softened by the light inside.

'Of course,' I said.

'Why did you surf alone? I told you not to surf alone. I tell you so much about the danger of the ocean, and it was like you did not listen to me at all.' He turned away for a second, like he was too frustrated to even look at my face.

'I thought I would be OK,' I stammered, taken aback by his anger.

'Margot. You almost drowned because you cannot follow a simple instruction.' He stood up and paced around on the wooden floor in front of me. He picked up a tin of board wax and turned it over in his hand.

'I'm fine!' I said, realizing how blasé it sounded as soon as it came out of my mouth.

'*Non!* You could have *died*! Do you understand? You could have died because you thought you knew better than *years* of experience.' He threw the tin of board wax across the room, and we watched it bounce on the floor.

'Why are you so angry? I thought you'd be happy that I'm OK!' Now I was getting frustrated.

'Why am I angry?' Antoine threw his arms in the air and looked at me. 'Because I am your instructor. I should have been there to protect you. And if some stranger had not been there to save you . . .' His hand was in his hair again.

'It wasn't a stranger,' I said. 'His name is Felix. We're . . . seeing each other.'

Antoine stopped pacing and stared at me, something turning in his head. But he didn't say anything, so I continued. 'He works at the campsite Brasserie, and he hasn't been in the water since his brother Gabriel died. But he did go in. To save me. And that means . . . I don't know . . . *everything*?' I could feel tears building again.

'Stop,' Antoine said, his tone replaced by something softer. More vulnerable. But I needed him to know what Felix did for me. People deserved to know.

'Stop what? Telling you that someone *else* is the hero in this scenario?'

'Margot, I said *stop*!'

His face went white. The fury still there, but it was mixed with something else. A raw kind of pain that exposed him. Exposed Antoine as being the same as everyone else. Not invincible after all.

He turned to look out the window, at the ocean that looked so beautiful and threatening at the same time. 'You are . . . with him?'

'Well, it's complicated.' I stood up too. 'We've been spending a lot of time together.'

'And you are sure that he saved you?'

'Yes.'

I watched Antoine's shoulders sink. Like some life just left his body. 'Go home, Margot.'

'Antoine . . .'

I stood up and walked towards him, but before I got there, he strode purposefully to the door and opened it, holding it ajar. And when I went past him, head up, shoulders back, I noticed that his eyes were glistening.

'Margot?' Antoine called when I was a few metres away.

'What?' I asked, the word sticking in my throat.

'If you are going to surf again, you need to find another instructor,' he said, before closing the door behind me.

26

I stormed across the beach. But instead of turning down the lane towards the campsite, I kept walking, along the long sandy stretch I hadn't explored before. I gazed out at the water, at the surfers, and felt it again. That magnetic pull to the ocean. This wasn't something I could just give up now. Not something that made me feel like that. I couldn't just give it up. I *wouldn't*. I didn't *need* Antoine. I kicked the sand.

I'd walked so far in my frustration that I didn't recognize this part of the beach at all. There was a beach café down here, pedalos, banana boats. Maybe it was attached to another campsite. And I was about to turn round when I heard a voice say, 'Margot!'

I spun round and looked towards the café, where I spotted Lili sitting with Delphine, both in sunglasses, at a little table.

Lili waved me over. And I was still so exasperated I considered pretending I hadn't seen them, but then Delphine waved at me too and I found myself waving back.

They both stood up and greeted me with kisses to my cheeks.

'*Un café?*' Delphine asked, motioning for the waiter.

'*Un coca, s'il te plait*,' I said.

Delphine ordered for me and the waiter came back almost immediately with my Coke, setting it down in front of me.

'*Merci*,' I said.

'How are you feeling?' Lili asked, reaching over and touching my hand gently. 'That was scary.'

'I'm OK,' I said. I watched them look at each other. 'I'm a bit sore, but now I really want to get back in the water, and Antoine has just told me he won't teach me any more.'

I squeezed the bottle of Coke as I took a drink.

Mum and Dad were trying to stop me surfing, Antoine was trying to stop me – it was ridiculous.

Lili was whispering something to Delphine and then they looked at me in pity.

'Are you sure you want to keep on surfing?' Lili asked. 'After what happened?'

Her black curls were pulled into a bun on top of her head and I could see her whole face up close for the first time. Her features were soft, with rounded cheeks that made her look younger than she was. She reminded me of a doll with her delicate red lips.

'I *need* to keep surfing,' I said without thinking. It was true, it was more than just wanting to surf. I hadn't cared about anything in my life for the last couple of years, not really, and now that I did, all those feelings I had when I was swimming – the rush of excitement, the pride of knowing how good I was – it was like a drug. And it wasn't just that. I knew who I was when I was swimming, like my life just made sense. And I thought I'd lost that forever. Until I got on that board. And

I wanted more. I shook my head. 'But Antoine has given up on me.'

Delphine looked me straight in the eye. '*Non*, he has not given up. He is scared. I have seen how he looks at you, Margot. You are not just a summer girl for him, and after that day, he is scared of you getting hurt. I know how he works.'

The way he looks at me . . . I had a sudden flutter of butterflies before the memory of what had just happened between us turned them all to dust.

'I get that he's worried,' I said with a sigh, 'but I made a mistake. Doesn't everybody make mistakes? I've learned from it. I want to keep surfing . . . I *have* to.' I took a drink of Coke, the sweet bubbles fighting with the bitterness in my throat.

Lili whispered something else to Delphine, who was just staring at me. Her brown eyes searched my face for something.

'Do you want to know what I think?' Delphine asked.

'Sure,' I said, with no idea what was coming. But I was broken anyway. Someone else telling me how much I'd messed up? Big deal.

'I think you have real potential. Unpolished. But true potential –'

Lili cut in. 'Delphine . . .' It was like a warning, but Delphine continued.

'I have watched you in the water. From the beginning. You read the waves better than students who have been learning for years.'

'Antoine said that too.' I shrugged.

'Antoine is complicated. And you being here, it is more complicated than you know, but sometimes it is best to not think of these complications and to focus on what you really want. And what you really want is to surf, *non*?'

'Yes,' I said immediately. I noticed Lili looking between us with worry in her eyes.

Delphine nodded briefly. 'The qualifier for *La Vague d'Or* is at the end of the week . . .'

Delphine let that hang in the air between us and Lili sighed and mumbled something in French.

'The end of the week? It's not long enough.'

'What if I told you it is just as long as you need?' Delphine didn't break my gaze.

'Delphine has helped a lot of people get ready for competitions.' Lili touched Delphine's hand supportively, like she'd abandoned any attempt to dissuade her.

'What do you mean?' I asked. I wanted her to spell it out to me, because in my head she was offering to coach me. And that was just too good to be true.

'I think you should enter the qualifier,' Delphine said matter-of-factly.

'But Antoine sai–'

Delphine waved away my words. 'Antoine is not the only coach in Biarritz. I will train you.' Her eyes were filled with determination. And it was contagious.

'Delphine trained me for my first competition,' Lili added.

'I could work with you every day this week. It would be intense, but you would be ready.'

And the butterflies were back. Thousands of them, colliding with each other in my stomach.

'You think I can really do this?' I looked at her for reassurance.

'Listen. Margot. I did not like you at the beginning.'

'Delphine!' Lili looked horrified.

Delphine shrugged. 'It is true. I thought you were just another tourist. One who would break the heart of Felix and one who treated surfing like a hobby. But I was wrong. I have really watched you . . .'

'And?' I asked.

'You are different. You have natural ability. And the fact that you want to get back in the water after your accident? It tells me everything I need to know.'

'Really?' I asked, fishing.

'You lack confidence and competition experience,' she continued. 'That is what I can give you.'

Emotion flooded my chest, making it hard to get the words out. 'Thank you. So much.' I pushed away thoughts of the disastrous last swimming gala.

Lili looked at me. 'Now you will have something that is just yours. Something that is not about anyone else,' Lili said.

Then Delphine's steely gaze was back. 'One week of intensive training. Dawn lessons, technique work, competition preparation, here, down the shore –' Delphine pointed along the beach – 'where Antoine doesn't teach. You will be ready, whether he agrees or not.'

And behind the excitement, doubts crept in. 'What if I fail?'

'What if you do not?' Lili smiled at me and a confidence surged in my stomach. I smiled back at her gratefully.

'Even if you do fail,' said Delphine, 'which you will not if you listen to me, you will fail doing something that matters to you. And that is better than not trying at all.'

I nodded at her. She was right. And it was nice, this space in my head where it was just about surfing. Just about me, and what I could do.

'Think about it tonight. If you decide to do it, then meet me at six a.m. tomorrow.'

Antoine's time.

I pushed him out of my head and bit my lip in concentration, already imagining surfing in my first competition.

'And, Margot?' Delphine broke me out of my thoughts.

'Yeah?'

'Never let someone else's fear decide your future,' Delphine said. And I could tell that she really meant it.

The walk back to the campsite felt like breathing space. A chance to focus on myself. On surfing. And to make my remaining time in France about my own goals and dreams instead of the constant gnawing guilt I felt about the mess I'd found myself in.

27

Back at the caravan, I was filled with optimism. I sat down at the outside table and took out my phone.

> **ME**: Hey . . . I've been thinking about our last conversation

> **ME**: I'm sorry. I was so pissed off about other stuff and it just felt like you weren't being supportive. But maybe, when I think about it, you were just worried about me?

> **ME**: Oh, and someone has offered to train me for this competition next week.

***PRIYA** is typing*

My stomach sank every time the writing disappeared as she started the message again and again.

PRIYA: God Margot! I was SO worried about you. You KNOW I'm living for the resurrection of Margot of Christmas past . . . Just promise me you'll be careful?

That made me laugh. God, I missed her.

ME: I will. But enough about me, what's going on with you?

PRIYA: Never mind me, tell me about this French boy you had a date with . . .

ME: OMG it's so complicated. But it turns out that he was the one who pulled me from the water . . .

PRIYA: Shut up! Are you serious?

ME: Yeah . . . but there's something else . . . There's this other French boy . . .

PRIYA: Oh here we go, of course there is

So I phoned her and told her everything. And it all just came out. Everything that had been in my head lately. My rollercoaster feelings for Felix, the chemistry with Antoine, and it ended with my head still a complete and utter mess. But I felt better than I did before.

I spent the rest of the afternoon helping Rue do her stretches, cleaning sand from her splints and sitting with her and Wren, watching cartoons and eating snacks.

I looked up women surfers on my phone and we watched YouTube videos of them tearing up the waves.

'That could be you, Margot,' Wren said, thankfully out of earshot of Mum and Dad. And I allowed myself to believe it, just for a second, because the daydream felt so damn good.

'Do you think it could ever be me?' Rue asked. And it brought me straight back to earth.

I put an arm round her and hugged her. 'I think whatever you do is going to be amazing. But you never know. Look.' I showed her my phone. It was a girl with cerebral palsy who'd won an adaptive surf championship. 'And Lexie got back to me, she said her boyfriend will be starting a disability team next season, so I'll get Mum to give her a call when we all get home. And maybe she can bring you down to Ferndale whenever you've recovered.'

I showed Rue the message and she grinned so hard at me her mouth must have hurt.

'Oh my God, Rue, that could be you!' Wren squealed excitedly at the screen.

I watched Rue's chest swell with pride as she watched the video over and over again.

'Margot?' Dad came inside and poured himself a glass of water. 'Are you sure you're OK to watch the girls tonight? You're sure you're feeling OK?' he asked, concerned.

'Yeah, course. And Felix said he'd come over.'

Mum and Dad had taken me up on the babysitting offer so that they could go to that restaurant in Bayonne that Felix had recommended.

'Yay!' Rue cheered, and Dad looked at me for a second before nodding.

'We'll be fine,' I assured him.

'Thanks, love. Not long left, girls! Make sure you make the most of the rest of the holiday.' Dad took his glass and went outside to Mum again.

I followed him and sat down opposite them at the table.

'I'm sorry,' I blurted out.

'What for, love?' Mum looked up, confused.

'For everything. For quitting swimming. For the way I've been acting this last year. I dunno, it was like I lost myself when I stopped swimming.' I glanced up at them, at Mum's gentle eyes and Dad's pensive expression.

'Oh, pet, you don't need to apologize. We could see that losing swimming broke your heart. And it wasn't about the parties and the curfews . . . you stopped talking to us. Stopped letting us in . . .'

'It was like we were just watching you throw away your future, and there was nothing we could do about it.' Dad's voice was thick with emotion. Like it had really hurt him. 'And then when we nearly lost you –'

'Dad –' I reached for his hand – 'I know. But you didn't.' He squeezed my hand and took a sip of water. 'I really am sorry for this year. Please go and chill out tonight.'

'Oh we intend to,' Mum said. 'With lots of wine.'

*

A couple of hours later, I heard Felix talking to Mum and Dad. Dad was laughing at something he'd said and when I went outside, they were shaking hands.

'Ah, Margot,' Dad said when he saw me. 'Felix was just giving us advice on what to order in Bayonne.'

'I am no expert,' Felix insisted. 'Only what I have learned at the Brasserie.' Then he found my eyes as I walked down the little steps.

'Well, you certainly know more than we do,' Mum said as she emerged from the caravan behind me wearing a floral maxi dress and smelling like a garden.

'You look beautiful, Mrs Ryan,' Felix said, with no awkwardness, no embarrassment.

'Oh, Felix, thank you. This is just something old.' Mum tangled her words and fixed her hair even though it was perfect as it was. But she was beaming too. The same effect that Felix had on everyone.

When Mum and Dad left, a silence hung in the air between us.

'Hey,' I said.

'Hey,' he replied, moving close and kissing me on both cheeks. 'Are your sisters inside?' He motioned to the mobile home. 'I have gifts.' He held up a fabric shopping bag with a baguette poking out of it.

'Felix!' Rue shouted when we walked into the caravan. The two of them were already in their pyjamas, sitting at the little table with iPads in front of them.

'*Bonsoir*, Rue and Wren,' Felix said. When they stood up, he leaned down and kissed them on both cheeks, just like he'd done at the Brasserie. The girls giggled.

'I brought you gifts,' he smiled, and they both grinned so hard it must have hurt. 'But first I thought we could make *le goûter*.'

I looked at the girls and pulled a confused face. They both laughed.

'Translation?' I turned to Felix.

'*Le goûter*. Hmm . . . Usually, children eat it as a snack, after school. *Goûter* means "to taste" in French.' Felix walked to the little kitchen and took out a baguette, a tin of what looked like hot chocolate and a bottle of milk. 'You want to try?' He turned back to us.

My stomach groaned in assent. 'We want to try,' I answered for everyone.

It turned out that *le goûter* could be any sort of after-school snack. But for Felix, it was buttered baguette and a bowl of hot chocolate. Felix explained that he used to dip his baguette into the hot chocolate.

'That's disgusting!' Rue shouted, and Wren agreed. But they tried it anyway and took back their words.

'You are ready to say that I am right? That it is good?' Felix teased them.

'You were right,' Wren admitted.

He had such an easy way with them. Rue didn't relax for just anybody. There was a comfortable rhythm, like he'd been part of our lives forever.

After we ate, Felix reached for his bag again. The girls were silent in anticipation.

'First, for Wren.' Felix passed a tin to her.

'Colouring pencils,' she said gratefully.

'They are from an art shop near my home. Do you like to draw?' he asked, and Wren smiled to herself before looking up at him. 'I love to draw. Thank you so much, Felix.' Wren turned bright red as she examined her pencils. Felix couldn't have known she adored drawing. It was the perfect present.

When he mentioned home, it all came back to me. His bedroom. His bed. The smell of his skin. The way I felt when he held me. Safe. Wanted. And now, looking at how my sisters were gazing at him made me see him in a different light. Like his gentle, steady presence was felt by all of us.

'And for Rue.' Felix reached into his bag again, pulled out a book and handed it to Rue. '*Le Petit Prince*. It is very special in France; every child reads it. But this one, it has both English and French.'

Rue was already looking through the pages, more carefully than I've ever seen her touch anything.

'I love it, Felix. I love it so much, thank you.' Rue hugged her book.

We watched *Miraculous*, a French cartoon, until Rue's and Wren's eyes began to close.

'I think you two should go to bed now.'

'No,' complained Rue, while Wren was already sleepily getting up.

'Come on, Rue,' said Wren.

Rue shook her head. 'Only if Felix reads us a story.'

Felix looked at me and I whispered, 'Only if you want to.'

'You would like to hear some of *Le Petit Prince*?' he asked. 'I will bring it in when you are ready.'

Rue and Wren disappeared and when they did, Felix

reached for his bag again. He pulled out a small jar filled with little pieces of coloured glass, tied with a blue ribbon.

'And for you.' He handed it to me.

It was beautiful. Even in the artificial light, the colours sparkled.

'Sea glass,' he explained. 'I used to collect it from the beach. I always liked how the broken pieces become something so beautiful.'

I stared at the jar, turning it round and finding new pieces every time I did.

'I love it. Thank you.'

He looked embarrassed. And I reached over and kissed his cheek gently. Then he put his hand on his face, as if to keep the kiss safe.

'It is nice here. With your sisters.'

And just as he said it, Rue shouted 'Ready!' from next door, and he got up, taking the book with him.

He turned to smile at me before walking into their bedroom. I smiled back, so utterly content that I knew I could spend forever like this, in Felix's company. Perfectly at peace. And then I waited for them to come. The hurricane of butterflies that made my heart malfunction. The way they did when I so much as looked at Antoine.

And as the realization of how I felt about Antoine dawned on me, consciously for the first time, a wave of sickening guilt replaced the hollow of non-existent butterflies I felt for Felix.

28

The next morning, I woke at five thirty. I was extra quiet, tiptoeing around and leaving doors slightly open.

The sky was a soft blue-grey when I walked to the beach, and I knew it wouldn't be long until the sunrise was burning golden on the horizon. I looked down to the hut, squinting to see if Antoine was there. And he was. Just standing there, staring out at the ocean in a way that had become so familiar.

I turned and jogged the other way, towards the beach café, looking for Delphine.

'Margot, you should have saved your energy for the actual run,' Delphine said with a hint of a smile when she saw me.

I'd forgotten how hard it was to run on sand, and I was already out of breath. 'Our run?! We're not going in the water?'

'*Pas encore.* Not yet,' Delphine said, stretching her quads. 'We will run. Every morning. What do you think? You are in?' Delphine barely waited for me to nod. 'Good. We go.'

I took off my sliders like Delphine had and we ran up the beach.

'You have good stamina,' Delphine remarked on our way back. And I smiled, even though I was gasping for breath and my lungs were burning. It wasn't until we got to the space in front of the beach café that I managed to speak.

'I was a swimmer,' I reminded her.

'Yes. Of course. This makes sense.' Delphine pulled off her T-shirt and put on a rash vest.

'Delphine?' I said, still out of breath. 'Do you have a spare vest?'

'You can borrow one of Antoine's.' Delphine reached down into her rucksack and pulled out a top. She threw it at me and the scent of it caught me by surprise. Spicy, salty, Antoine. I held it to my chest before I pulled it over my head, breathing him in as I did.

'That looks good on you.' Delphine nodded in approval, and I looked down at the rash vest that fell over my bikini like a dress.

'Thanks,' I said, smiling.

'*Alors, allons-y.*' Delphine grabbed her board. 'I brought you another board. I thought that maybe you would not want to use the same board as before . . .?'

Delphine's words trailed off into the air as I took the board from her. An unexpected lurch in my stomach shocked me as I touched it.

'You are OK?' Delphine asked as we walked towards the water.

I nodded. 'I'm ready.' *I want this.*

'We do it then.' Delphine smiled, and I followed her into the ocean. The last time I'd been here this early I'd almost drowned. The water splashed round my waist. *Déjà vu* as we walked a bit deeper. I could feel Delphine's eyes on me as my heart began to race.

'It is OK if you want to stop,' she said.

I shook my head. 'No. I need to do this.' And with that, I jumped on to my board, paddling out and showing the water that I wouldn't let fear win.

We surfed wave after wave, and Delphine was harsh but fair, critiquing my technique and making me do something repeatedly until I got it right.

When we took a break, taking turns to dive deep into the sparkling water, I decided to dig a bit more into her life.

'So, tell me about *La Vague d'Or*,' I said. 'What happened last year?'

'I came fourth, by half a point. So I did not qualify for sponsorship last year. That's it,' Delphine said.

'Oh, OK,' I said, wondering if she would elaborate. I'd seen her surf – there was no way that there were three people better than her. She looked at me like she was deciding whether or not to share. Then she sighed.

'One of the competitors was the daughter of the judge. The points went in her favour. But I cannot use that as an excuse for my whole life. I just need to train harder,' Delphine said. I respected that. How she was trying to move on from a ready-made explanation as to why she didn't make it.

'No bullshit,' I said.

And Delphine smiled. I don't know why she didn't smile more, because her whole face lit up. '*Exactement*,' she replied, 'no bullshit,' and splashed me from her board. 'You keep training like this and you will definitely be ready for *La Vague d'Or*.'

'You really think so?'

'I know it. Really.' Delphine rolled her eyes and splashed me again, and my chest almost burst with pride. Coming from Delphine, this was huge. 'Why else do you think I would be training you for the qualifier?'

'*La Vague D'Or* . . . it's in September?' I asked.

'Yes.' Delphine nodded.

'I mean, I'm supposed to be leaving soon, but . . .' I said, thinking about the possibility.

'But? You are eighteen, *non*?' Delphine offered.

'*Ouais*,' I replied.

'You can make your own decision,' Delphine said, like it was simple. 'But think about it. I think you will qualify. You are a natural.' Then she paddled hard towards the shore and caught another wave, leaving me floating in salted bliss, imagining competing in a surf competition. Me?

I surfed another few waves then followed Delphine out of the water and we sat down, exhausted, on the sand.

'I will see you back here later? Five p.m.? For strength work. And there is a barbecue tonight, at South Cove. You should come. All the hopefuls for *La Vague d'Or* will be there. And all the hope-less too.' Delphine grinned, and I laughed in shock at her telling a joke.

'I will come . . . but will Antoine be there?'

Delphine shrugged. '*Bien sûr.* But I will cover for you. If you are serious about this?' She looked me in the eye as I squeezed salt water from my hair on to the sand.

'I'm serious,' I said without hesitation.

'*Bon.* I will see you later. In the meantime, I need you to eat properly. Real food, a lot of protein.'

'I remember. From swimming.' I thought back to all the spaghetti, the Greek yoghurt, the eggs, the smoothies.

Delphine nodded briefly. 'Good.'

'Why are you doing this for me?' I asked, genuinely curious. 'Because I nearly drowned?'

Delphine exhaled. 'Ah *non*, all surfers will have a scary experience.'

'Then why?' I pushed.

'Your sister,' she said, before pulling the rash vest over her head.

'My sister?' I repeated. Confused.

'I have a cousin with *la paralysie cérébrale*. It is much more severe than Rue. It impressed me. How you are with her. How you do not treat her differently. It can be hard. And I understand that there is a difficult balance, so that you might not want to shine too brightly. A guilt maybe? I am not sure, but I have felt it too. And when someone saw potential in me, they trained me and let me focus on myself even though I had been raised to always put family first.'

'I didn't know –'

'I did not tell you. And I am not saying that it is the same for you. But I thought that maybe, just in case, I would show you.'

I'd never thought about it that way. And I was overwhelmed with guilt then, because I *hadn't* always put family first. Definitely not over the last year. Before this holiday, it really had been so long since I'd spent any proper time with my sisters. Had I ever? Ever since they were born, they kind of came as a package. The kind of package that didn't say my name on it, so I didn't bother paying it any attention. Or tried not to.

But I was wrong. This holiday, in the confinement of a mobile home, seemed to hold up a magnifying glass to our lives, zeroing in on all our personalities. I remembered Antoine's names for the girls.

Rue, *la guerrière*. That's exactly what she was. What she always had been. And Wren, *le petit oiseau*. Watchful but cautious, startles easily, quiet except for when she's in a safe space. Which was why her laugh surprised me so much. And the full-on hysterics that took over her entire body when Antoine made her laugh. He was a safe space for her.

And now, because of the surfing, we all had something to share.

But surfing had given me something else. Hope that I could really find myself again. After that detour. Maybe I hadn't ruined my life with the shitty grades that would no doubt be waiting for me. Delphine had made me see that my life was just beginning.

29

I walked slowly back to the campsite, exhausted. Back to the Brasserie, where Felix was setting up tables.

I watched him as he lifted down chairs with Yves, the early morning sun shining on his hair, making it look even more golden than it was. He looked beautiful. And I thought about taking a photo to capture this moment. The way he smiled at something Yves said. And then he pushed his hair back. A habit now so familiar that it made me smile.

'Margot!' Felix walked over. 'You were surfing?' I nodded, and he looked at me with concern. 'But not alone?'

Felix left the words in the air for me to elaborate.

I shook my head. 'Not alone. With Delphine. She's training me for *La Vague d'Or* qualifier.'

'You are staying for *La Vague d'Or*?' Felix's brown eyes lit up.

'I don't know yet. I don't know what I'm doing. But it felt good, getting back in the water.'

'You are very brave, Margot. But I cannot say that I am not worried.' He pushed his hair from his face.

But he didn't make me justify my choices.

'Promise me that you will be careful?'

'I promise.'

'And I am happy, of course, that you might stay,' he added.

'I *want* to. I mean, I haven't worked anything out. And I might not qualify anyway.' The prospect of staying in France was a total pipe dream, but one I let take over my thoughts.

Felix waved away my negativity. 'That is not what Delphine said last week. She said she cannot even be jealous because you are so good.' He raised his eyebrows, and I wanted to kiss him. But I didn't. After last night with my sisters, my feelings for Felix were confused. It was beautiful, what we had. Supportive, safe, comfortable. But was it more than that? Really?

'She really said that?' My heart swelled.

He nodded. 'And I told you she had a problem with *la jalousie*.' He laughed. 'So maybe I will not have to say goodbye?' Felix reached for my hand, raised it to his mouth and kissed my knuckles gently, brown eyes still on me.

'I'm not ready to say goodbye to France,' I said, scanning the Brasserie, the trees, the sun that burst through the branches, then I watched Felix's expression drop.

'And you, obviously, I am not ready to say goodbye to you,' I added. And the side of his mouth curled into a smile. 'But I will have to qualify first. And I will have to convince my parents that I need to stay.' Saying it out loud sent waves of excitement through me, making it impossible to deny that this was something I really wanted to do.

'You know, Lili's parents rent out a room in their home, for students. I think that someone left recently so they might have space.' Felix raised his eyebrows.

'Really?' My whole body fizzed with excitement. The possibility of staying here, in France. It was intoxicating.

'Would you like me to ask? And you will need a job if you are going to stay. I will speak to Yves, and we will speak to Lili. I think it is an excellent plan.' Felix smiled, genuinely happy.

And then, despite everything, I kissed him. The excitement at the prospect of staying in France, of competing in a surf competition, of training with Delphine, of spending more time with Felix. All of it. He kissed me back like he always did. Slow, gentle, safe, wanted. I chose not to think about everything else. The fact I hadn't told my parents, or my feelings about Antoine. I just put it all out of my head.

'Yuck,' called Delphine, who'd just shown up to work with still-wet hair. I broke away and laughed. 'Here, take these for your family.' Delphine handed me a paper bag filled with pastries. 'You can tell them that you left early to get breakfast. Not to have illegal surf lessons on the beach.' She winked at me.

I licked my lips. 'Thank you!'

'They are not for you. For you is something healthy,' Delphine said seriously. 'Give them to your sisters.'

'Ugh,' I complained and savoured the smell of the pastry. The least I could do if I didn't get to eat any.

'Felix, are you coming to South Cove tonight?' Delphine asked.

'South Cove . . .' he said apprehensively.

She nodded and he stepped back slightly before running his hand through his hair.

'You are going?' Felix asked me.

'Yeah,' I said.

'Maybe it is time, Felix.' Delphine's words were more gentle than I'd ever heard from her before. 'And tonight is . . .' She cut herself short.

I watched him contemplate what she was saying. But I couldn't bear the fear on his face.

'Or I can stay with you, and we can hang out here instead?' I offered.

Felix inhaled. 'I do not think I am ready to go back to the beach.'

I reached over and squeezed his hand, and he found my eyes.

I nodded, then stood on my toes and kissed his cheek, breathing him in as I did. The calming lavender and vanilla sending peace through my veins.

'Do not forget our training later. Five p.m.,' Delphine said.

'I won't,' I replied, then took the forbidden pastries back to the mobile home.

Rue and Wren cheered when they saw me walking down the dusty path with a paper bag. They were still in pyjamas.

Rue grabbed it from me and looked inside.

'I want the apple one,' she said.

Reluctantly, I handed them over.

'Where were you this morning?' Dad asked as he walked outside to us with a coffee.

'I was just at the Brasserie getting breakfast.' I grinned. And I'm not sure if he believed me or not, but I was wearing my own T-shirt instead of Antoine's rash vest and my hair was pretty much dry again from the morning sun.

'I've been practising my paddling, Margot,' Rue said, and showed me her best cupped fist paddle through the air.

'Brilliant!' I replied.

'Rue, we talked about the surfing,' Dad said gently.

'*You* talked about it,' Rue said sulkily.

'Dad said we can't do lessons any more,' said Wren sadly.

And it would have been so easy for me to agree. Because the last thing I wanted was to see Antoine. But Wren's expression broke something in me. It just wasn't fair.

'Dad, come on. I will be there. Nothing will happen. It's different to me going out on my own. They'll have at least two adults watching them at all times.

I could tell he was wavering when he didn't immediately shut it down. He used to find it really hard to say no to me, but he found it even harder to say no to Rue.

'Please, Dad,' she begged.

'Please, Dad,' I repeated.

'Fine. But seriously, Margot, you watch them like a hawk and if *anything* happens to either of the girls – anything – that's it. No more surfing.'

Rue and Wren cheered, and I saluted Dad before we sat at the table and I enviously watched them eat my pastries.

On our way back to the beach, Wren spotted Felix, who was untying an apron from round his waist.

'Felix! Felix!' Rue shouted. Loudly. Shamelessly.

He looked up, smiled and walked over to us.

'I've been drawing this morning with my new colours,' Wren said, beaming.

'That is fantastic!' Felix smiled and she leaned into my side.

'Come with us to our surf lesson!' Rue tugged on his hand.

'Oh no, I do not really go to the beach,' said Felix cautiously.

'Why not?' Rue pushed.

'Rue! Felix, we'll see you later? I will anyway.' I pulled Rue away, but she turned back towards Felix.

'Please?' she begged. 'You can see how good we are at surfing. Mostly me. I'm really good.' She grinned extra hard. And I mouthed 'sorry' at Felix, who was clearly trying really hard to think of a way to say no.

'OK,' he said.

I noticed Delphine flick her head towards us when he agreed.

'Are you sure?' I asked, feeling bad for letting Rue pressure him. But in my defence, I didn't actually have any control over Rue. Getting Rue to do what you wanted required thought, time and a lot of reverse psychology.

'Yes. I will be OK,' he said. But the look on his face said otherwise.

30

It wasn't until we were halfway down the sandy lane that it struck me how awful this could be for him. Going to the same beach his brother died on. The exact same stretch where he'd pulled me out of the water.

'Felix, are you sure about this?' I asked, concerned, when the girls were out of earshot.

He inhaled. 'I think so . . .'

I nodded, followed his lead, and matched his slow steps, just as reluctant as he was to go to the beach, but for very different reasons.

I spotted Antoine a mile off, in his black rash vest, board shorts and black aviators, lining up surfboards.

I looked back at Felix. The girls had taken one of his hands each and he was smiling at whatever they were saying. But behind the smile, he looked edgy. His shoulders were high and tense, and he walked with slow, reluctant steps.

'Wait until you see me, Felix. I'm going to be a real surfer like Margot,' Rue shouted.

And as we got closer to the hut – to Antoine – my heartbeat sped up. Antoine was waxing a board on the sand. And then, when we were a few metres away, he looked up. And for a split second, he stopped what he was doing before scrubbing the board again. Harder this time.

'Antoine! Antoine!' Rue called and walked over to him.

'*La guerrière et le petit oiseau!*' Antoine said, then stood up. But the smile that Antoine usually reserved for the girls was missing something.

He stared at Felix. Then turned to me. 'I did not know we would have an audience today.'

'It's a free beach,' I replied, and I was met with a brief nod.

Then Antoine turned to the girls and bent down on his haunches in front of them.

I turned to look at Felix, who stood awkwardly on the sand, and I hated Antoine for making him feel like that when it had been so hard for him to come. There was no need to be so rude.

'You are ready for the waves?' Antoine asked. They both nodded enthusiastically.

'I have a surprise for you both.' Antoine went to the rack, where he pulled out a board. But it wasn't a normal board. There were foam bumpers along each edge as well as a handle built on to the front.

'You can both use this board. We will take turns. Look at this handle.' He pointed at it. 'Sometimes the pro surfers use this to learn new techniques.'

'Wow,' said Rue. 'I'm going to be a pro surfer.'

I looked at Wren, who was smiling. 'It looks much safer.' She sighed, probably with relief.

Antoine caught my eye, and I mouthed, 'Thank you.' And it was only the slightest nod, the tiniest acknowledgement, before he turned back to Rue and Wren. 'Who wants to try it first?'

Rue put up her hand straight away.

'*La guerrière.* Of course! OK, come with me.' Antoine held out his hand and Rue grabbed it before they walked towards the water. Wren waited on the shore.

Felix and I sat down on the sand.

'Are you OK?' I asked. It was so brave of him to come here at all.

'I think so. If I stare too much at the water, it makes me feel sick. So I will not look.' He started tracing the sand with his finger.

'I'll look for you,' I said, my eyes settling on Antoine.

I commentated on the whole lesson for Felix, making him laugh when I told him about Rue's failed attempts to push Wren off the board. He seemed to relax a bit. He held my hand, and by the end, the tension that had almost crushed my fingers had nearly disappeared.

The girls had so much fun, and they were both more stable on the board. Even Wren begged for another go at the end.

I watched Antoine help Wren on to the board for her final turn. She held on to the handle and lay there as the wave rushed her to shore. She stepped off into the shallow water, excited, turning to bring the board back for Rue's go.

I watched as he held on to the board the whole time, helping to paddle it out and steadying it as the waves swelled beneath them. Rue's squeal of delight made me laugh as it pierced the air. Antoine swam, and then ran to catch up with her, having lost her on the wave. He had a huge smile on his face when he reached her, and I found myself smiling too.

'What is it?' Felix asked. I turned to him.

'What is what?' I said.

'You were smiling at something.'

'Oh, just Rue and Wren, how happy they are. It's nice. You know, Antoine has been amazing with them. Especially Rue. When I first met him, I thought he was just some arrogant surfer. Which he kind of is, but he's so good with kids.' I was staring at him again. At the easy way he talked to the girls and made them laugh so much.

'He is . . . skilled,' said Felix. My eyes followed his hand to the sand, where he was digging into it with his fingers. Hard.

'Time goes so fast here,' I mused, sighing in the heat of the sun.

'Yes. Time moves differently in Biarritz. Especially in the summer,' said Felix. But it was as if his voice had lost energy. Like he wasn't actually paying attention. I wondered if it was all too much and he wanted to leave.

And then the girls were slowly coming back up the beach, with Antoine carrying the board behind them. I stood up to greet them, while Felix stayed on the sand.

'Did you see us, Felix?' Rue asked, out of breath, deliriously happy.

'I did. You were incredible,' he said, smiling.

I could feel how close Antoine was before I looked. It was like my body reacted to his presence with goosebumps that raced over my skin. I glanced up to see him drop the surfboard at his feet.

'They are becoming good,' Antoine said to me. 'Like their sister.'

I almost smiled, despite everything. Even though *he* wasn't smiling, it wasn't conscious. Just this automatic smile reflex, a side effect of receiving a compliment from Antoine.

'But I kept falling off,' Wren cut in, upset.

Antoine crouched down in front of her. 'The falling off is the most important. Because that is how you learn. And how many times did you get back up and do it again?'

Wren held up eight fingers and Antoine smiled, then winked at her, making her grin. He ruffled her hair and stood up, then walked over to the hut. To my left, Felix cleared his throat, jolting me out of my head.

'Do you want to go back?' I asked. 'I can stay here, with the girls?'

He stared at me for a second, and I held out my hand to pull him up, but he didn't take it. He just dragged himself to his feet and brushed the sand from his shorts as he looked at me.

'You light up when you are near him,' he said.

'What? Who?' I asked.

'Antoine. You become more . . . vibrant. It is hard to explain.'

Felix's brown eyes searched mine for their reaction.

'I don't know what you mean,' I stuttered, hoping he couldn't hear the thud of my heartbeat against my rib cage.

'Yes, you do,' he replied with a sad smile.

And just as he turned to walk away, we were distracted by Rue's voice. 'Did you really see me, Felix?' she said. Then she came and wrapped her freezing, wet arms round him.

'Of course I did. You were amazing. So was Wren.'

The girls and Felix found a spot on the sand to sit down. I watched them for a moment, before instinctively turning round to find Antoine watching me. Unsmiling.

I walked closer to him, conscious that Felix was still in earshot.

The tension was palpable. Vibrating angrily between us. I didn't *light up* around him at all.

'Thanks for the lesson, Antoine, they really enjoy them,' I said, trying to take any emotion out of my voice.

'They take instructions well . . .' he said. An obvious dig. Wren and Rue were play-fighting with each other. Antoine took off his rash vest and I forced myself to look away, because I was seething and didn't want to be distracted.

'They're children. They need instructions.'

Antoine laughed and walked towards the hut. But he turned back to say, 'Are you going to South Cove tonight? I am sure that Delphine has told you? She tries to get everyone to go to South Cove parties.'

'Maybe. Why?' I shrugged, conscious of Felix nearby. His silence, awkward and loud all at the same time.

'Because South Cove is not just a party. It is where competitions are discussed. Arrangements are made . . .'

'Why are you telling me this? What does that even mean?'

'I just mean that you should be careful if you come tonight. Be careful who you talk to. What you agree to.'

And that made me snap. 'I don't need you to protect me.' I spat out the words.

'I think, from seeing you a few days ago, you *do* need me to protect you.' He said it seriously, making sure to find my eyes, with no hint of a smile.

'That was a mistake. Have you never made a mistake before?' I asked, trying to keep my voice down with Wren and Rue so close, but it was almost impossible. He was so exasperating. I pushed back hair that wasn't even in my eyes.

'Mistakes? Of course. But yours? It was avoidable.'

I turned away and then felt Antoine's grip on my wrist. I wrenched it away.

'One more thing. Your ... Him.' Antoine nodded over at Felix, who was playing a game with Rue and Wren on the sand.

'What about him? And he has a name. It's Felix,' I raged, furious at the lingering tingle of heat that was sweeping through my body.

'Do not bring him,' he said, staring at me through his sunglasses.

Another order, setting my gut on fire. 'You can't *dictate* who ... I'll make my own decisions about who I spend time with!' I could barely get my words out.

He smirked, then shrugged. 'Yes. It worked well the last time you made your own decision. *Non?*'

'Margot, can we go now?' Wren was at my side, tugging my hand, so I couldn't scream at Antoine and tell him how pissed off I was, a feeling compounded by the guilt of Felix calling out the way I reacted around Antoine. The shame of Felix seeing, clear as day, what my body had known the very first time I'd met Antoine. I guess it just took a while for the rest of me to catch up.

Antoine turned his back and walked into the hut, slamming the door behind him, leaving me on the sand as Felix and Rue joined me and Wren, wondering what was going on.

'I *hate* him,' I said, under my breath. But when I looked up, I was staring straight into Felix's sad brown eyes.

'That is not true.'

31

My second training session with Delphine was brutal. And it was all on the sand. Stretches and bodyweight exercises, over and over again. But despite the exhaustion, I loved it. And we didn't talk about Felix or Antoine or anything except surfing. She corrected my technique, over and over, explained the competition set-up and gave me tips to impress judges.

But one exchange hit home more than anything else . . .

'Do you really think I have a chance to qualify?'

'I would not waste my time if I did not.'

I walked back to the caravan in a daze after that, buzzing from what she'd said.

And then I had some time alone. I shut myself in my bedroom, lay on my bed and finally let myself think about earlier. What Felix had said about Antoine. And it was like all the signs had been telling me the same thing. The butterflies, the chemistry, the constant daydreams. But it took Felix saying it out loud for it to really sink in.

And then came the guilt. Like a slow leak that wouldn't stop, overflowing and seeping into my bones.

I covered my face with the pillow, as if hiding would make it all go away. This mess of feelings. How it was clearly so stupidly obvious to Felix, and after all that he'd been through, I'd put him through this too.

I'd apologize to him tonight. I'd stay with him at the campsite and I'd tell him I was sorry.

I put on my shortest denim shorts and my Bikini Kill T-shirt, then I lay back down on my bed and found myself opening Priya's messages.

ME: Remember I told you there were two guys? . . .

PRIYA: Yeah?

ME: Things are kind of complicated now . . .

PRIYA: Tell me!!

ME: Felix is sweet and thoughtful and way nicer to me than Theo ever was. But I think I've kind of just realized that we might be better off as friends . . .

PRIYA: He sounds really sweet

ME: He is! He's perfect. But there are like no butterflies. At all. I mean, there were at the beginning, when I first met him, but they've just gone! Do you still get them with Cal?

PRIYA: Every time I see him . . .

ME: OK hold on I'm going to call . . .

Something lifted in me when I saw Priya's smiling face. 'OK, yeah. Like zero butterflies with Felix now, and I feel like such a bitch, like I've led him on, but he's just so nice. You know?'

Priya nodded in understanding. 'Totally get it.' Then her eyes lit up with a grin. 'OK tell me about the other one.'

And I couldn't help but smile as his face filled my head. 'Antoine. My surf instructor. He totally drives me crazy, and can be seriously patronizing, but makes me feel more alive than I've felt in years! Like every time I see him I get goosebumps and my heart goes mental . . . but he's refusing to teach me to surf any more, so now Delphine is training me secretly –'

'Hold on. Secretly? Why?' Priya's forehead creased in confusion.

I rolled my eyes. 'Yeah. Mum and Dad don't know, and the fight with Antoine was because he said I wasn't ready to surf properly after I got into trouble in the water. So Delphine offered to coach me for the qualifier for this competition in September –'

'September?' Priya's voice was getting increasingly high-pitched.

'She said I might be able to qualify for it.' I'd lowered my voice. On the off-chance someone was outside my door.

'And you're going to stay? In France?'

And my heart melted when Priya said it the way she did. Like it really was my choice. And a real possibility.

I bit my lip. 'I don't know.'

'Jesus.' Priya exhaled. 'Drama. Intrigue. Secret training montages. It's pretty much your standard teen sports movie at this point.' She laughed.

'Help me, P. Tell me what to do. *Please*,' I begged.

'Surf the qualifier, enjoy the rest of your holiday. It sounds like you've already decided on which boy will solve your boy problem though. Oh, and one last thing. Update your best friend on every detail.' She smiled.

'*That's it?*'

'What did you expect? I'm not that philosophical. It feels like you're making everything way more complicated than it needs to be.'

'Maybe you're right.'

'I usually am. Actually, I do have one more thing. Maybe I *should* be a philosopher . . . Maybe it's not really about your French boys. *Maybe* it's about running away from decisions. Like swimming, like our friendship. Maybe it's time to stop running?'

I stared into the screen and let her words settle in the silence.

'You OK?' Priya squinted at me through the screen, then tapped it with her fingernail.

'Yeah. Thanks, Aristotle.' I smiled.

Priya grinned. 'What do *you* actually want?'

'When did you get so wise?'

'Maybe it happened the same time you went AWOL? Jokes. I've always been wise.'

I had a lot to think about. We hung up and I put the phone down on my bed.

What *did* I actually want?

And when I thought it over, it wasn't Felix's or Antoine's face that filled my head. When I closed my eyes, it was the rush of the waves that took over my senses. The hairs on my arms stood on end as I imagined the cool salt water around me. The sound of the waves roared in my ears, and mock adrenaline shot through my veins. I needed to stay true to that. To stop running, stop reacting. Surfing was what I was here to do, and there was nothing that could shake that.

I walked to the Brasserie to find Felix. I had it all in my head what I was going to say – I'd tell him I thought that we were better as friends. I'd changed into my little black dress, with a baggy, faded black jumper over it.

He was wiping a table when I got there, and when he saw me, his face lit up. My stomach lurched. He was in a white shirt and black jeans, with his sleeves rolled up and a cloth in his hand. He put it down and kissed both my cheeks.

'Do you want to hang out for a bit?' I asked, steeling myself for our conversation.

He took my hand and led me away from the busy Brasserie, far enough that we could hear cicadas chirping around us.

'I will come tonight,' he said, like he'd been building up to say it all day.

'To South Cove? Are you sure?'

'I am sure,' he said.

And he seemed so adamant that I didn't question him any further. 'We will go on my Vespa?'

I smiled and nodded, and once he'd finished cleaning the tables, I let him lead me towards the reception.

'Wait,' I said, halfway there. I couldn't just go to this party without telling him. It wasn't fair. Not when I'd finally understood it in my own head.

'Is something wrong?'

'I need to talk to you about something.' I tried to keep eye contact, but it was too painful, so I let my gaze fall to the floor.

'Is it about Antoine?'

Then I looked up. 'It's about us. I think you're amazing, Felix, I really do –'

'But I am not him,' he said sadly.

I shook my head. 'No, it's not that. You feel like family to me.' I took his hands in mine, and he let me. 'Like the brother I never had. And that's not like some consolation prize or something, I really mean it.' Tears pricked my eyes as all the emotion swelled to the surface like a wave. I squeezed my eyes shut, forcing tears away.

'It is OK.' Felix put his hand on my cheek, and I leaned into it. 'I do not want you to be sad.'

'I didn't want to hurt you,' I said, unable to keep the tears in any more, and a few rolled down my cheek, over Felix's hand.

'I know. But I would rather have you as a friend than nothing at all.'

I hugged him then, burying my head in his shoulder and breathing in the scent of this beautiful, sweet boy.

'We should go now?' Felix whispered into my hair, and I nodded my reply.

We walked to the Vespa and he handed me a helmet.

I wrapped my arms round his chest and watched the French countryside fly by in the soft blue twilight. We drove towards the coast, along winding roads, the wind still warm on my legs.

Felix parked on a hill and helped me off. I pulled the helmet from my head and handed it to him.

'We are here. The South Cove, but there is nowhere to park down there,' Felix said. I wasn't really listening. I'd walked over to the edge of the hill to look at the view.

The sea looked beautiful, endless as it blended with the darkening sky. Felix stood beside me, and I leaned against his shoulder.

'Are you OK?' I looked at him as he watched the water, wondering why he was putting himself through this. Another beach.

'I will be OK. It is important for me to be here tonight.'

'Why?' I asked.

'Gabriel,' Felix replied. 'But we should go before I change my mind.'

We walked side by side down a steep path and I wondered if this had been Gabriel's favourite beach or something. I didn't want to break the comfortable silence between us, so I didn't ask. I could hear voices from the top of the hill. The path opened up into a little cove, already full of groups of people sitting around driftwood fires. The sound of someone playing a metal drum gave a backdrop beat to the night.

A barbecue was set up way back from the water. I could feel Felix's hand tense in mine as we walked towards it.

'Are you really OK?' I asked. But he didn't have a chance to answer.

'Felix!' Sébastian called out, louder than the music, the chatting, and the hiss of the waves on the shore.

Sébastian was at the barbecue and his face lit up as he held up his hand to wave Felix over to him. Felix's hand tightened its grip, and I took a deep breath, as if I was trying to inhale some of his anxiety.

We walked over, through little groups of people who all turned to look at Felix. No wonder he was nervous.

'Felix.' Sébastian put down his barbecue tongs and pulled him into a hug when we reached him. Felix let go of my hand, and I stood there as they had their moment.

'I will speak English for Margot. I am so happy you came,' said Sébastian.

'Thanks,' replied Felix, hand in his hair.

'Felix!' Lili came out of nowhere, her dark curls bouncing around her shoulders, and behind her, Delphine. Lili threw her arms round Felix when Sébastian let him go. 'Do you remember the first barbecue, when everyone was sick?' Lili laughed.

'Unfortunately, I do remember.' Felix smiled and stepped a bit closer to me. 'Maybe I should do the barbecue tonight?' Felix looked at Sébastian with raised eyebrows and he glared back at him, before bursting into a huge smile. 'I thought you would never ask.' Sébastian handed Felix the tongs and they switched places, so Sébastian was standing beside me. 'I will get you a drink, Margot.' He disappeared to a barrel filled with ice and came back with a can of beer.

'Thanks,' I said.

'How are your legs?' Delphine asked. Her hair was pulled into a messy updo, and a cardigan was draped over her elegant shoulders, revealing a dark summer minidress.

'Tired,' I admitted, thinking back to our run, then our lesson.

'Good. We will do the same again tomorrow?' she asked.

'Delphine,' Lili warned, then she touched my arm gently. 'Sometimes Delphine is too strict. She makes people work too hard.' Lili spoke to me, but she was looking at Delphine with a smirk. Delphine rolled her eyes.

'It's OK. I like to train hard,' I said, and Delphine smiled smugly back at Lili.

'And you will come to the qualifier, Fe?' Sébastian asked Felix, who was turning burgers.

'One step at a time,' Felix replied, staring into the barbecue.

Then I heard Lili say 'Antoine' when she was talking to Delphine in French. The name caught my ear like it was meant for me. I followed their gaze towards the water, and there he was. A figure standing with his back to us, hands in pockets, just looking out at the ocean.

I looked back to Felix, who was surrounded by people I didn't know. All of them smiling, talking to him, delighted that he had come.

So I slipped away towards the water, my full can of beer still in my hand.

I walked between the groups of people, dragging my feet through the cooling sand, towards Antoine. He was wearing a white T-shirt and dark board shorts, his tattooed arms still jammed in their pockets when I reached him. I nudged him with my shoulder. '*Le flic de la plage.* Still checking the water?' I looked up at him and the side of his mouth twitched into the beginning of a smile that never actually materialized.

I had the urge to take his hand then. To squeeze it in mine, like this connection between us was so strong that it superseded everything else. Like how patronizing he'd been and the things he'd said, how it all just faded away.

But Felix was on the beach. And despite our conversation, I couldn't do that to him.

So I just stood there, beer in hand, with the charged salt air fizzing with tension between us.

'I hope you are not planning to drink that near the water.' Antoine nodded at the beer can in my hand.

'I wouldn't dream of it,' I said.

'Good. I have arrested people for less.'

I gave him a side eye and smirked.

'Why did you come tonight?'

'Because Felix wanted to.' I shrugged.

'He is here? Felix?' Antoine glanced towards the crowd spread across the beach.

'Yep,' I answered.

Antoine sighed and scanned the crowd, as if to look for him.

'Is that the only reason?' he asked, letting his words hang in the air as he stared back out at the ocean.

He inhaled, and in those seconds, I couldn't hear the rush of the waves, the bang of the drum or the chatter of French teenagers, because it was like everything was silent. Like it was just us on the beach.

'No,' I said. And I didn't mean it to come out. Or maybe I did. Priya *did* tell me to be honest.

And he was about to say something. He opened his mouth and, desperate to hear what he had to say, I moved closer. But something had caught his attention behind us. He turned, and I watched the muscles in his shoulders immediately tense.

I followed his gaze. Felix. Far away, but unmistakable. His square-shouldered silhouette watched us from the glow of the bonfire beside him. Antoine turned to me, his expression hard, jaw set, and I wondered what condescending words would come out of his mouth.

But he just shook his head in frustration, then stormed away from me, up the beach, towards Felix. I jogged after him but was stopped by Sébastian, who held out an arm.

'Be careful, Margot. It is better not to get mixed up.' He looked down at me with pleading eyes beneath his blonde mop of hair.

'What's going on?' I asked.

But I couldn't hear his answer, because a crowd had gathered around Felix and Antoine, who were shouting at each other in French. French that was far too fast for me to attempt to translate. I looked between them. Felix looked angrier than I'd ever seen him. His brown eyes flashed in the light of the bonfire, embers sparking around them, like even the universe was expecting a fight. Antoine stood tall, holding his head up, chest out, seeming bigger than he was. He paced on the sand in front of Felix as they fired angry words at each other.

Sébastian bent down and whispered into my ear. 'Antoine is asking why he is here. He says that he lost the right to be here when he walked away three years ago.'

'I don't understand.' I looked at Sébastian, confused. But he was listening again and hadn't heard me.

'They are talking about Gabriel now,' Sebastain explained.

'Gabriel. Felix's brother?' I asked. No answer.

I watched them again, and everything around me blurred, as a sickening revelation passed through my body. The bone structure. It was the same. The same defined jawline and high cheekbones. The eyes – same shape, different colour. Square shoulders, olive skin, toned but lean.

Gabriel was Antoine's brother too.

I reached for Sébastian's shirt beside me and tugged it. He bent down so he could hear me.

'Felix and Antoine. They're brothers?' I looked into his eyes, hoping he'd shake his head, prove my stupid theory wrong.

But he nodded, his eyes still on them. 'You knew . . . *Non* . . .? They have not spoken for three years. Not since Gabriel died.' Sébastian translated again: 'Antoine says that he was supposed to be there that day. That he felt guilty. And Felix is saying that it was him who took Gabriel out to surf, that it was all his fault, and that Antoine has blamed him ever since.'

I stared open-mouthed at Felix, whose pain was so visible that it was hard to watch. Sébastian kept translating. 'I never blamed you. I blamed myself. You walked away. From me. From the ocean. I lost two brothers that day.' He mirrored the painful animation in Antoine's voice.

My hand moved reflexively to my mouth and a lump formed in my throat.

'Felix says that he could not stay. Not with the ghost of Gabriel. Not when he thought Antoine hated him.' Felix's words were stilted, like he was about to cry.

But I couldn't take any more. I pushed my way back through the crowd and sat down on the sand. My head was spinning. I'd found myself in the middle of this awful family tragedy. I should have seen it. The similarities, which were just so painfully obvious now that I knew.

And I had never felt more stupid.

32

I left the crowd and started to walk down the beach, the light and heat of the bonfires getting further and further away. Then I heard a voice.

'Margot. Wait!'

I turned to see Delphine jogging after me.

'Do you mind if I join you?'

I shook my head.

'Do you want to sit?' Delphine motioned to a semi-flat rock beside us.

I nodded and sat down, pulling my knees to my chest and staring at the ocean.

'I am sorry that you found out like this. Felix, he did not want you to know. He thought it would make everything more complicated,' Delphine said gently. 'He sometimes does not make the best decisions.'

'More complicated? It would have been better than this.' I didn't even know where to start to try to make sense of it all.

'I have known the Laurent brothers my whole life. We all grew up surfing together. Me, Antoine, Felix, and eventually Gabriel. They were like family to me.'

I leaned my head on my knees and turned to her. She was staring out at the ocean, twisting a piece of hair in her fingers. 'When Gabriel died, it broke something in all of us. Especially Felix and Antoine, of course. And it was like they shattered, and the fragments scattered in opposite directions. Antoine started to teach, and Felix, he kept his distance from the water.'

'They should have told me. *Someone* should have told me.' Although I wasn't sure what good that would have done. If I'd known, would I have stayed away from Antoine altogether? Maybe that would have been better.

'*Bien sûr.* Everything makes more sense when you look back.' She shrugged. 'But for what it is worth, neither of them has looked at anyone the way they look at you. Not since before Gabriel.'

'What do you mean?' I turned to her, and she glanced at me this time and smiled.

'I mean that Antoine had just been going through the motions, teaching, surviving, but not really living. With you he becomes alive.'

I shook my head. It just added to the confusion about how I should be feeling. And it was exactly what Felix had said about *me* when he saw me with Antoine. That I lit up around him.

'And Felix? He has not let anybody be close to him since Gabriel. And, Margot, he went into the water. For you. Do you realize how huge that is?'

The weight of what Delphine said felt like a thousand bricks on my shoulders. 'But what now?' I asked, hoping she'd just give me the answer, knowing full well it wasn't as easy as that.

Delphine got off the rock and stood on the sand, looking out to the sea again. 'Now it is up to you. Walk away, from Antoine, from Felix, from surfing, or you can stay and see it through.'

And I thought about what Priya had said. About me running away from hard decisions all the time. How I had to figure out what I wanted and just go for it. And she was right. But everything had just got so much more complicated.

'I will leave you to your thoughts. And I hope I will see you tomorrow morning for training.'

I gave her a half smile, and sat there for another twenty minutes, letting everything settle in my head, until the chill in the air forced me to walk back towards the bonfire.

The drums were playing again, and the chatter of all the little groups had returned. I wished we'd been at the campsite beach where I could have just slipped away with nobody noticing, but Felix had driven me, so I was stuck. I pulled my jumper around me and walked towards the closest bonfire to get some heat.

'Margot?' A voice from behind me, a hand on my waist.

I spun round. Antoine.

'You came back.'

I shrugged. 'I didn't know where else to go.'

'I should have told you. About Felix . . . About everything.'

'Why didn't you?' I asked.

His hand was in his hair. 'Saying his name. It hurts. It feels like opening a wound that has not healed properly.'

I nodded. I got it. I really did. But that didn't mean it didn't hurt me too. And while I was thinking about what to say, someone else touched my shoulder. I turned to see Felix looking at me with concern on his face. 'You are OK?'

'Yeah, I'm fine,' I said with a sad smile.

'You went away. I was worried. But Delphine, she said she found you.'

'She did.' I nodded.

'I am sorry, Margot. For not telling the truth.'

'We both are,' Antoine added. Felix looked at him and I watched as Antoine gave him a brief nod. Like there was some new understanding between them.

'And what about you two?' I asked. They looked at each other. They didn't smile, but they didn't look like they wanted to kill each other either.

'One day at a time,' Felix said. Antoine simply nodded.

A girl with braids nudged me and handed me a cardboard cup filled with wine. I looked around to see that everyone had a cup and then I saw Sébastian standing on a rock, looking even taller than usual.

'I will speak in English, because we have English-speaking company.'

That got some boos, but I was thankful.

'Tonight is our annual bonfire. Year number three, when we, the surf community, gather to celebrate the life of the spectacular Gabriel Laurent. For three years we have been missing him at every surf session, every bonfire that he was too young for, and every sunset, when he said the water looked like magic.'

And now it made sense. Why Felix wanted to come tonight. Why this 'party' was different.

Sébastian took a moment, inhaling deeply then taking a drink of his wine.

'I do not think I have told anyone this before. But one week before he died, Gabriel was at my lessons and he told me that his brothers taught him better than anyone else. And that they did not agree on anything, except the waves. He would tell everyone that his brothers were the best surfers in Biarritz. Which was quite rude because I was right there in front of him. But he was a Laurent. And so it was impossible to be angry at him. So tonight, we do not just remember Gabriel for who he was. But for what he loved the most. The ocean, the surfing community, his family.'

'Gabriel,' everyone said together. I could hear people crying, and when I looked at Antoine and Felix, both sets of eyes were glistening with tears. My heart ached for them. I took a sip of wine.

After that, everyone started to leave, and Antoine hung back to make sure all the fires had been put out properly.

'Would you like me to drive you home?' Antoine asked as I stood there, feeling awkward watching him.

I pointed at Felix, who was chatting to Delphine. 'Felix drove me,' I said. And at the sound of his name, he came over.

Antoine said something to Felix in French and he nodded before looking at me.

'It will be cold on the Vespa. Maybe you should go back with Antoine tonight,' he said.

'Are you sure?' I asked, concerned about him driving alone after so much emotion.

'I will take Delphine.' Felix smiled. 'But I will see you tomorrow?'

'Of course,' I said.

As Felix and Delphine walked away, it felt like I'd made an unconscious choice. There I was, alone with Antoine and a million different thoughts, all contradicting each other.

But there was one thing that hadn't changed. The electricity in the air.

33

Antoine's van was just as messy as it had been the last time I'd been in it. I breathed it in, the scents of salt on damp clothes, board wax and engine oil, which to me were just the smells of Antoine now. The smell of all those lessons at the cove.

I twisted my curls in my fingers and rested my other hand on the gear stick. He turned on the engine and didn't even ask me to move; he just put his hand on top of mine and shifted the gear stick in a sure, smooth motion. And I didn't pull my hand away, because I liked it, the warmth that radiated right down to my bones and the familiar throb in my abdomen that I'd grown to expect whenever he was close.

'Why did you come with me?' he asked bluntly as we drove back towards the campsite.

I was taken aback by the directness of his question. But I knew the answer – more clearly now than ever, that Antoine drew me towards him like a magnet, with some invisible force that I didn't really understand. 'Because it would be cold on the Vespa.' I smirked.

'So you are able to listen to advice now?'

'Very funny.'

I turned my head and gazed out the window, breathing on to the glass and moving my hand from the gear stick to doodle my name in the condensation.

'You and Felix . . .' Antoine said.

'Me and Felix what?' I replied, turning back.

'You are still together?'

I shook my head gently. 'Me and Felix are better as friends.'

'Sometimes that becomes clear.'

'Yeah,' I agreed, as a fizz of nerve endings ignited themselves in my body.

'And what about me? We are just friends?' he asked, breaking his gaze on the road for a second to look over at me. And when I looked back at him, I had to force myself to stay on track. Even in the dark, his eyes were disarming, messing with my head, scrambling my thoughts.

'It's complicated. Don't you think?' I asked.

'Complicated can be good.' I caught the edge of his smile before he turned back to watch the road.

'I still don't understand why you didn't tell me that Felix was your brother when I told you I was seeing him. I understand not talking about Gabriel, of course I do. But Felix?' A new wave of frustration rolled through me.

'I was jealous,' Antoine said simply.

'Jealous?'

He gripped the steering wheel with both hands. 'I knew that Felix could give you things that I could not. Normal conversations. Normal human interaction. I am better in water than I am on land,' he admitted.

I took in what he'd just said. I used to say the same about myself. Yeah, Priya got me, but I'm not sure anyone else did. Not really.

'Maybe we're more similar than you think,' I said, and put my hand back down on the gear stick, only for him to put his on top again.

We'd just pulled into the campsite when I decided to tell him.

'I've been training since our fight . . .'

He pulled his hand off mine, on to the steering wheel and looked at me. 'Training? With who?'

'Delphine.'

He didn't say anything for a second.

'She's coaching me for the qualifier,' I continued.

'*La Vague d'Or* qualifier?' Antoine asked, then shook his head.

'What? You don't think I can do it? You don't think I can qualify? Delphine said I had potential.'

Antoine turned to me with the twitch of a smile on his lips. 'I did not say that at all. Delphine does not say that lightly. She is right.' He nodded.

'We had two sessions today –'

'Two? Your arms. They should feel like spaghetti now.' He reached over and squeezed my bicep. I tensed it.

'They do. But I like it. It reminds me that I'm getting stronger again. That's the plan. Two sessions a day until the qualifier.'

Antoine smiled at me, as though he understood where I was coming from, but also like he didn't know what to say. Then he turned right, into the campsite car park and turned off the engine.

'You are really going to do this? The qualifier?' he asked with a sigh, knowing that I wasn't about to change my mind based on his opinion.

'I am.'

He took his hands off the steering wheel in mock surrender.

'And I'd like you to be there,' I said.

'As your coach?'

'Delphine is my coach,' I reminded him. 'Just as . . . whatever this is.' I motioned between us.

'Whatever this is . . .' he repeated.

'Complicated is what it is.'

'You like that word. Complicated.'

'It seems to come in handy here,' I said. He'd moved closer, so he was inches from me, and I was staring straight into his blue eyes. 'Delphine says that my technique has really improved, and that I have really good . . . instincts.' I whispered the last part.

Antoine nodded, intrigued. 'And what do your instincts tell you now?' he asked, his voice rough from his fight with Felix.

'That maybe some waves are worth the risk.'

And with that I opened the door, before turning to face him again. '*Bonne nuit*, Antoine.' I got out of the van.

'*Bonne nuit*, Margot.' And our eyes held each other's gaze for longer than necessary. Or maybe not long enough.

I closed the door and walked back to our mobile home, feeling his eyes on me until I was out of sight.

Everyone was asleep when I got in, which I was happy about. I didn't want any questions, or to have to try to come up with answers when my head was a tangled mess of new information, painful realizations, guilt, secrets and a yearning, so strong that when I went to bed, Antoine was the only thing I was thinking about.

I wondered what it would be like to kiss him. And that was kind of why I didn't, right there in the van. I liked the not knowing, I liked creating a whole narrative in my head of us kissing on the beach, against the soaking, salty rocks at the surfer's cove. His hands, coarse from the surfboards, gentle but firm on my lower back, pulling me into him.

And then I fell asleep to the lullaby of the ocean and the unmistakable growing waves of desire.

34

It was hard to wake up the next morning. The dawn sessions and late nights were catching up with me, and when my alarm beeped at four thirty, I almost reached over and turned it off. But then I stopped myself. I wanted this. *I* wanted to surf, *I* wanted to compete. So I needed to get up.

I dragged myself out of bed, put on a bikini and the borrowed rash vest, then sneaked out the door, more quietly than ever.

Delphine grinned when she saw me. And I'd never seen it before, Delphine smiling like that. She waved at me from down the beach and when I reached her, she kissed me on both cheeks.

'Margot! You came. Antoine told me that you said that I am your instructor. Now we can train back in the usual spot. Unless you do not feel like you can?' Delphine looked into my eyes, searching for fear. Fear that wasn't there. I'd rationalized it in my head. I knew the qualifier would be held at that same stretch of beach, so I'd made myself think about it logically. There was no difference where I surfed. All water could be dangerous in the wrong conditions. And I'd rather practise where the competition would be.

'Let's go,' I agreed. And she nodded.

'I was not sure if you would come back after last night. It was a bit intense. *Non?*' she said as we walked along the sand.

When we got to Antoine's hut, Delphine went straight to the rack and pulled out a surfboard. Antoine's black surfboard.

'Oh no, that's –' I protested.

'I told her to use it.' I heard Antoine's voice before I saw him. Then he emerged from the back of the surf hut, a length of rope slung round his neck. And, for the first time, my words got properly stuck in my throat. So I coughed.

'Oh, thanks,' I said, heat rising through my body as I remembered all the things we'd done in my head last night. I turned away, hoping he wouldn't catch my blush.

'Antoine is only watching. So do not worry.'

'I wasn't,' I said, reaching for some board wax and crouching down to scrub it on the board.

I concentrated on it, trying not to miss anything. But my mind kept flicking to last night. The tension, the electric air, the daydreams . . .

'You have missed a bit, *Princesse*.'

I looked up to see Antoine beside me on his haunches. I sighed dramatically, then chucked him the board wax. 'Do it for me then,' I said, then stood up as Delphine laughed.

'Yes, Margot!' she sang, and Antoine gave her a side-eyed glance.

Delphine walked a few metres away from the hut and held out her arms. 'Minimal wind. Perfect. What will you do, Antoine?'

'Board repairs. And I will watch.' And when he said the word 'watch' he was looking straight at me. I shivered and picked up my board, walking towards Delphine.

'Margot. What are you doing?' She looked at my board.

'What?' I asked.

'We run!' she said. 'The same as yesterday.'

And she was right. Yesterday we'd gone on a beach run followed by stretches before we even set foot in the water. I was blaming Antoine for that. Messing with my head. I glared and him and he smiled back, tilting his sunglasses down slightly, and I rolled my eyes before dropping the board and running after Delphine, who'd already taken off.

The training session was harder today. Which was good. It didn't give me any time to worry about what Antoine was looking at back on the sand.

'Your tail slide. It needs some work,' Delphine said when we finally got in the water. 'All of your weight, it must go on the front leg. You are not doing that.'

So I did it again. And again, until Delphine was happy.

We emerged from the sea exhausted. Antoine greeted us with bottles of water.

'You looked good out there,' he said.

'Thanks,' Delphine answered with a smile.

'You both did.' He took my board from me and put it on the rack. 'Margot, you are more ready than I was for my first competition.'

I glowed with pride.

'I am taking all the credit for her.' Delphine put her arm round Antoine's neck.

'I think she can take all the credit herself,' Antoine said, then chucked a towel at me.

And I blushed at that as I covered my face with it.

I squeezed it through my hair gently, trying to get it to dry as quickly as possible before Mum and Dad saw.

When I threw the towel back to Antoine, I noticed Delphine looking at the sky. She mumbled something in French.

'I think they were right. What do you think, Antoine?'

'The storm? It is coming, for sure. Lucky you had a session already.'

'A storm? No!' I complained. I was so looking forward to uninterrupted surf lessons.

'You will be OK, Margot. You can do some push-ups in your caravan,' said Delphine. 'Oh, I must go and help Felix set up. I told him I would be there today.'

I waved goodbye to Delphine and turned to Antoine. 'So, what did you really think?'

He stopped tidying up for a second and studied me. His eyes rested on my face before tracing my body. And it was like I could feel them, as if he was touching me with his fingertips.

'Your bottom turn. You are dropping your back shoulder,' Antoine said, his eyes on mine.

'Oh really? Delphine didn't mention it,' I said.

'It is subtle, and sometimes Delphine does the same thing . . . I can show you?' He raised his eyebrows. 'Yes?'

I nodded, and he took the board back off the rack, lying it on the sand. 'Lie down,' he instructed.

I hesitated, before lying down on the board as if I was going to paddle out. Then he was next to me, leaning on the sand.

'OK, pop up.'

So I did. And he watched. Inches away from me. Then his

hands were on my shoulders, gently repositioning me. And there was that current. The one that I knew so well but still seemed to shock me. I inhaled. Desperately trying to hold on to the moment and concentrate at the same time.

He guided me through the movement. One hand on my shoulder, while another moved to my hip, and I had to bite my lip to distract myself from the craving in my abdomen. 'Do you feel how your weight shifts?'

I nodded, swallowing hard.

'When you come out of the bottom turn it is about connecting your upper body to your lower body.' The hand that was on my shoulder joined the other one on my hips. He turned me slightly and then put his hand on my stomach. 'The core. The power comes from here.'

My breath was shallow. 'I think I get it.'

'Good,' he replied and let go. But the feeling didn't disappear – my skin was still alive, almost vibrating from where he'd touched me.

'I better go. Before my mum and dad get suspicious.'

'OK. Just remember that the storm is coming. Be safe.'

'I will.'

I walked away, with my skin still burning from his touch.

Mum and Dad were outside eating breakfast when I got back to the mobile home. My hair had already dried in the sun so it couldn't give me away.

'Morning, Margot,' said Mum. 'Did you go for a walk?'

'Yep, just down to the beach. It's a really nice morning.' I kept my voice cheery.

‘It really is. We are planning a trip to Saint-Jean-de-Luz for lunch after the girls’ lesson – would you like to come? Or have you other plans?’

‘Sure,’ I said. I didn’t have any other plans; Delphine had cancelled our extra training because of the imminent storm. ‘But there’s a storm coming. Did you know?’

‘It says that it’s not due until this afternoon, so we *should* be OK.’

‘She’s really coming?!’ I heard Wren shout from inside.

And that made me smile.

It was hot in Saint-Jean-De-Luz. Like really hot. The humidity was making my T-shirt stick to my skin and I noticed Rue fidgeting with her splints even more than usual.

Saint-Jean-De-Luz was just how I’d remembered it from when I’d come here with Felix and we’d had such a lovely day. And as soon as Felix came into my head, so did the guilt of all the thoughts I’d been having about Antoine. I’d been so sure at the beginning that it had been true passion with Felix. He’d been so nice to me. And maybe that’s what made me confused. Theo had never been like that, and it was intoxicating. Just being with him made me feel so good about myself. And then I felt selfish. Like I’d somehow used him. But I hadn’t. Not intentionally. I didn’t trust myself to think about Antoine when I was with my family. It felt wrong, having those thoughts. So I pushed them both out of my head.

Dad gave Rue a piggyback through the town, all the way to the little pizzeria that Felix and I had eaten in.

And after we ate, Mum’s phone rang.

'No caller ID. Hospital?' Mum mumbled at Dad, and my stomach lurched, as it did every time the hospital phoned. Because it never meant something good.

I looked over at Rue to see if she'd noticed, but she was busy showing Wren something she'd drawn on a napkin. Mum stood up and I watched her walk outside into the humidity. Dad followed her and I just studied the two of them, trying to work out what was being said.

Mum put her hand over her mouth, and I still couldn't tell. She didn't look upset. Maybe Rue didn't need to have her operation because they'd got some test results back and she'd been miraculously cured?

Now Dad had his arm on Mum's shoulder. She was still on the phone, and it looked like she was asking loads of questions. She wiped sweat from her forehead, then hung up the phone and just looked at Dad.

Then they hugged. And I still had absolutely no clue what was going on.

They stayed outside talking for a while before coming in.

'Why did you take so long?' Rue demanded to know when they walked through the door. 'We need to order ice cream.'

'Ice cream, of course,' Mum said, when it was clearly the furthest thing from her mind. I glanced at Wren, who was looking nervously between Mum and Dad, like she knew something was coming.

Mum ordered ice cream, then both she and Dad sat down.

'We have some news,' she said. She was looking at Rue when she said it, then looked at both me and Wren.

'Good news?' Rue asked with a huge smile.

'*I* think so,' Mum said.

My stomach twisted.

The waiter came back and set down bowls of vanilla ice cream in front of Rue and Wren.

'*Merci*,' I said for them. 'What is it?' I asked Mum, getting impatient.

'Well, it's about Rue's operation,' Mum said. Everyone looked at Rue, who just stared into her ice cream. 'Remember that it was supposed to be in September?'

'Yeah?' I nodded, scared for what was coming next.

'Well, we just had a phone call from Doctor Malone. She said she had a cancellation and can do Rue's operation early,' Mum said carefully.

I glanced at Dad, who just looked at Rue with pain in his eyes.

'How early?' I asked.

'Next week,' Mum said. 'Which means we'd have to leave on Friday to get to Liverpool on time. And they said there'll be space at the Ronald McDonald house, so we can stay there.' Mum tried to sound bright and cheery, but her voice wavered and gave her away.

Friday.

The day of the qualifier.

35

Nobody spoke on the way home. Not even Rue, who had just gone quiet. Mum put on Taylor Swift for her, and we all listened, pretending that we loved the music when I'm sure everyone else's brains were spinning as much as mine.

It was great news. Rue would get her operation early, and maybe it would help. Her legs might be less stiff, and she'd be more mobile. But her recovery would be tough. The pain would be so hard to watch. Mum and Dad would be terrified that something would go wrong, as they always were when Rue had to go to hospital. They thought they hid it really well, but a few days before any of Rue's procedures, Mum would start cleaning the house. Like properly tearing it apart, throwing stuff out, scrubbing tiles, and trying to pretend it was normal.

I got it. I felt sick when Rue had to go in for any sort of treatment, and it must be even worse for Mum and Dad, but sometimes I thought all you needed to do was take one look at Rue, who showed up with them to the hospital, who held out her arms and feet for needles without so much as complaining.

I reached over for her little hand and squeezed it. She squeezed it back and I listened to her hum to Taylor Swift all the way to the campsite.

And by the time we got back, the storm had started. The wind blew hard into the tents that lined the little paths, and people were rushing around bringing in clothes and toys so they wouldn't get destroyed. A lot of other tourists clearly hadn't expected the storm to be here already, or maybe just hadn't heard about it at all.

'I *love* storms,' said Rue. 'I hope there's thunder.'

'Thunder?' said Wren, sounding scared.

Mum turned round to calm her down. 'Don't worry, love, let's get inside before the rain starts. It will give me a chance to get on with some cleaning before we leave,' she added for Dad's benefit.

My breath caught in my throat, and I was scared I might cry as I got out of the car, so I refused to think about it.

'I need to go somewhere. I'll be back soon,' I said.

And I left before they could convince me that it was too dangerous. Even though I heard them calling, and Dad telling Rue that she couldn't follow me.

I walked through the campsite, with the wind determined to push me over, and headed straight for the Brasserie.

The storm was picking up, and soon it would be raging, but it didn't matter. I couldn't think about one thing before something else crashed into my head, pushing it away. Rue's operation, the qualifier, Felix, Antoine. The electricity that appeared from nowhere when he was near me, how when he touched me every nerve ending buzzed with excitement and longing. And Felix. Perfect Felix. He'd been so kind, so understanding, despite what he was going through. And now I had to say goodbye. My hand moved reflexively to my mouth as tears fell. I shook the thought away. I loved spending time with him. I truly did. I kept my head down, thoughts twisting, fuming at the unfairness of it all, then feeling disgusted at my own selfishness. There was Rue, who had to go for an operation, and I was crying about some surf competition and a couple of boys?

I kicked a tree stump and it hurt. But I didn't care. I deserved it.

'Margot?'

I looked up and noticed I was just outside the Brasserie. I saw Felix standing in the rain, umbrella up, just staring at me.

And it just made me cry more. Seeing him standing there in the rain, his beautiful face full of concern. He rushed towards me, putting the umbrella over us both and pulling me into a hug with his other arm. And it almost made it worse, as I remembered the thoughts I'd been having about Antoine last night.

'What are you doing out here? It is not safe. You should be inside.' Felix led me inside the Brasserie where Yves was sitting down at one of the tables with a glass of beer.

'*Bonsoir*,' I choked out.

'*Bonsoir*, Margot. *La tempête, c'est mauvais, non?*' he said.

I glanced at Felix for the translation. 'He said the storm is bad.'

'*Oui*.' I nodded and sat down at a table with Felix.

He took both my hands in his. 'You are very wet,' he said. 'Why are you outside in the storm?'

And I couldn't help it. I felt my face crease as I started to cry again.

'Margot, *non*! What is wrong?' Felix put his palm gently on my cheek and I leaned into it.

'I have to leave France.'

'What do you mean? Because you do not want to do the competition? You do not have to do it.' Felix shook his head, like this was obvious.

I shook my head. 'Rue. She is having an operation, and it got moved forward, so we need to go home.'

Felix leaned back in his chair. 'Ah, I understand,' he said sadly.

'And I feel so guilty and selfish because I'm devastated. I should just be thinking about Rue. And of course she needs me. I'm a horrible person.' I shook my head, barely able to get the thoughts straight.

'Horrible? Margot, because of you I have been able to go to the beach again. And I have seen you with your sister. I wish I had been as nice to Gabriel.' And the way he said it was like he wasn't looking for sympathy, but that he really believed it. 'This, it is not horrible. Unless horrible means something else in English.' He raised his eyebrow, and I gave him the tiniest smile I could manage. Then I shook my head.

'Felix, I . . .' I what? Have been dreaming about your brother every night since I met him? Have used you and your endless kindness? 'I should go. I can't. I'm not who you think I am . . .'

I got up and started to walk away when I felt him grip my wrist. 'Margot.'

And the pained look on his face made it impossible to pull away. So I didn't. I sat down again and put my head in my hands. 'Felix . . .' And I just couldn't get it out.

'You do not owe me any explanation,' he said, then he reached for my hands again and pulled them away from my face, holding them gently in his.

'But I do, I –'

Felix shook his head. 'Margot, we had our time together, and it was beautiful, but then it was clear to me that you belonged to someone else. Even if I did not want it to be true.' He smiled sadly and I blinked back more tears.

'It's not like that. I don't belong –'

'You do. And it is OK. Like I said before, you light up when you look at him. You light up when you talk about him. And the light has become brighter this last week, has it not?' Felix looked at me and I nodded, unable to lie to him any more.

'I didn't mean to hurt you,' I whispered.

'I know.' He reached over and brushed a tear gently from my cheek. 'So it is hard for me to be angry.'

'I don't deserve this. You're being too nice,' I said as his hand found mine again. I squeezed it.

'Maybe you are too hard on yourself,' he said, letting the words settle in the air between us.

And then we just sat there for a moment, in the comfortable silence that I would miss so much. But I couldn't sit there any more, because I knew if I did, it would just make everything worse. Looking at Felix's perfect face, drowning in his kindness. It wasn't fair.

'I should head back.' I stood up and tried desperately not to cry again. He stood up too.

'Can I get you anything before you go? *Chocolat chaud?*' He gave me the saddest smile. I shook my head before throwing my arms round him, breathing in the lavender-and-vanilla scent I'd come to know so well.

'Thank you,' I whispered. 'For everything.'

'*Au revoir*, Margot,' he whispered.

'Goodbye, Felix,' I said, before turning and walking towards the door.

'Oh, Margot?'

I turned, and he hesitated. Then he said, 'Whatever happens with my brother. Make sure to look after your heart.' He pressed his hand on his chest. 'You have told him yet? That you must leave?'

I shook my head.

'It is where you are going now?'

I nodded, walking out the door before the tears came back, in the thick of the furious storm.

36

The rain was blowing sideways as I reached the sand. It fell in thick droplets that soaked me right through in seconds. I breathed in the wet, salty air as a deep sadness filled my gut. I couldn't leave here. I couldn't leave *him*.

Thunder roared through the darkening clouds, and I looked towards the ocean. Huge waves with violent peaks crashed to the shore like they were just as furious as I was.

And I *was* furious. The disappointment had long since turned to anger as I stormed across the sand towards Antoine's hut.

And he was there. Of course he was there. Bringing things inside, securing the hut against the violent gusts of wind that were growing stronger by the second.

He didn't see me until I was almost beside him. Then he turned and shouted over the noise of the wind and waves.

'Margot! What are you doing here? It is not safe!' He pulled the rack of surfboards closer to the hut and started tying them together with some rope. Lightning flashed over the ocean and the thunder roared again as another torrent of rain followed.

'I have to leave.' I shouted over the beat of the rain on the roof of the shack and the waves crashing behind us.

'Yes, you do, it is not safe!' Antoine repeated, more frantically this time.

'France! I have to leave France,' I yelled, more desperately than I'd meant.

Then he stopped what he was doing and just stood there, staring at me in the rain. Water ran down his face and he didn't wipe it away. His dark hair sat flat against his forehead, but his eyes seemed even more blue. Like they'd come alive in the storm.

He flicked wet hair away from his eyes. 'What do you mean, *Princesse*?'

But he didn't wait for an answer; he just grabbed my hand and pulled me into his hut, which creaked and groaned from every angle.

'I have to leave,' I said. My voice was choked, and I told myself it was from the rain in my throat, but that was a lie. 'My sister. Rue. She has to have an operation and it's been moved earlier, so we need to go home.'

I forced myself not to cry, even though the disappointment consumed me like a wave.

'That is . . .' Antoine pushed his hair back again and turned away briefly before looking back at me. 'Your sister. She needs you. When is the operation?' he asked.

'Next week. But we need to get to Liverpool. The hospital there is one of the only places that does it.'

Antoine nodded, slowly, like he wasn't really listening, and I just stood there, with no idea what to say next.

'The qualifier. You know you would have been ready. Don't you?' He said it with such sincerity that when I nodded my reply I couldn't hold back tears any longer. He stepped forward and I leaned into his soaking-wet chest and cried. I thought about the wasted opportunity, how I'd finally found something that I loved. That lit me up, that I was *good* at. And that would be it. Gone forever.

But he was right. Rue needed me. There was never a question of me staying. But that didn't mean that it didn't hurt.

I was shivering now, and when I looked up at him, my teeth chattered. I shook my head.

'And what about us? We are just friends? Or it is still complicated?' He looked down at me, his sea-blue eyes intense with the question. I just stood there for a second, hesitating, frozen and aching for his touch. So I kissed him, giving him an answer he couldn't misinterpret. And it was like nothing I'd felt before. Kissing Felix had been sweet, glowing embers. Kissing Antoine was a frantic, hungry fire that rushed through my body like my veins were laced with lighter fuel. He picked me up and I hooked my legs round him, and the desire grew into something I didn't just want, but *needed*. Antoine set me down and pulled my soaking-wet dress over my head before taking off his own T-shirt. I gazed at his tattoos before tracing my hands over his chest. Over each tattoo, gently, like I was committing each one to memory through my fingertips.

'You are sure, *Princesse*?' He looked down at me.

'I'm sure,' I replied.

The rain beat hard against the windows, and the roar of the waves just added to the atmosphere, which was charged with something inexplicable. It was like the universe had brought me here and it was proving with all its furious energy that this moment had been predetermined.

We moved so my back was against the cold wooden wall. The rain was even louder here. Its rhythmic thuds let me know that we were safe in here, in the confines of the hut. He gently threaded a finger through the strap of my bra, letting it fall over my shoulder. He kissed his way down my neck, before reaching round my back with one hand to unfasten the clip. It fell to the floor, and he looked down briefly.

'You are so beautiful,' Antoine whispered.

My breath caught in my throat as the ache in my abdomen grew. I gazed at him. *He* was beautiful. His dark, wet hair, the stubble that lined his jaw, the tattoos that covered his chest. All of it. I wanted all of it.

I put my hand on his jaw and pulled him towards me, letting my other hand reach for the hardness beneath the wet material of his shorts. His kisses were more forceful this time. Hungrier. And I gave them back, with even more power.

Sex with Antoine was like an out-of-body experience. Like I wasn't controlling any of it with my mind. My body just knew what to do. As if we were built to be together this way, each movement of his body triggered a response in mine, before pleasure surged through me like an explosion, bringing me back to earth with a satisfaction that I'd never felt before.

Out of breath, we relaxed on the couch, a worn red blanket over us both. Antoine leaned over to give me a salty kiss.

'Margot ...' Antoine looked at me. 'I will not be here tomorrow. I am taking a group up the coast to scout conditions.'

This was it? 'But . . .' I started. I didn't know what else to say.

Antoine put his hand on my cheek, gently, and stared into my eyes. 'You have made me believe in something again.'

I sniffed tears back and he continued.

'After Gabriel, and everything with Felix, I stopped believing in anything good.'

I leaned my cheek against his hand.

'But then there was you. This beautiful, stubborn Irish girl who looked at the ocean the same way I did before. Like it was full of magic. Who looked at me . . . like I was not just a surf teacher. That I was maybe worth more than that.'

'Antoine,' I said, unable to hold back tears any more. He wiped one away with his thumb.

I bit my lip.

'You gave me back my heart, *Princesse*, even if you are taking it back to Ireland with you.'

I smiled at that, and kissed him again, tasting the salt from my own tears. I pulled away, wiping my face with the blanket. 'Antoine, don't you see? You've done the same for me. You've made me remember what it felt like to be me – the *real* me.'

'You are spectacular, Margot.' His voice was a whisper.

I shook my head. 'I'm just glad I got to have this. To feel this much, to want this much, even if it breaks my heart.'

And we kissed again until the rain subsided.

We got dressed and walked outside into the aftermath of the storm and I stared at the one person who made me feel everything, so deeply, all at once.

A million different words stuck in my throat.

But he spoke instead. 'Take care of yourself, *Princesse*,' he said, trademark hand in his hair. 'The sea will still be here. If you ever come back.' He smiled. But it was a sad smile, one I never wanted to see. Not from him. Not from Antoine, who was so impossibly sure of himself.

But I couldn't think of anything to say. There were no more words. None that wouldn't bring another flood of tears.

I turned and walked across the beach, which looked peaceful now that the worst of the weather had passed. A stark contrast to the weight of the storm clouds inside me that felt like they'd never lift.

37

The next morning, I woke up at five thirty. Not to train, but because I owed it to Delphine to tell her in person that I couldn't stay. And that I wasn't doing the qualifier.

When I got to the beach, the sun was attempting to rise and Delphine smiled when she saw me.

'You are late, Margot! We need to make up for our missed session yesterday.'

I slowed down, reluctant to have another conversation that just left me feeling empty.

I didn't go straight to the rack of surfboards like I usually did, didn't dump my stuff in the usual spot. I just stood there trying to work out what to say.

'What is wrong?' she asked, putting down the tin of board wax in her hand. 'You are OK?'

I shook my head. 'I can't do it.'

'You can, Margot! You are brilliant,' she said.

I wished so hard that's all it was. A crisis of confidence.

I shook my head. 'My sister, her operation has been moved forward, and we have to leave. Tomorrow.'

'Oh . . .' Delphine said as the information hit home. 'Family. It *is* important.' Her voice was laced with disappointment.

I nodded.

'But so are *you* . . .'

'It's for the best anyway. I mean, it was unrealistic to think that I could qualify and stay in France by myself. And Felix and Antoine, it's all such a mess.' Now I was the one with my hand in my hair. It got stuck in my tangled curls.

'Margot! *Non!*' Delphine said with conviction, and it made me look up at her in confusion.

'No?'

'If I can say one thing it is that you should *never* make your decisions based on boys. It is *you* and *your* life. They might be a part of your life, but we must make our own decisions. You are eighteen, *non*?'

I nodded.

'Well then you must make your own decisions. You are an adult now, and you must act like one.' She'd gone back to the frosty tone I knew from a couple of weeks ago. 'Your sister. That is a different decision, but do not let Felix or Antoine influence what you want from your life. Do you understand what I am saying?' She paused. 'I can tell you a secret?'

'Of course.'

'I nearly quit surfing because of a boy . . . Antoine . . .'

I looked at her in shock. 'Seriously?'

'Very seriously. When we broke up, everything reminded me of him, and I stopped surfing for a few weeks. But then I realized that it was a stupid way to live. Things, they change, people change, but it does not mean that you must lose everything connected to a bad experience.'

I nodded in semi-agreement. I got it. I really did. But Rue's operation was still happening, and what kind of sister would I be if I wasn't there too?

'Just think carefully before you make any decisions. I will not take your name out. Not yet. I will see you for your sisters' lesson?'

I nodded.

When I got back to the mobile home, Mum and Dad were rushing around like mad, packing up our whole holiday ready to leave tomorrow. Rue and Wren were sitting at the table eating breakfast. There was stuff everywhere. My heart sank. I sat down beside them as Dad paced around us. And I could tell by his fake cheery voice that he was really stressed.

'Just think, girls, soon we'll all be staying at the Ronald McDonald house. Burgers all around,' he said.

Usually Rue and Wren got ridiculously excited about the prospect of McDonald's, but they didn't say anything.

Antoine's face flashed in my head. His wet hair and how his T-shirt clung to his skin yesterday. How he'd held me as I cried.

How I longed to be back on the beach with him.

I had a shower and put on Antoine's rash vest again. I don't know why I did it, maybe because I was so reluctant to let go – of any of it.

When I stepped out, Rue spotted me first.

'You're going surfing?' she asked, with the first smile I'd seen since we'd been told we were leaving.

I shook my head. 'No, I just like the shirt.'

'But what about that competition in September?' Rue asked, and Wren looked at her, remembering that I'd made them promise not to tell Mum and Dad. Not like it mattered any more.

'What competition?' Dad asked, conveniently coming in from outside holding a croissant.

Rue looked at me. 'Oops,' she said.

'It's fine.' I waved away her apologetic look and turned to Dad. 'It was just a surf competition that Delphine thought I should enter.' I shrugged and picked up a phone charger, desperate for something to fidget with.

'Oh, Delphine thought, did she? What did she think about you almost drowning? Was that just a rite of passage?' Dad was fuming and trying desperately not to explode completely.

'No, Dad. It doesn't matter. It's not happening, we're going home tomorrow,' I said, my voice wavering, betraying me.

'Hold on a minute. Rue said September?' Dad stared at me, demanding an answer.

'It was just a thought. There was a qualifier tomorrow, and if you do well enough you can compete in *La Vague d'Or*. That's the name of the competition. And yes, it's in September.' My voice got quieter and quieter. And so did the room.

'So what was your plan, that we would just leave you here in France?' Dad shook his head in disbelief. 'With these people you barely know? To do something that almost *killed* you?'

'Dan.' Mum came in and put her hand on Dad's arm. But he was still staring at me like he genuinely could not believe what was happening.

'Sweetheart, I understand that you've loved learning to surf, but a competition? After what happened in the water?'

And I don't know what it was, but the way Mum said it lit something inside me. Something that made me adamant that they had to understand where I was coming from. Because from where I was standing, they still didn't understand anything at all.

'I don't just *enjoy* it. I'm good at it. *Really* good. And Delphine saying I could qualify for *La Vague d'Or*? It's a big deal. A really big deal,' I said, my jaw tense and my eyes fixed on Dad when I said it. 'And yeah, I wanted to stay in France until September, but I decided to come home with all of you.'

'You're talking like it was ever up for discussion, Margot . . .'

'Dad, I'm *eighteen*. I don't have to ask your permission for everything any more, but your support would be nice.'

Dad just stared at me – less angry, more shocked.

I stormed into my bedroom and tried to distract myself by watching TikToks. Everyone left me alone, and I didn't emerge until it was time for the girls' surf lesson.

'Wren, grab your shoes. Rue, put your splints on.' I looked at my sisters and nodded for them to get up off the sofa.

'Where are you going?' Mum asked.

'I'm taking them to the beach for their last surf lesson. They deserve that much.' Rue and Wren went outside, past Dad, who didn't try to stop them.

'Let them go, Dan,' Mum said gently.

'We'll be back in an hour or so. Then . . . then we can talk about tomorrow.'

I just about stopped myself from crying as I walked outside. We headed down the path and after a few metres, Rue stepped into me and wrapped her arms round my waist.

'I'm sorry, Margot. I didn't mean to tell,' she said.

And when I looked down, her big eyes were filled with tears. I knelt down beside her and gave her a hug.

'Don't worry, it doesn't matter now. Who wants to surf?' I asked them both.

'Me!' they said together.

'Good, let's go.'

We made our way to the beach, with me giving Rue a piggyback for the last ten minutes of the walk. It was hard to walk on the sand with her on my back, so it slowed me down.

'*Les filles!*' Delphine spoke directly to Rue and Wren when we reached her. 'You are here to surf? There is no Antoine today, so it will be me. Is that OK?' Delphine smiled warmly at them and when they nodded, she walked over to the rack.

'The most special board.' Delphine pulled out the board that Rue had used before. The one that Antoine had got for her. My heart swelled at the memory.

'You are ready?' she asked my sisters. Delphine acted like it was a normal lesson. She didn't ask me if I'd made up my mind yet and didn't bring up our earlier conversation at all.

And I just stood on the sand and watched as she took them on wave after wave, with the sound of Rue's laugh making my eyes well with tears.

I walked to the water's edge and studied them both, but especially Rue. How hard it was for her to get into the same positions as Wren, how it must have hurt her legs, but you would never have guessed she was in any pain, not by the smile on her face.

She fell off. Again and again. And she got back up, again and again.

La guerrière.

When they were taking a break, Delphine walked over to me.

She nudged me gently with her elbow. 'Your sister. Rue. She never gives up, even when it is hard.'

'She's amazing,' I said, pretending not to pick up on the double meaning.

'Do you know what I see out there?' she asked. 'It is difficult for her. Much more difficult than it is for you or for me. But she does not use that as a reason to quit.'

'This isn't about quitting. It's more complicated than that,' I said, trying and failing to put conviction into my voice.

'*Bien sûr.* Of course it is. Life is complicated. But do your family need you to give up on something that you love? Something that matters to you?'

I didn't know what to say to that. But it seemed like Delphine had enough words for both of us.

'I told you that when I first met you, I thought you were just another tourist playing at being a surfer. I do not want you to prove me right.' Delphine went back into the water, leaving me standing there, the weight of her words crushing me.

I tried not to cry as I watched the girls surf, my eyes on Rue and her determination. If she could fight that hard for something she loves, how the hell could I give up so easily?

38

On the way back home, Rue was exhausted but buzzing. She couldn't stop talking about each wave she surfed, dissecting it and sharing her excitement with Wren.

'Are you going to win the competition?' Rue asked when we were close to the Brasserie.

It caught me by surprise, and I laughed, which lightened the darkness in my head for a moment. I stopped to answer her, shaking my head. 'I'm not doing the competition,' I said hesitantly. Delphine's words were turning in my head. 'I'm coming back with you,' I explained, even though I thought she knew this. She was far from forgetful.

'But why?' She tilted her head on its side and Wren looked at me too, waiting for an answer.

When I didn't give one, Wren jumped in. 'Delphine said you are, like, *really* good. And she doesn't even like people.'

Perceptive as always.

Rue started again. 'If I could surf like you, *I'd* stay. I'd do *all* the competitions and win *everything*.' She flexed her muscles and made Wren laugh. They were like a tag team.

But I didn't laugh this time. I had too many thoughts. Contradictions, complications.

'But . . . it's not that simple. You need me at home.'

Rue considered my words and Wren watched her, the two of us just waiting.

Then she shook her head. 'Nope. I'll have Mum and Dad *and* Wren.' Wren put her arm round Rue's shoulders and Rue grinned at me. 'And plus! It would be so cool to tell everyone at school that my sister is a *real* surfer.'

I just stood there, marvelling at how easily she could cut through all the adult bullshit that made everything so complicated, and how she just saw things the way they were. The way they should be.

She grabbed my hand. 'Let's go and tell Mum and Dad!'

I pulled a face, and my stomach lurched as I imagined how that would go.

'You should stay. I'll be OK,' she said.

I squeezed her hand in response. And in thanks for making the impossible feel . . . maybe *not* so impossible. But that was what I should be doing for *her*. I was the big sister. And instead, here she was, teaching *me* things.

When we got back into the mobile home, all the bags were packed, and Mum and Dad were cleaning counters.

Rue and Wren went outside, and I took a deep breath. 'I should have told you about the competition, I'm sorry.'

Dad sighed and stopped cleaning. He turned round and Mum looked at him, giving me the impression that they'd discussed things when we were out.

'Margot, I know you love surfing, but after everything that happened, and Rue's operation –'

'I know,' I said, holding up my hands in peace. 'But hear me out. This isn't just about the surfing.'

Mum and Dad sat down on the little sofa to listen. Dad gave me a small nod.

'Do you remember when I used to swim? The early mornings, the galas, how I was before I quit?' I asked.

'Oh, I remember.' Dad smiled at a memory. 'You loved it so much. I couldn't understand how someone could enjoy getting up at four thirty to get into a cold pool.'

'Exactly!' I said, like Dad had got an answer right in an imaginary quiz. 'And after I quit, I felt, I dunno, lost. Like I didn't know who I was any more. Rue and Wren's sister, your daughter, someone's girlfriend. Never just Margot.'

'Oh, love,' Mum said, looking troubled. But I continued.

'When I'm in the water, I feel like *me* again. The real me. Like I've discovered something that's mine. And that I happen to be really good at.' My voice wavered. 'This isn't about abandoning my family, because I would *never* abandon Rue and Wren. It's about the fact that I found a part of me that I lost.'

Mum looked at me. Her expression soft, sad. 'You're serious about this, aren't you? It's not just a summer thing?'

I shook my head.

Dad looked at his hands, which were twisting round each other.

'Dad?'

He looked up and, for a second, I thought I saw the shine of tears in his eyes.

'I told Margot she should stay. I want her to.'

I turned to the doorway. I hadn't even noticed Rue come in.

Dad looked between us, then Rue went over to sit beside Mum.

Then he looked at me. 'I'll need to speak to your mum but if – *if* we consider this, there would have to be rules. Daily check-ins. A proper place to stay. *Plans*, Margot.'

He'd barely finished speaking before I rushed over to him and gave him a hug. And then I hugged Mum too. The excitement, it was like nothing I'd ever felt before, because it wasn't just for the competition, it was for the future, the potential.

Dad put the organizing on hold for a couple of hours. I messaged Lili for her parents' phone number and Dad spoke to her mum, who sent him links to the room she rented out.

I sat beside him as he made the call, my body fizzing with excitement as he wrote down details.

'OK,' Dad said when he hung up the phone. 'We are all meeting Lili's mum, Mrs Moreau, this evening. She will take us to the house to see your room, where you'll be living – one of the students has just gone back to Germany, so it's good timing . . .' His voice trailed off, like it was all just hitting him now. 'Margot, are you sure about this? It's a big step.'

'Dad. I'm ready,' I said, unable to contain my excitement. 'And if it doesn't work out, or it gets too hard, I can always come home.'

Dad smiled and put an arm round me. 'It's going to be so quiet without you.'

'I think those two are capable of making enough noise that you won't even notice I'm gone.' I nodded outside towards Rue and Wren.

'I still remember you being that age like it was yesterday.' Dad smiled sadly to himself.

'Me too,' I said, seeing myself there at the little plastic table with a bowl of Nesquik cereal, my skin plastered in suncream.

'Change is hard,' he said.

'But sometimes it can be great,' I replied.

I stood up. 'I'm just going to tell Felix my news.' He was the first person I wanted to know I was staying.

'And *I'm* going to take the girls to the supermarket,' Dad decided.

'Margot?' Mum called as I started walking down the path. I turned round. 'Could you get the number of Felix's mum, please? I'd like to speak to her before we leave.'

'Sure,' I said, smiling.

I jogged to the Brasserie and crashed straight into Delphine.

'Sorry!' I said as she stepped back and gave me a quizzical look. 'Can I still compete tomorrow?' I could barely get the words out in the right order.

'The qualifier? Of course. I never took out your name. You will be there?' Delphine asked, trying not to grin.

I nodded. 'Is Felix here?' I asked.

She didn't say anything, just nodded towards the bar.

I rushed past tables full of customers to the covered bar area, scanning it for Felix. And when he saw me, there was a sadness in his expression. But it didn't last long. I was smiling so hard that he creased up his face in the cutest confusion.

'Why do you look so happy to leave me?' he asked from behind the bar. I sat on a stool and twisted a curl in my finger.

'I'm not leaving,' I said.

And his face lit up, eyes and all. 'You are serious?'

I nodded and smiled.

Felix just stared at me in disbelief, his eyes twinkling. He filled a glass with ice then poured lemonade into it. 'One minute, I will be right back.' He picked up the drink and walked across the bar.

I turned on my seat to scan the Brasserie. I could not stop smiling. I would be staying here, in France. A world away from my life in Belfast.

I caught Delphine's eye as she carried a tray of glasses back towards me.

'So you really are staying?' she asked.

'I'm staying,' I confirmed.

'This is good news. And do not worry that our training got interrupted. You are ready. I promise.' Delphine gave me the smallest smile before walking off out of sight.

Felix appeared a few minutes later. He kissed both my cheeks.

'I have a break now. We should walk,' he said, and I followed him out of the Brasserie.

'I spoke to Yves, he would be happy to give you a job here, with me and Delphine, if that is something you would like?'

I threw my arms round him. 'Oh, Felix, thank you. I'm so happy I'm staying.' I looked at him when I said it, and he smiled too, but not with the same intensity as me.

'What if I don't qualify?' The thought hit me out of the blue.

'You can still stay,' Felix said, like it was obvious. 'You can train with Delphine and Antoine, you can work with me, you can find out who you want to be . . . in France?' He cocked his head slightly, and looked unbelievably cute.

'In France.' I smiled back at him.

'Does Antoine know?'

I shook my head. 'I haven't seen him since the storm.'

And when Felix had said his name, the feelings were back, the ones that spread like wildfire, before fizzing and exploding like fireworks when I leaned into them. I thought about his dark hair, the blue eyes, him calling me *Princesse.* And I ached to hear him call me that again.

'He will be happy,' Felix said simply, without any visible hint of jealousy. 'As I am,' he added.

'Me too.' I leaned over and kissed him on the cheek. 'Oh, and my mum was asking if she could have your mum's phone number? My dad has already phoned Lili's mum and sorted the room at hers.' It still felt like a dream.

And he smiled back. 'Of course.' Felix took out his phone and I gave him mine to type in his mum's number.

When I got back to the mobile home I gave Mum the phone number, then sent a message of my own.

ME: I have some news . . .

PRIYA: Tell me

ME: I'm doing the surf competition

PRIYA: Serious? That's amazing! But promise me you'll be careful

ME: And there's something else

PRIYA: Let me guess. It's about one of your French boys?

ME: Nope. Even better

PRIYA: You're coming to swim camp with me?

ME: If swim camp is in France?

PRIYA: Wait, what?

ME: I'm staying in France. I'm doing the qualifier, and then I'll stay for the competition in September. And even if I don't qualify . . . I kind of really like the thought of staying here . . . working, figuring out what to do next . . .

PRIYA: . . . I'm actually speechless

ME: That'll be a first

PRIYA: This is huge! So you're actually going to be LIVING in France?

ME: Yep. Living. Surfing. Hanging out with French boys

PRIYA: "hanging out"

ME: Ha! That too . . . But P, maybe you and Cal could come and visit? It might be nice for us to start over, somewhere that doesn't have memories everywhere?

PRIYA: A summer holiday in France? I'm down. Starting over? Down for that too :)
It's nice to have you back

ME: It's nice to be back :)

And I still had some left-over bravery when I'd stopped messaging Priya. So I sent another message.

ME: Hey Ari. Staying in France a bit longer while my parents come back early for Rue's surgery. Competing in a surf qualifier tomorrow (yes SURFING). Found something out here that I thought I'd lost forever. So it turns out you and Theo might have done me a favour. And I forgive you. Not because it's OK, I'm just too busy catching waves to carry that shit around with me. Take care of yourself. M

I typed out exactly the same message to Theo and hit send on them both before I could overthink it or change my mind. And when I did, it was like a ton of bricks had been lifted right off my shoulders.

39

Lili's mum's house was perfect.

It was right on the beach. Just ten minutes from the campsite.

There were flowers in little baskets beside the door, and wind chimes hung over the surfboards that were propped up against the wall.

I inhaled, taking it all in. This was going to be my home for the next couple of months. And it was nice to see my new room with Mum, Dad, Rue and Wren, like they were leaving a part of themselves with me. Wren bounced on what was going to be my bed and Mum and Dad asked Lili's mum a million questions. And when we left, they seemed happy.

Back at the mobile home that evening, Mum laid the table with little tea lights.

'Look, Margot, isn't it beautiful?' Wren asked.

I looked again at the table and saw that it had been decorated with shells too, dotted all over the white plastic.

'We did it for you!' Wren said.

Mum came down the little metal steps carrying bowls of

spaghetti and Dad followed with more. They set them down on the table, pushing candles and shells gently out of the way to make room.

I couldn't help feeling sad. Our last night. The last time I'd see my family in I didn't even know how long.

'Thanks for dinner, Mum,' I said.

'I thought you should eat pasta, give you energy for tomorrow. Oh, Margot, are you sure this is what you want?' Mum looked at me with worry all over her face.

'I'm sure,' I said. And I was even more sure after seeing the house on the beach just then. It felt *right.* Like this was where I was supposed to be.

'I'm sorry.' She shook her head. 'It's all just a lot.'

'I made you this.' I turned to see Wren standing beside me holding a folded piece of paper. She handed it to me, and I opened it out. A map of the campsite that she'd drawn.

'A map, so you won't get lost when we're gone,' she said.

My eyes filled with emotion, and I hugged her. 'Thanks, Wren, I'll use it every day.'

'And here, you can have this!' Rue said, pushing a shell towards me from across the table.

'A shell. Thanks, Rue.' I smiled.

'Not just any shell. A *lucky* shell,' she corrected.

I held it in my fist, then slid it into the pocket of my shorts. 'Thanks, Ruthie.'

'You're sure about this, Margot? Really sure?' Dad, who'd been so quiet, gazed over at me.

I nodded. 'I wasn't looking for this. I didn't come to France looking for *anything*. But I found this, and I need to see where it leads,' I explained.

Dad nodded at me briefly in understanding. 'Wren, why don't you give Margot her present?' Dad nudged her and Wren grinned.

'But you've given me presents,' I protested.

'This is from all of us,' Mum said, and got up with Wren and walked behind the mobile home.

They emerged carrying a surfboard. A bright pink one with painted black waves on it.

'Oh my God,' I said, getting up.

Wren could barely contain her excitement. 'Do you like it?'

'I chose it,' said Rue.

'I did!' argued Wren.

'They both did,' said Dad. 'The woman in the shop told us it was perfect for someone starting out in competitions.'

There was a lump in my throat, and I could barely get the words out without my voice shaking. 'Thank you all, so much. Wait. When did you even get it?'

Dad smiled. 'Remember when I said I was taking the girls to the supermarket, just before we went to look at your new room? Well, we actually went into town.'

My heart swelled at the thoughtfulness.

'Can we play that game again?' Wren asked.

'What game, love?' Mum said.

'The one where we say what we're grateful for,' she said quietly.

Dad glanced up at me and I remembered the last time we'd played, the better part of a month ago. I cringed again. Not because of the game, but at how angry I'd been the first time.

'Yeah, let's play,' I said.

'OK, me first!' Rue shouted. 'I'm grateful for the surfing lessons, even though I fell *a lot*.' Rue grinned.

'You didn't fall *that* much,' Wren offered. 'I'm grateful that I got to see how brave people can be. Like Rue going surfing even though it's hard for her, and Margot staying here all by herself. And Mum and Dad letting us try new things even though they're worried,' said Wren.

I looked over at Mum, whose eyes were shining. She put a hand over her heart. 'That was lovely, Wren.' She cleared her throat. 'And I'm grateful for seeing my beautiful daughters discover new parts of themselves.'

Dad reached over for Mum's hand. 'And I'm grateful for this holiday. For making us all see each other a bit differently.'

A wave of emotion rolled through my chest. What was I going to do without my family?

'Margot?' Dad asked.

'I'm grateful for . . .' I hesitated. The lump in my throat was still there, and my voice wavered. I coughed. 'For this place. The ocean, and everything it taught me. For new friends, and for you all, supporting me.' I took a deep breath. 'For you, Rue, for showing me what never giving up looks like, for Wren who always notices what people need. For Dad – thank you for letting me do this even though it scares you. And Mum –' I found it hard to look directly at her, so I settled my gaze on the top of her head in case I collapsed into floods of tears – 'for believing I can do this.'

'And I need a super-fast recovery so I can be a real surfer

too,' Rue said, jumping in, making me laugh, and making me even sadder that they'd be gone in a matter of hours.

Mum laughed. 'Let's not get ahead of ourselves.'

We finished dinner, then Dad brought out a plate of desserts they had bought in the supermarket. *Tarte au citron*, *les éclairs au chocolat* and *les mille-feuilles*, the same kind that Felix had shown me. He'd cut them all up into tiny pieces and we shared them as the sun set, with the sound of cicadas singing in the grass around us. It couldn't have been more perfect.

But this was it. This was goodbye. Tomorrow, I had to get up at five thirty a.m. and be at the beach by six. There wouldn't be time for extended goodbyes. And I needed to get to bed, to rest before the competition.

Back in my room, my phone buzzed.

ARI: Surfing . . . that's unexpected. Turns out Theo is a piece of shit to everyone, not just you. He dumped me for Carrie Richards a couple of days ago. I fucked up and I know it. Sorry. A x

And I didn't reply. I didn't have the headspace. Not with everything else going on. So I just put my phone down and went to sleep.

40

Something felt different the next morning. I woke up with a knot in my chest that I couldn't shift. And it tightened when I heard the stir of Mum and Dad loading the car with luggage, trying their best to be quiet.

I got dressed. Bikini, rash vest, T-shirt, shorts, hoody and towel to keep me warm after I'd been in the water. I left my hair down. The blonde curls, bleached lighter by the sun, bounced around my chin. No make-up. I had even more freckles now, and my face was the light golden colour of perfect-for-me toast.

I took a deep breath. Leaving this room was more than just that. It was my family leaving me, staying here alone, competing without them watching from the sand. The plan was that I'd stay here until the following week, on my own, and then I'd move into the room at the beach house.

My eyes welled but I closed them and took more deep breaths.

I could do this.

When I got outside, Rue and Wren were standing beside the car, hair sticking out, eyes still half closed.

'Margot!' Wren ran towards me. 'Do you still have your map?' She looked up at me.

'Of course,' I said. I pulled it out of my back pocket. 'How else would I be able to get to the beach?'

Wren grinned at me and I looked down to see Rue staring at me with the most serious look on her face. 'You better win,' she said, matter-of-factly. 'I want to tell all my friends.'

'Of course I'll win. Look at my new board!' I said. Wren pulled away and Rue launched herself at me. One of her splints dug into my shin, but I breathed through it. Her arms were so tight round me that it took everything in me not to cry right there. For Rue, who had to leave her holiday to have an operation, for me, wishing so hard I could be there *and* do the competition.

'Have you got your lucky shell?' she asked. And when she pulled away, there were tears streaming down her face. I went down on one knee and pulled it out of my pocket.

'Always,' I whispered.

'Good, because you can't win without it.' Her words were choked.

'Listen, Rue, you're the bravest kid I know. Never change.' And she threw her arms round my neck and hugged me again.

'Ruthie, love, we have to go.' Mum's voice was gentle as she pulled Rue away. Rue walked to the car and got in beside Wren, but didn't look at me again.

I braced myself and looked at Mum. She smiled, taking away some of the nausea that consumed me.

'Oh, Margot,' she said, tilting her head slightly. 'Look at you.'

I smiled, closed-mouth, trying not to cry.

'You'll be *brilliant*. You *are* brilliant,' she said. And before I could reply she hugged me, and I breathed her in, trying to memorize the scent.

'Thanks, Mum,' I whispered.

She got in the car, and then it was just me and Dad. Dad, who looked more worried than Mum. He was pacing around on the dusty ground in front of the car.

'You know if you want to leave you just need to make a call and we'll get you on the next flight, it's not a problem,' he said, like in his head he'd come up with a million different solutions to a million different disaster scenarios.

'Thanks, Dad,' I said.

'I mean it. Any time. And you can call night or day. Just because we'll be busy with Rue's operation doesn't mean that we won't be available for you. We –'

'I know, Dad. Thanks. And I'll be fine. I promise.' I smiled and walked over to him.

And I thought his hug might break me then. He held on, even when my arms went slack. Then he cleared his throat and put his hands on my shoulders.

'We're so proud of you, Margot. So proud.'

'I know,' I whispered back. 'You'll phone me after the operation?' I asked.

He nodded. 'And a million times before that.'

I watched them drive away, standing there until the car disappeared round the corner in the almost-light.

And then there was one.

And just after they'd gone, my phone buzzed. It was still so early, and home was an hour behind, so I was shocked to see her name pop up on the screen.

PRIYA: Good luck today! If you surf like the old Margot swam, you'll kill it . . . Oh and me and Cal are already planning our trip. Hope you have space on your floor xx

My heart swelled.

I could do this.

And then my phone buzzed again.

FELIX: See you at the beach. Good luck today. You will be brilliant x

I *definitely* could do this.

The beach was unrecognizable when I got there. A covered judging platform had been set up on the sand. There was another tent beside it, maybe for other officials and sponsors. My stomach flipped and I looked towards the water. Coloured buoys floated in the waves, which were already looking big. To me anyway.

I hadn't noticed that I'd stopped walking, like my body had frozen in anticipation of what was to come.

But then I heard my name. 'Margot!'

I looked down the beach, scanning the crowds that were already gathering, and I saw Sébastian waving at me. 'Margot, over here!'

My heartbeat calmed and I walked towards him. As I did, I saw Lili too. The two of them had set up camp already, a cool box between them and little chairs with binoculars hooked over the edge.

'Are you ready, Margot?' Lili asked, getting off her chair to kiss me on both cheeks.

'Nope.' I shook my head.

'But of course you are!' Lili said and grinned. 'Do not tell her I told you, but Delphine is very jealous of your skill.' She put a finger to her lips, and gazed towards the water, where Delphine was standing, just staring out at the ocean.

'Well, she has nothing to be jealous about.' I laughed at how much had changed in the last few weeks. How jealous *I'd* been of Delphine when I thought she was with Felix.

I walked towards the water and stood beside Delphine. 'Do you get nervous?' I asked.

'Not any more. What will be will be,' she said. 'Just remember to watch the waves. Pick the best one. I cannot help you when we're out there.'

I nodded, understanding. I looked towards the ocean, to the waters that felt like a second home and pushed everything out of my head.

I took a moment to breathe in the salted air and to just enjoy where I was. Right at this moment. Where the sun was about to rise over a glittering ocean, where my new friends supported me from the sand. I was about to compete in a *surf* competition. I smiled to myself. It felt too good to be true.

Someone testing the PA system made me jump.

I walked back up towards Sébastian and Lili when someone else caught my eye.

Felix.

He'd come.

When he saw me, his face lit up. 'There you are!' he said.

'And you! Thank you for coming.' I smiled as he kissed both my cheeks, and I did the same back.

'Of course. It is your first competition,' Felix said.

'It means a lot that you're here,' I said, looking into the brown eyes that I'd come to know so well.

'I will not go too close to the water, but it is a big deal for you,' he said, his hand in his hair.

'Thank you,' I said. 'Seriously.'

Felix pulled his phone from his pocket and looked at the screen. I watched his face as he raised an eyebrow at it. Then he put it away and looked at me.

'He did not believe me when I told him,' Felix said.

'What? Who?' I looked around, wondering if he was talking about someone on the beach.

'Antoine,' he replied.

And there it was. The butterfly explosion.

'He didn't believe what?' I asked.

'That you were staying here . . . He's on his way back from the coast.'

And it was a thousand things all at once. It was the fact that I'd be surfing in front of Antoine, making the pressure increase by about one thousand per cent. It was the fact that Felix was messaging him, like a brother. It was the fact that there wasn't any jealousy, no acknowledgement of a situation that could be awkward and complicated. There was none of that. He looked happy. Or maybe just happy for me. It said a million things about our friendship that I could never put into words.

'OK, Margot, *viens ici*!' Sébastian called me over and I walked towards him and Lili, with Felix beside me.

'Delphine has gone for a little run. Maybe you should go too? Do you know how it works?' Sébastian asked. He was serious this time. He stood up and put his arm round my shoulder. 'I will show you.'

Sébastian led me around the beach. He pointed to the judge's platform. 'Here is where the judges sit. They mark you out of ten for each wave. Only the two highest waves count towards the total.'

I listened intently to everything Sébastian had to say. We probably looked related as we strolled along the beach, with our blonde hair almost the same shade, his longer than mine and a lot less curly.

My chest swelled, taking in all the faith he had in me as he explained the competition in detail. How there would be four rounds, and in each heat the best two surfers would progress to the next round. In the final, the top four competitors would all qualify for *La Vague d'Or*.

'And Antoine will be here?' Sébastian asked, jolting me out of competition mode.

'I think Felix said he was coming, yeah.' I tried to make it sound casual, even though every time someone said his name my whole body tingled.

'You have been like a lucky charm for the Laurents,' said

Sébastian. And I felt a surge of gratitude for him, for putting into words something I didn't even know I needed to hear. 'A lucky charm' – like me being here, in France with the boys, truly mattered. That maybe I'd changed something, not just for me, but for them too.

But I needed to concentrate. So I put my hand in my pocket and pulled out the shell that Rue had given me.

'This is *my* lucky charm,' I said, showing him.

He took it from my hand and kissed it. 'And now it is more lucky. We should get you your vest.'

Sébastian and I queued up at the officials' table and he spoke to them in French, before one of them handed me a black rash vest with 'Biarritz 2026' on it in bright white print. I held it up in front of me and stared at it as we walked back to Felix and Lili.

The sun had risen now, and the heat was already warming my skin.

I got changed behind a screen, removing my shorts and taking the shell out and squeezing it in my hand before putting it away carefully. I put on my vest with pride, smoothing it down over my skin and inhaling deeply as I stepped back out into the sun.

I walked over to the hut and had to take a moment to myself as images of the last time I was inside raced through my head like an X-rated movie. I shook the thoughts away and hoped that nobody had noticed the flush of heat in my cheeks.

It felt different here without Antoine. I wanted to tell people to step away, to stop leaning on the walls and looking in the windows, that this belonged to Antoine. But instead, I picked up some wax and held it in my fingers, remembering the day Antoine showed me what to do, how he leaned over my shoulder, his hand on mine, his breath in my ear, hairs standing up on the back of my neck.

I waxed my board then carried it back to Sébastian and Lili. Felix and Delphine were there too.

Delphine still wasn't smiling.

'The conditions. They could be better.' She sighed. Then a voice rang out across the beach.

My heart raced. It was in French. I had no idea what they were saying. I looked in panic at Felix who waited until they'd finished speaking before looking me straight in the eye.

'OK. It is the first heat. And both you and Delphine are in it.'

I could barely hear what he was saying because of the thud in my chest. This was it. An actual competition. I squeezed my eyes shut for a second and thought of Rue. What she'd said. How she expected me to win. And how brave she was.

Today I'd be channelling Rue.

I picked up my board and walked towards the water with a racing heart and a determination that I hadn't felt in years.

41

There were four of us in the first heat. Everyone picked up speed as we neared the water, breaking into jogs and looking straight out to the ocean. I glanced at Delphine as she threw her board on to the water and started to paddle. I followed her.

We all paddled out. No talking, only the sound of the ocean and the hum of the crowd on the shore. I felt sick. These girls knew what they were doing. They looked almost professional, the way they paddled, the way they watched the waves.

And then one girl went for it, paddling hard and catching her first wave. She was amazing. And the hole in the pit of my stomach grew.

Delphine took the next wave. My heart was in my throat when she surfed, hoping she'd do well. And she did. Perfect form. A perfect wave.

I kept watching the waves, but I found something wrong with all of them. Until it came. The most beautiful swell I'd ever seen. And I knew it, I knew this was the one. I started paddling hard, then almost fell off my board as a girl cut right across me, taking the wave.

'Hey!' I said. But nobody did anything. That was *my* wave.

And she surfed it beautifully. I kicked the water, my heart beating harder than ever.

I saw a yellow board in the corner of my eye. Delphine was back.

'Fear is excitement without the breath, Margot. *Breathe.* This next wave is yours.' I glanced at her, and she winked at me.

I took a deep breath. She was right.

I took my eyes off the shore and focused on the next wave. I paddled hard. Harder than ever, then popped up, and there it was, the rush of adrenaline, the cool water on my hand and the exhilaration that I'd only ever felt on the board.

I cut back into the wave and did my best to keep my form as I finished.

I was so in the zone that the cheer from the shore sounded distant, like it came from miles away. But I couldn't stop smiling as I paddled back out into the water to catch more waves.

Delphine was incredible. Every wave she surfed was perfect, and like Sébastian had said, it was the best two that counted. There was no way she wouldn't make it to the next round.

I surfed four more waves, and by the time we'd all returned to the shore, I was exhausted. Sébastian and Lili met us at the water and took our boards. Lili and Delphine kissed in celebration and Sébastian high-fived me. 'That was amazing, Margot! You were so much better than the other two,' he said far too loudly, as we both looked at one girl in my heat who threw her board on to the sand.

'Thanks, Sébastian,' I said, smiling.

We walked back to their little camp where Felix was waiting. He kissed me on the cheeks, and I hugged him in response.

'I am so tired.'

'Well, you will probably have to do it all again.' Felix nodded towards the judges' table where one of them was standing up with a microphone. And as she spoke, Felix translated for me.

'Conditions were challenging today, with cross-shore winds affecting wave selection. All competitors have demonstrated remarkable skill. The judges have now deliberated. It was an extremely close heat with only eight points between first and fourth positions. The results will now be displayed on the scoreboard.'

I grabbed Felix's hand as the numbers flashed on the board. 'I can't look.' I turned in towards him and closed my eyes. 'You look.'

'I think you want to look, Margot,' said Felix. And I could tell that he was smiling.

And when I stared at the board, I couldn't believe it. 12.50. I'd come *second*! And Delphine was first.

I threw my arms round Felix, and he lifted me up.

'Delphine!' I called when I was back on the sand. And she grinned at me, with Lili holding up a bottle of beer in her honour.

She walked over to me. 'We still have a long way to go, but it is a good start. Well done, Margot. I knew you were something special.'

And when she said it, I saw Felix glance at me with a smile.

'We are the champions!' Sébastian sang as he joined us.

I laughed and sat down on the sand, watching the next heat, with the sun beating down on me.

My good luck didn't end with round one. My next round finished with Delphine in first again, me in second, but it still didn't guarantee qualification to *La Vague d'Or* – there were more rounds to come.

Lili had made us sandwiches. Baguettes with cheese and ham, which we ate gratefully after round two.

The next round was tense, with the stakes getting higher each time, and you could feel it in the water, the way the other competitors were silent as they watched the waves. There were no smiles and no conversation, not even with Delphine.

I scored 14.10 and Delphine dominated with a 16.23. Second place by the skin of my teeth.

Even Lili and Sébastian had started to tire, with Sébastian actually falling asleep on the sand. There was no sign of Antoine. But I wasn't disappointed. Today was about surfing, *not* about boys.

We rested in between rounds, but by the time the semi-finals came round, I was still completely exhausted.

'I can't do this,' I whispered to Felix.

'Of course you can. Only this round and the final, and then that is it. You belong out there.'

I looked at him, into his steady eyes as I took a deep breath and stood up. Then our next round was called.

'Good luck, Margot! But you will not need it.' Felix smiled.

I would one hundred per cent need it, but he'd calmed me, if only for a minute. And I was grateful.

The wind was different now. And as I sat on my board watching the waves, I found it harder and harder to pick out the best ones. They were unpredictable, choppy, with huge lulls between sets. But the other girls seemed to know what to do; they rode the waves like they were perfectly formed. And when I tried? Everything fell apart. I lost control, falling off mid-wave. I swam back, slamming my hands into the water as I paddled.

The microphone blared across the shore in French. Delphine paddled towards me. 'It is about you. They said the competitor in black needs a significant score. The conditions are deteriorating and wave selection is critical.'

Fear is excitement without breath. Breathe. I repeated in my head what Delphine had told me earlier. I took a deep breath.

'Thanks, Delph–'

But she had gone, taken another wave, and surfed it like a pro.

I thought about Rue again. How she fell and fell again and still got back up. So that's what I did. I surfed the next three waves like I had nothing to lose.

But I felt sick when we waited for our scores. I saw Delphine's first. 16.6, first place. And I was so happy for her. She deserved it. Then I saw my score: 13.93. *Fourth* place.

I sighed in disappointment, trying to hold back tears. Lili ran over to hug me.

'Margot! The finals!!' she squealed.

'What? I came fourth. I didn't get through.'

Felix appeared beside me. 'They're taking four, the top four qualify, and the final is used for seeding position,' he said. I couldn't believe it. I could barely contain my excitement. I hugged them both with aching arms.

Then I walked down to the water, just to look out at the ocean, the thing that had almost killed me but made me feel more alive than ever. My chest swelled with pride. I'd done it.

I'd got into the finals of the qualifier. Nothing could feel better than this.

'Nice moves, *Princesse*.'

The hair on my neck stood up before I even turned round. I closed my eyes, scared to open them in case it wasn't real.

But I could feel him. The heat of his body standing behind me, the warmth of his breath on the side of my face. I turned to face him, and it was like he'd become even more beautiful since that night in the storm. No top, just his black board shorts.

'Thanks,' I said with a smirk.

'I leave for two days, and you steal my moves? That cutback? *Parfait*.'

'I had a good teacher.'

'Thanks.'

'I was talking about Delphine.'

'Oh yeah?' He grinned and moved even closer to me. I bit my lip and found myself staring at the tattoos on his chest. I reached out and pointed to one where his heart was.

'What does that mean?' I pointed at the quote, *En art comme en amour, l'instinct suffit*, brushing my hand against his smooth skin.

'Ah,' he said. 'It means "In art as in love, instinct is enough." Anatole France. He was a writer.' Antoine's voice was low and soft, and it melted into my ears as the noise of the crowd behind us disappeared into nothingness.

'Do you think that's true?' I asked with a slight tilt of my head.

And he answered by kissing me, pulling me into him, his hand in my hair, our mouths salty and in sync under the French sun.

42

As we walked back towards the crowd, my face flushed as a group of people cheered. I turned to Antoine.

'You've distracted me before the final.' I pretended to be annoyed.

'I wish that I could say I was sorry,' Antoine replied. He tugged my hand to stop me before we reached the group. 'I did not just come back to see you compete. I came back to see if you felt it too. That it was not just a dream.' He stared at me with blue eyes a few shades darker than mine, and the intensity sent a jolt of lightning through my veins.

'It's not a dream,' I said. And then he was grinning like he'd just won the lottery. 'But I stayed for the surfing. Just to put that out there,' I said. I couldn't have him thinking I'd just stayed because of him.

'*Bien sûr.* But it was not you who made the decision.'

'Excuse me?' I challenged him playfully.

'It was the ocean. She decided that you belong here, and who are we to argue with the ocean, and Rue, *la guerrière*?'

'*Le flic* is here!' Sébastian called out to us. 'And what is this I hear about you moving back home? The Laurent boys have finally reconciled?' Sébastian grinned at Antoine, and I looked up at him for clarification.

He pushed his hand through his hair. '*Ouais*, I think it is time. Felix?' He looked past me and I turned round to see Delphine, Lili and Felix standing there. Felix smiled at him and gave a slight nod.

'I'm sure your mum will be happy,' I said.

'She is already planning a party at the house,' Antoine said. 'You will come?'

'I will come,' I said, nodding. He kissed me again without warning, leaning me backwards, my hand moving reflexively to his stubbled jaw.

Then I picked up my board and walked towards the ocean, feeling awkward that Felix must have seen us kiss. And there he was, watching me with quiet contemplation. He gave the tiniest shake of his head, as if he was trying to get rid of a thought. 'Remember that you have already qualified, this is just for seeding. Do not be nervous,' he said. And although he smiled, I could sense a sadness behind it.

'Thanks,' I said gratefully.

'Good luck, Margot. You are already incredible.'

And with that I turned and paddled out after the other competitors to take part in the final.

I'd been given a second wind. Whether it was the break, or Antoine showing up that did it, I'll never know, but I concentrated so hard on every wave that I thought my head might explode. Aching arms, aching legs, salt water in my throat, in my eyes, up my nose, but I didn't care. This was it. My last chance.

I thought of everyone watching from the shore. Felix, Lili, Sébastian. And Antoine. I wanted to give them a show. But it wasn't for them. It was for me – for the me that thought I would amount to nothing after I quit swimming. The fire that had been given back to me after all this time was raging in my gut. I'd do it for Rue and her bravery, and for my whole family, who put all their trust and support in me.

I surfed six waves and was utterly drained.

I collapsed on the sand, with Delphine dropping down beside me in a heap.

'We did it!' she said, smiling up at the sky.

'We did it,' I repeated, out of breath.

And then we were surrounded by Lili and Sébastian, pulling us off the sand and into hugs.

We walked with them up the beach to where Antoine and Felix were talking. And I hung back for a moment just to watch. They stood close, but not too close. And they were talking like they knew each other, but only just. Like they'd met by some strange coincidence. Felix laughed and it was the nicest sound in the world.

'Margot! Margot! Margot!' They all cheered when I finally joined them. I looked across at Antoine, who winked at me, and I had to stare down at the sand to try to stop myself blushing.

'The scores are in,' Felix said, giving me an encouraging smile. And I felt sick.

They all came up at once, and I scanned the board desperately for my score. Then I found it. 15.20. Fourth.

Delphine was celebrating, and Sébastian and Lili were dancing over to me.

'We are going to *La Vague d'Or*,' Lili sang.

Then Antoine was in front of me. 'Congratulations, *Princesse*.'

'I'm going to *La Vague D'Or*!' I threw my arms round his neck and squealed in excitement. He picked me up and I hooked my legs round him, kissing him hard. And in that moment, it was just us. Me, breathless, exhausted, still wet from the sea; him, hot skin, rough, firm hands on my back and thigh. My fingers tugging on his dark hair, my heart racing in a heaving chest.

When he set me down, he was breathless too. He just stared at me for a second as a smile crept slowly across his face. He took my face in his hands. 'Margot, you were spectacular. Tell me again that this is real.' He spoke quietly, so only I could hear his sexy French whisper.

I bit my lip to tame the grin that desperately wanted to take over my face.

'Real as those waves out there. I'm not going anywhere,' I said. And I was still smiling when he kissed me again.

Euphoria.

This is what it felt like.

When Delphine and Lili came over to talk to Antoine, I excused myself to make a very important phone call to Liverpool.

And as I listened to the beep of the European ringback tone, I gazed out at the glittering sea again, and whispered a silent thanks to the water for bringing me back to me.

Acknowledgements

So many people were involved in the making of this book, it seems wrong that there aren't a million names on the front cover.

To my (former ☹) editor, Ruth Knowles, thank you for everything. To Joanna Moult, my agent. To the copy editors and proofreaders. Sorry about my aversion to timelines, and thanks for the eyes on my rusty French. To everyone at Penguin who worked on this book in any way. Thank you.

To Janelle Barone who, once again, brought my characters to life with her brilliant art.

To my friends from University of Liverpool MFII (and their lovely extensions), especially Ciara and Alex, you made a year in Paris so much less terrifying for someone who was permanently petrified. Ciara, everyone should be lucky enough to have a friend like you, and Alex, you have the most calming presence of anyone I've ever met. Life always felt more manageable with you.

To the French boys from those summers in Pézenas, and to Karen, Robyn, Jane, Sarah and Lucy, who made those summers unforgettable. Thank you for the memories. (And the inspo.)

To Fi Scarlett. My friend across the border. I genuinely don't know what I would do without your friendship.

To my SCBWI friends, always.

To the VWG and NIYA writers, your support is invaluable.

To Aimée and Rachael Murray. I know Northern Ireland is small and all (and I'll never say out loud that I believe in fate), but the overlaps in our lives have become ridiculous. I couldn't be more grateful to know such a wonderful family. I am constantly in awe of how much you do for other people. Thank you so much for the early reads, and Rachael, thank you so much for that lunch and all the info.

To Marta, your enthusiasm when you ask about my books is so appreciated. *Gràcies*.

To Bill and Colette, I am always so thankful for your support.

To Rosemary Ireland, who loved to read. And to my own grandparents, who I wish were alive to see these books.

To my mum and dad, thank you for all the French summers. Those holidays were perfect. Thank you for all your endless support (not just for the writing), and for acknowledging that I am your favourite child without ever having to say it out loud or actually acknowledge it in any way. Don't worry. I know.

To Chris. My best friend. I'm so happy I get to spend my life with you. Thank you for everything you do for us (although you could probably buy me more gifts).

To Lyla, my favourite daughter, who has always had her own mind, and never fails make me laugh. You are perfect, exactly how you are.

To Rory, the best, most thoughtful son. If only the world had as much empathy. You are extraordinary.

I could not love either of you more.

To Children's Books Ireland and to all the wonderful booksellers (especially Jo and Chris at The Secret Bookshelf), thank you for all the support. It means so much.

To my readers (with a special thanks to Max), your time is precious – thank you so, so much for spending some of it with me, and in the worlds I create.

More from Jenny Ireland . . .

Love triangles, grumpy x sunshines and just a couple of enemies to lovers . . .

'Full of warmth, growth and romance' *Paper Lanterns*

'Romance with substance' *Irish Times*